PARADISE IN MOURNING

Book 3
Crescent Moon Chronicles

L. E. Towne

Literary Wanderlust | Denver, Colorado

Other Books by L.E. Towne

Knight of the Crescent Moon
Battle for Daylight

Copyright 2021 by L.E. Towne

Published in the United States by Literary Wanderlust LLC, Denver, Colorado.

www.LiteraryWanderlust.com

ISBN Print: 978-1-942856-81-8
ISBN Digital: 978-1-942856-89-4

Cover design: Pozu Mitsuma

Printed in the United States of America

Dedication

For Sarah, Matt, Isaac, and Maggie.

If one only has a small family, it's preferable to have an exceptional one.

Prologue

Marlowe's Third Journey to Philadelphia

From under the manuscript pages, the metallic ping of a cell phone interrupted the loft's peaceful atmosphere. Izzy shifted on the couch and shoved a heavy stack of papers to the side—Renaissance works and photocopies of rare scripts in Marlowe's own hand.

She turned toward the man in the kitchen. "It says unknown, you want me to get it?"

"Sure." He put a kettle of water on a burner and flicked the gas on.

Izzy answered. "Angelo Volpi's phone."

"Isabelle?" The man cleared his throat, and his next words came across clearer. "Is it you? God's blood, I'm relieved to hear thy voice."

"Marlowe?" Izzy pressed the speaker button and held the phone out.

"Kit, where are you?" Angelo asked as he hurried into the

living room.

Marlowe's familiar accent echoed through the phone. "I hath not a clue, old friend. But you need to make haste to the Fair Ridge Cemetery. If I am correct, Tamberlyn is in dire circumstance. Something may be very amiss."

"We'll come get you."

Izzy handed him the phone and pulled out her own to call her sister, knowing that for once, Tam wouldn't mind the interruption.

"Cemetery, first." Marlowe's tone was politely insistent. "It's imperative. I am without transport and will not arrive in time. I've borrowed a fair lady's speaking device. I shall wait here for thee." There was a muffled question, and he came back and gave Volpi his location. The call ended.

"Tam's not answering." Izzy pocketed her phone, wondering what her sister had gotten herself into this time. The kettle started its tentative slow whistle, and she hurried to turn off the flame. She watched Angelo slip a fixed blade Bowie knife into his trench coat pocket as he waited for her.

As Marlowe feared, Tam was indeed in some dire circumstance. At the cemetery, the crescent moon and old streetlights created more shadow than light, but Volpi's flashlight illuminated almost too much.

Tam was on the ground, backed against a headstone, with an assemblage of bone and rotting flesh towering over her. The large human-like figure was a sickly gray color and almost translucent in the sparse light. It lunged at Tam, its curved claws jutting outward from bony fingers. Angelo's whistle pierced the night, and the beast turned at the sound.

"Watch the entrances," he commanded as he ran toward the thing. Izzy held her breath, almost afraid to look. Logically, she knew both Ange and her sister could handle themselves, but the monstrous thing was, well, monstrous, and she breathed a sigh of relief when it collapsed on the ground, Ange's large knife in its heart.

A faraway sound made her jump. She'd forgotten about watching for others. Having studied ghouls as part of her supernatural being research, she knew they traveled in packs. Likely, there were more on their way.

Izzy searched the shadows of the cemetery, finding the rest of the pack weaving their way between mausoleums to get to their downed pack-mate. Ange helped Tam toward the entrance as she cradled her arm against her side, her face scrunched up with pain. She tried a smile at Izzy. "How did you know?" Not answering, Izzy hugged her sister gingerly, careful of her injury.

"We'll take my car. We can get yours later. You should let Ange look at that."

The fight with the ghoul must have been something because a normally protesting Tam nodded and got into the back seat of Izzy's used Volvo. Angelo climbed in after her, ripping open the med kit and staunching the blood flow from Tam's arm. Izzy took a deep breath and got in the driver's seat, pulling out from the street in her usual careful way. In her side mirror, she saw the shapes circling the fallen ghoul.

"You sensed me again, didn't you?" Tam's eyes met hers in the rearview mirror. Izzy focused on street signs and the GPS.

"Not this time," Volpi answered for her. "We had a little help. Why didn't you tell us you were out hunting?"

"Because I wasn't hunting. I was coming from X and Connie's—"

"Tuesday night dinner," Izzy said, finally glancing in the rearview mirror.

"Yeah. And I saw this guy, he looked odd, had the typical gait of a ghoul, so I followed him."

"Alone?" Volpi's voice was stern. "Knowing they travel in packs and where there's one, there's—"

"A shit load," Tam finished for him. "He was headed toward a residential neighborhood. I couldn't just let him go. Ouch." She pulled her arm from Volpi and glared at him.

"This needs stitches." His tone was brusque, but Izzy knew

it masked a genuine concern for her sister.

"I have surgical glue at home. I'll be fine." Tam turned toward the front. "Where the hell are we going? The loft is north of here. Iz, I swear, for a smart person, you can't navigate for shit. Even with a GPS."

"We're making a pit-stop." Izzy glanced in the mirror again, not at all bothered by her sister's jibe. In fact, she was excited to be able to reunite Tam and Marlowe. Until Marlowe came along, Izzy had thought her sister would end up the crotchety spinster at family dinners.

Marlowe was the perfect match for Tam's standoffish bravado. He was *the* Christopher Marlowe—a literal Renaissance man.

"We're here," Izzy said as she pulled the car to the curb. The street was empty, and the intersection shrouded in shadows. She peered through the side window as she shifted the gear into park. "Do you see him?"

"See who?" Tam asked.

In response, Volpi jumped out to look around, leaving the back door open. Tam was abnormally quiet. In the rearview mirror, she slumped against the back seat, appearing even a little faint, and Izzy turned to check on her, receiving a pained smile and a quick nod to her unasked question.

Suddenly a man smelling of mildew, damp, and things Izzy did not want to think about entered the backseat. A voluminous black cape covered most of his frame, and he laid a long scabbard and sword on the floorboard before turning to Tam. Unruly brown hair framed his face and reached to the tops of his shoulders, a fierce smile broke through a badly trimmed beard and surrounding stubble. The smile was all for her sister, who sat immobile on one side of the car.

"Fair Tamberlyn, tis so good to see—" He got no further. Tam reached for him with her good arm, pulled his face toward hers, and kissed him. Izzy's smile rivaled Marlowe's in its broadness as Ange climbed into the passenger seat beside her.

"You're alive," Tam murmured in Marlowe's embrace. "And here. I thought I'd never see you again." Izzy heard something she hadn't heard from her sister in years, not when their father died or even the bad breakup before college. Tam was crying. Marlowe pulled her closer into his shoulder.

"Tis been a short time for me, by heaven. This is only my third moon since leaving you last." He turned toward the front seat, still holding Tam close to him. "Mistress Isabelle. How fares thee on this wonderful eve?" His segue gave Tam some time to compose herself.

Izzy smiled at the man who knew her sister so well. "Far better now, Master Marlowe. I trust thy journey was without mishap?" She answered in the same vein, the words coming from her as naturally as talking with her cohorts in grad school.

"It's been years for me." Tam huffed, ignoring her sister's words. "Two years since you left. God." She pulled away from him, irritated at the unfairness of time travel. "I'm even older than you now."

Marlowe chuckled at her frown. "Art thou willing to overlook my youth and inexperience? I assure thee, I would be a most appreciative student with such a teacher, with thine obvious wisdom and skills." His voice dropped into a sexy baritone at the last word. "How many years between us? Three? Four? 'Tis of no consequence, as you are as beautiful and as ageless as the moon that brought me to you."

"I'm twenty-eight and you're what, twenty-three now?"

Marlowe kissed her again, and she said no more on the subject of their age difference.

Izzy smiled at her sister's very human insecurity. Tam was so sure about everything. Always forging ahead, busting through life like tissue paper on Christmas morning.

Izzy not so much. She worried about everything; her sister's safety, the hostiles invading Philly on a regular basis, Tam's relationship with Marlowe—who only appeared on the random phase of a crescent moon, even Izzy's own relationship with

Angelo Volpi.

Angelo was a good man, and despite their age disparity, Izzy had fallen completely in love with him, but she could never quite tell if he felt the same. She had tried talking to her sister about it, but Tam could avoid touchy subjects with the finesse of a diamond cutter. And Volpi's and Izzy's romance was a very touchy subject.

"Take Platte Street." Angelo broke into her thoughts.

"Why? Aren't we going back to the loft?"

His handsome profile registered a rare smile as he gave her thigh a squeeze. "No. Drop them at Tam's place. We'll meet up in the morning."

"Ange, we need to work," Izzy protested, her own sense of logic kicking in. "He can tell us what he's found. It will save months of research. And maybe this time we can..." Her words faded as Tam giggled in the backseat. Marlowe was murmuring words Izzy could not hear, but the tone was intimate enough that she remembered her reason for wanting Marlowe back— her sister's happiness. She made the turn onto Platte Street.

Marlowe spoke to Ange as the car pulled up to the curb. "Thank you for heeding my call, friend. The last time, it was I who chanced upon her in the cemetery. But time changes all things, and this time I was too afar to reach her."

Izzy peered at him as they stood on the sidewalk. "This is the future journey you spoke of. The cemetery? You knew about the ghouls. We should talk about—"

Angelo's hand tugged gently on Izzy as he spoke to Marlowe. "We'll give you a chance to clean up, rest, and Tam needs to see to that wound. Meet at the loft in the morning?"

"We'll see you soon," Tam said, pulling Marlowe toward her apartment building. Izzy looked at Ange as he watched them walk away.

"You know it's unlikely they'll show tomorrow, right?" she asked, knowing her sister.

∞

Three days later, Marlowe appeared at the door to Volpi's loft.

"Where is Tam?" Izzy asked after they'd settled onto the couch, hot mugs of tea in their hands.

"She is at the constables building." Marlowe's voice was steady but guarded.

Since meeting Marlowe and knowing his plight, Izzy had studied everything she could get her hands on about time travel theory. She knew every action in the past has a reaction in the future, so likely this time around was different. Better or worse they wouldn't have known, but judging from Marlowe's world-weary expression, it was worse.

His hazel eyes regarded Izzy. "You know of her partner, Xavier?" He paused for breath as though the very act of breathing hurt his lungs. Izzy extended her hand and a tiny spark of blue arced between them. She gasped, jerking her hand back. Marlowe's time in the modern world was short.

After a moment, he found his voice. "I tried to thwart the danger by changing the locale, but I failed. I should not have tried." He faltered. "In the past, deliberately altering the events has been disastrous. This was no less so."

"X died?" Izzy asked, somehow knowing that this was true. Tam's police partner was gone, and this wasn't the first time. She rubbed her temples as memories arranged in her mind. After a moment or two, she raised her eyes. "The Strigoi Mort?" she asked.

"Dead," Marlowe replied, somewhat surprised. "You know of this?"

She nodded sadly. "The premonitions have increased. It's not just sensing when Tam is in danger anymore, but..." she hesitated. "It's hard to tell what's what, but Detective Hernandez died the first time around too, didn't he? Only you couldn't tell her."

"You saw this? A vision?"

Izzy shook her head. "No, they're more like memories—different timelines. It's very disconcerting. Is Tam okay?"

"Tamberlyn is upset with me. She has every right to be." He sipped at his tea. "The moon is changing. Let us work while we can."

"Tam must know that X's death is not your fault. She's got to understand that."

"I kept things from her, Isabelle. I betrayed her trust. About someone very important." His tone was morose, almost broken. "Please, let us to work. I cannot speak of this any longer."

Chapter 1

Tamberlyn
(Months later)

I loved the snow. Loved the pristine cleanliness it gave to my city, even if it was just a temporary illusion. Tomorrow the streets would be full of dark slush and sooty heaps on the corners. But tonight the world was breathtaking and serene, with a clear, cold moon shining down on all the white, and I shivered with the nagging anticipation of death. Hopefully not my own.

"Tam!" The gruff voice of my mentor, Angelo Volpi, crackled in my ear. "You sleeping up there? They're coming."

"I know," I murmured, keeping my voice low. Wearing a single earpiece plugged into the phone in my breast pocket was a low tech way of communicating with the group. From my position at the north end of Tambery Bridge, I thought about the concept of being part of a team. I had a team now. A quirky, exasperating, odd collection of people that helped me do what I do, which is hunt monsters—human and otherwise.

I'm a cop by day, working in Homicide Division, and in my off time, I do what I can to protect the unsuspecting humans from the more supernatural forces out there. I have a team for both jobs. Tonight we were hunting down a group of wraiths.

Now *wraith* is just the Scottish word for ghost, and ghosts are limited in their ability to harm humans. Even vengeful spirits have their impediments, and if you know what you're doing, they're not difficult to handle. However, the creatures I'd encountered a couple of days ago had developed the ability to remain semi-corporeal—at least parts of them. Especially solid were the three-inch claws and fangs.

The human-looking creatures were large, between six and seven feet tall, with claw-adorned hands sporting only four digits, each sharp enough to rip through flesh. They craved adrenaline, could smell it like bloodhounds and would shred their victims in order to get at the adrenal glands. Too technical I know, but the point is, they're a different brand of ghostie and much harder to get rid of.

"You see 'em yet?" A male voice pierced the darkness, and my skin prickled inside my jacket. I shivered.

"X!" I hissed and muted my phone. "You scared the crap out of me. Don't sneak up on a girl in the middle of a hunt. And no, not yet. You?"

"I feel 'em, but can't tell you from where."

"Volpi said they were headed this way." I stared out at the parking lot, the sparkling snow topping the chain link fence, the soft mounds of parked cars covered and resting like extinct dinosaurs in a tar pit. X was right, there was not a sign—no sound, no smell, nothing.

Xavier Hernandez had been a burly fellow with a linebacker build and a soap opera smile when he'd been my partner in Homicide. His appearance was pretty much the same to me. His dark eyes still crinkled, he still smiled, but less so these days. X was the big brother I never had. He interfered in shit that wasn't his business and was way too overprotective, but he also made me laugh and could be trusted in a pinch.

In many ways, he still was all that, though only for me. For everyone else, X was dead—killed in a shoot-out by a dirty cop. Now, he appeared whenever I needed a shoulder to cry on—which I would never admit to—or if there was a case, supernatural or otherwise. Whether he was just in my head or literally materializing in some non-corporeal form, I didn't know. Lately, things had happened when he was around—things that could only be explained by X figuring out how to navigate this plane of existence.

"There," I said, spotting a blur of motion at the far end of the lot. "You guys ready?" I unmuted the phone. Three answers came back. Check, check, check. I turned to X, but he was gone.

Pulling the double-edged sword from its scabbard, I tested the grip with my leather glove. I wasn't as proficient with the weapon as I'd like to be, but it would have to do.

Volpi and my sister, Izzy, were working to contain the wraiths. Trap them in the small lot so they couldn't revert into their ectoplasmic form again. If they stayed as flesh and blood, they could be killed. And that's where Ziggy came in. She had devised some chemical base compound that would adhere to their physical form and lock them in that state. The rest was up to us.

Bottles of the compressed compound, looking like the propane you used for a camp stove, were rigged with tiny battery-operated detonators. The rub was they had to be close enough to the wraiths in order to disperse the chemical properly. Too far away and the substance would dissipate harmlessly into the air. The wraiths would be hurt but not significantly weakened. I was the bait, distracting them long enough for the canisters to be placed.

The blur of one wraith turned into two, almost side by side, ghosting over the slick surface and leaving no tracks as they closed in on me. I stepped farther into the open space of the lot, my feet crunching on the cold white ground. My hope of facing them one at a time faded as they closed the gap.

Turning, I held the sword in an overhead two-handed stance John McEnroe would have approved of. I was aiming for heads and hands. The two wraiths moved apart, and I could see the third not far behind. Great, all three at once.

Suddenly, the wraith on the left tripped and fell end over claws in a ball of mist and snow, and I heard X's chuckle in the distance. Like I said, X was always good in a pinch.

The first wraith came within spitting distance—literally as I felt cold slimy mucus eject from his gaping maw and land on my cheek. I swiped at my face with a sleeve as I swung the big sword at him. He parried my first blow like swatting a fly, and I ducked, narrowly missing his claws. I spun completely around, sword swinging for all I was worth, and struck again. My attack was too low, slicing through the wraith's ectoplasm like butter, a low raspy sound emitting from him. It sounded oddly like a laugh.

The creature heaved his ghostly body at me, his friend not far behind. I shifted to the side, thrilled at my quick footwork. That lasted a microsecond. My back foot slid down the ice, putting me in the most graceless stance ever. I toppled over like a toddler in tumbling class, sliding along the snow-covered lot.

A claw caught my lower leg and I felt my boot catch in his hand. The heavy leather saved me from a vicious wound, but I wasn't going anywhere either. I kicked at him with my free leg and saw wraith number three flanking me. I twisted as much as I could to keep an eye on him, still kicking at my captor who'd also sprawled on the ice but held fast to my ankle.

A swirl of snow and ice whirled up from the ground like a tiny cyclone and pelted ice crystals into the wraith's eyes. The wraith, its eyes closed against the stinging snow, roared its displeasure and loosened its grip on me. I kicked away, rolling to my knees and swinging the sword to my left. This time it connected at the base of his claws. Long, curved nails fell onto the icy ground. The beast howled.

"Tam, get out of there." Volpi's voice came not over the phone but from the north side of the parking lot. The canisters must be in place.

I turned to the north, slashing my way through the other wraith as I went. Another claw caught my ankle, and I was pulled to the ground and dragged along my stomach toward the others.

With a sharp popping sound, a shimmering blue net surrounded my assailant, holding him fast against the ground. It was temporary, but it gave me enough time to twist and sit upright. I hacked downward toward my ankle, hoping I wouldn't miss and chop off my own foot. The sudden release flattened me against the ice. I glanced down, relieved to see my foot still attached to my leg. Attached to it was a dismembered hand, its long claws imbedded in my leather boot. Kicking and scraping along the ice, I scuttled away, crab-like.

I felt Volpi's hands under my armpits as he dragged me up and helped me find my feet. We ran for cover behind one of the snow-covered cars as he shouted to Ziggy.

The chemical tanks went off with a flash and a roar, followed by splattering and howls as the creatures writhed under viscous green gunk. They flopped on the ground like dying fish, and Volpi and I went back into the goo, hacking and slicing until they were hunks of blood and ectoplasm. It was hard, exhausting work, and I was glad for the help.

For years, I'd worked alone, thought I was alone, and like the legend of Buffy Summers, only I could save the world from monsters. Three years ago, I found out otherwise, and my world suddenly became inclusive. Not for everyone, mind you, but these few had stepped up and basically saved my ass on numerous occasions. Working with a team had its drawbacks. One had to constantly worry about their safety, their opinions, and their feelings, but clean up was a snap, and you always had a ride home.

A few hours later, my phone rang as I slipped into the hottest bath I could stand.

"Izzy," I answered, pressing the speaker button. "I'm decompressing—leave me alone."

"I'm just checking on you." Her young voice chided. My sister and I hadn't been close since we were kids. She was four years younger, and until our father died almost three years ago and the evil and weirdness of the world came rushing in on us, she'd had no idea what I did. When she found out, Isabelle Paradiso comported herself much better than I'd ever thought she would.

"I'm fine. You know that, so why are you really calling me?"

She chuckled. In the background of the call, I heard soft strains of a jazz piano—a usual choice for Volpi after a stressful day.

"Angelo wanted you to meet us at Pinkie's tomorrow." Angelo. I knew better than this. Meeting up was my sister's idea, but she figured using Volpi's name would have more incentive. Sometimes her enthusiasm for her research was exhausting, but she was right about adding my mentor to the invite. If she'd convinced him it was something, then I would go.

"I have a real job, you know." I sipped at the Dewar's in my glass and scrunched lower into the water. My barely olive skin was pinking up with the heat of it.

"Yes, and sometimes you get to be a homicide detective too. After your shift will be fine."

"Fine. I'll be there. Something up?"

"Nothing that can't wait until tomorrow," she said, her voice throaty as Volpi said something I couldn't hear. She giggled. I was tempted to hang up. Last thing I wanted to envision was my advisor, an age-defying, anti-social half-wizard putting the moves on my sister. It was an unlikely relationship, and quite frankly, I couldn't see my sister's attraction. Volpi was brilliant, and could charm bubbles out of champagne, but he also loved the sound of his own voice and basically hated everyone who disagreed with him. Izzy had him wrapped around her little finger.

Izzy's tone was sympathetic when she spoke next. "We could have used him tonight."

"Yes, but we made it."

"I know you miss him. We all do, but—"

"I've got to go, Iz. I'll see you tomorrow." I hung up the phone before I could hear another word about Christopher Marlowe.

Chapter 2

Isabelle

Izzy ended the call and curled next to Angelo on the couch. He was freshly showered and warm enough that she felt her bones finally lose their chill from the night out in the cold.

Copious empty mugs sat on the floor and end table respectively. Books and sheaves of curled paper, spiral notebooks, and sketching pencils were arranged over the couch and table in a haphazard fashion. Across the loft, a small fire popped in the woodstove, the sound mixing with the throaty sax rifts of Coltrane coming from the old fashioned turntable.

Since Marlowe's last visit, this had been their usual research method—working from his scratched leather couch, pouring through Volpi's voluminous library, and searching for a clue that would enable Marlowe to control his travels.

Angelo sipped his whiskey. "Did Tam seem okay tonight?"

"No weirder than usual. She's on edge, probably because of the crescent moon. Marlowe could be here anytime now. She always gets this way, hoping he'll show up and then waiting for the duration of the lunar phase. When he doesn't show, she's pissed, grumpy, and even harder to live with."

"Precisely why I asked. She hasn't mentioned him since he left."

"Xavier died, Ange. Her partner died. As strong as she is, she's still not over that. I wish there was something we could do."

"And you think dragging her to Pinkie's bar will do something for her?"

"The portal—" she began.

"Is dangerous." He interrupted her. "And no guarantee that we'll find anything."

Two and half years ago, Izzy discovered a strange—she didn't know what to call it at first—a vibration, an entity, a feeling. But she followed it into a dive bar within walking distance of Angelo's loft. In the basement storage room of Pinkie's, a gateway opened, and against all her better judgment, she had gone through. Tam had followed her.

"I may have come up with something," she said.

The idea had formed while she watched Tam skid her way through a fight with the ghostly wraiths. She'd slid on the ice, her boot connecting with the ectoplasm of the wraith, but instead of sliding straight through, her trajectory was deflected. Not as much as striking a solid being, but her path had changed. On the way back to the loft, Izzy had mulled this idea around like a snowball, shaping and crunching it in her brain.

"It's not a solid object," she said.

"What's not a solid object?" Angelo looked at her profile, and she felt the moment he realized her track of the conversation. They often did this—only half-finished thoughts and ideas— words becoming an obsolete method of communication. "It has to be an artifact." Angelo disagreed. "The energy needs a focal point or else it spirals out, which is what causes Marlowe's travels to be so random." He plopped his feet on the coffee table next to hers. She took in the warmth throughout the length of him, their hips and thighs in constant contact.

"Maybe the focal point is like a deflector—altering the path of the traveler, but not severely," Izzy explained. "It can be a code, a line of text, an incantation, anything. There are travelers and guides. We know pretty much how travelers do their thing."

Their research had taught them about the genetic disposition of people like Tam and Marlowe, which made them more sensitive to the gravitational pull of the moon cycle. Marlowe's travels seemed random, but were tied to the moon's crescent phase, when the space-time fabric was thinnest. This allowed him to pass through to where he was needed and kept him there until he was snapped back to his origins.

"But guides need the code, a marker in both time and space," Izzy said.

"If you wanted to kill Hitler, you'd need a marker to pinpoint where and when."

"But the coordinates have to be fluid, because—"

"Time is fluid. I wonder why someone hasn't." Angelo turned to smile over at her.

"Hasn't what?" she asked.

"Gone back and eliminated Hitler."

Izzy's shoulder rubbed against his. "Maybe they have. Maybe he died in obscurity and never came to power. Or Hitler is alive and well and living in Mallorca."

"Even if this marker isn't an artifact, that doesn't mean the ancients had the answer."

"Remember what you said when Tam and I came back home."

"Something along the lines of what the hell were you thinking?" He rattled the ice in his glass before taking a last sip of the whiskey.

When she'd traveled through the portal, Izzy had lived with an ancient clan of people, learning the old ways, the old language. "When we came back from the portal you mentioned the spoken word as being very powerful. It's how ideas are expressed; how we form bonds with one another, find commonality, and also divisiveness."

Volpi nodded. "Words can turn the tide of nations, from despair to hope, or fear to hate, depending on who's speaking them." He placed his empty glass on the end table.

"And who listens," Izzy interjected. "I'm just really slow at listening. But Marlowe's translation, from the last time he was here." She flipped to the pages of her notepad. *The Tree gives way to song. Of life and time and worlds abound.* "We know this is the Tree of Life, a symbol from our ancestors. But whatever the song or rhyme is, there is nothing in all of our research about it."

Volpi's response was a long sigh, but he eased himself from the couch to stand in front of the enormous wall of books at one end of the loft. He looked weary.

Izzy stretched out her legs. "This would be so much easier if Marlowe could just send us a letter, float it through time, or something."

He turned to her. "Now you sound like your sister. I'm afraid our friend is much too clever to be that direct. He knows that whatever clue he leaves us has to survive four hundred years of translations and mishandling by scholars."

Izzy liked his use of the present tense for Marlowe, as though the man had not been dead for hundreds of years. A death that had already happened. Soon, Marlowe would come to the end of his natural short life, and they would see him no longer. Time was not their friend.

She wrenched her attention back to the conversation. "Similar to Nostradamus hiding his predictions in couplets and refrains. I agree. But we're looking even farther back than Marlowe's time—ancient upon ancient times. And not to translate what the words mean, but what the words are. It may be—"

"The spoken word." Volpi finished for her. "It's the song we read about." He looked at her sharply. "Izzy, we've talked about this. Portal travel is far too unpredictable and dangerous. No. Just, no."

"But I've learned so much since then. We've been over every possible Marlowe related document. It could be that he hasn't found anything. The portal may be our only way."

He rose and stretched, turning this way and that, gazing out at the middle distance past his loft windows. Light from the moon highlighted the faded sign for Goodrich Tires, painted on the building across the parking lot.

Izzy had been fascinated with the man since Tam called her for help some years ago. Izzy had arrived at the loft to find Marlowe, Tam, and Angelo Volpi working on a math equation. At the time, she'd had no idea it was related to time travel. In fact, her memory of that day was mostly of Volpi. His dark blue eyes as he'd watched her work at the whiteboard. His quick intelligence and trim physique. Even the way he moved with such energy and light. The way he looked at her as though she were the only one in the room.

Izzy's life had changed so much from then on. Not only were she and her sister closer than ever, but she'd fallen for the older man. The age difference had been one stumbling block. Her sister's reaction was another.

"You can't date Volpi. He's too old and way too weird for you. And he's grumpy, anti-social, and pig-headed."

"You do know that you've just described yourself." Izzy had reminded her.

"I can be that way. We're not dating."

"The heart wants what it wants, sister." Izzy had never been one to let anyone talk her out of anything she wanted, and she wanted Angelo Volpi. For both of them, the age difference had mattered little—they connected at some deeper level.

As the fire in the woodstove died down, Angelo turned back to her. "Are you staying over? It's getting late."

Izzy nodded sleepily. She'd been at his loft almost more

than her own place lately. Both of them often worked late into the night, reviewing equations and ancient legends of charms, swords, and guardians.

"Let's go to bed." He reached out. "We can solve the world's problems in the morning."

She took his hand, letting him pull her up off the couch and toward his curtained-off bedroom on the other side of the loft.

Chapter 3

Tamberlyn

Work mornings are a bitch. I can say this with every fiber of my bitchy self. Most of my compatriots know to stay away until I've downed a third cup of caffeine. But this particular morning, I was up early, had one cup, and even jogged a couple blocks around the neighborhood before heading to District 21 of the Philadelphia Police Department.

A successful hunt makes me feel like all is right, and the world, or at least my little corner of it, is safe once more because of me. Sounds a little egocentric when I put it that way, so I'll re-phrase, because of us—the team. Italian Protectors, Team Paradiso, though both Hernandez and Zigfield would probably object to that. Okay, so we don't have a cool name, but if I had to describe the team it would be like Black Widow, her sister, Jean Grey, Merlin, Casper, and the Oracle.

I walked into the Oracle's lair, better known as the police forensics lab, with two cups of coffee—Americano light cream for me and a frilly concoction for the lab supervisor. My friend was an exotic combination of African, Jewish, goth, and nerd, all blended together in a uniquely cool person whom everyone called Ziggy.

The Coffee Hut around the corner had something known as the Ziggy Special, which she ordered at least twice a day. I never asked about the ingredients of the special, I just paid for it about half the time. I figure it was the least I could do for Zig saving my ass as much as she did.

Jane Zigfield was the only lab tech and forensics specialist in the department with an actual medical degree and license to practice. She occasionally assisted the coroner with some of the autopsies, but for the most part, she analyzed evidence—blood and tissue samples and chemical compositions of all sorts of things. She'd also covered up the more supernatural elements of our world when needed so as not to panic the general public.

"Hey Zig," I spoke loud enough to be heard over her earbuds. She turned toward me, pulling one out, and I could hear strains of Linkin Park blasting from the tiny speaker. I handed her the coffee. "Thanks for the wraith bombs last night. Worked like a charm."

Ziggy took the coffee, turned, and spat a huge wad of pink gum into the trash before sipping the drink. Behind her square-framed glasses, her eyes closed in appreciation, heavy black eyeliner edging toward her temples.

"It was fun. I don't get to see much of my projects in the field."

"Fun, huh?" I smiled at her, remembering how long it had taken me to wash wraith gunk out of my hair. I changed the subject. "You get any trace evidence off the body?"

Our current case was the death of a senatorial intern from Harrisburg. She'd been in Philly assisting a state senator for his meeting with the gaming commission. My money was on a slick mobster named Balfour as a prime suspect. With ties to both New York and Chicago crime families, Balfour's outfit had been on our radar in the past few years.

Ziggy picked up a report and read over the pages. "The sample came back with trace elements of *Conium maculatum*." She leaned back in her swivel chair, crossed her boot-clad ankles, and sipped her coffee.

My blank stare was intentional. "Okay, I give. You say that as if it's something significant."

"On the eve of his marriage, a bartender asked Hemingway what he would like to drink, and Hemingway responded, 'a glass of hemlock, sir.'" Ziggy's dark red lips broke into a sardonic smile. "Needless to say, the marriage didn't last." Setting her coffee on the counter, she pulled her salon-relaxed dark hair from its tight bond, smoothed it back from her forehead, and retied it into a tail.

"Hemlock? You're saying our victim died of hemlock poisoning?" I frowned, knowing what she was going to say before she said it, and I didn't want to hear it.

"Could be that Balfour's not our guy," she said. "Not on this one, anyway. Sorry."

"Who the hell kills people with hemlock? Besides Macbeth, I mean."

Ziggy smiled.

"What? I read. See a play now and then." I frowned at her.

"I didn't say anything." She widened her deep blue eyes for emphasis.

She didn't have to. We both knew that prior to Marlowe showing up in my life, my preferred entertainment was Neil Gaiman graphic novels, the occasional Stephen King book, and Die Hard movies. Since then, I'd become fairly educated in Shakespeare and playwrights of the Renaissance Era. How could I not? Tamburlaine the Great was written after Marlowe's first visit to my timeline and my first name is Tamberlyn. This is not a coincidence. When someone has Christopher Marlowe using poetic license to work their name into a play that's been around for four hundred years, one tends to look that shit up.

"Hemlock seems personal," Ziggy said, her tone deliberately business-like. "It's not an easy thing to acquire as poisons go, and there's certainly far deadlier and easily administered poisons if someone wanted to kill a politician. Aconitum, thallium, potassium chloride, cyanide. Most of these we test for. Others create symptoms contraindicative to heart attack prior to death, but hemlock? Takes too long." She ticked off her fingers. "Forty-eight to seventy-two hours depending on the dose. It attacks the central nervous system, causes tremors, vomiting, movement problems. So she could have easily gotten medical help, and with the proper diagnosis, she would have lived to tell the tale."

"Then why didn't she?"

Ziggy shrugged again. "I'm still analyzing the evidence from the room: a fruit basket, water glasses, the coffee carafe, etc. It was hemlock, for sure, but another compound acted as a catalyst, making it far more potent and fast-acting. Regardless, hemlock doesn't seem like Balfour's M.O. I know you've wanted to make a case against him for a long time."

"So it turns out he didn't kill Cynthia Wu, but only because Munson got to her first." My mouth contorted at the sound of Munson's name—the dirty cop who killed not only Balfour's girl but my former partner as well.

"We'll nail the bastard, Paradiso. Just maybe not on this case."

I turned to find my new partner filling the doorway of the lab. Six-foot-four inches and two hundred pounds of muscled dark skin and shoulder length locks, he had an attitude worse than mine on Mondays, and that's saying something. .

X had been a large man also, but where he was a jovial, easy-going fellow, Damian Cobb had the personality of a surly crack dealer. Cobb was a good cop, smart, efficient, but I didn't trust him as far as I could throw him.

Which wasn't far. Due to my extra-curricular activities, I can hold my own in a fight, but there are limits. I'm small in stature—five-foot-four if I stretch, and I tip the scales at 115 on donut day. I wouldn't want to be on the bad side of Cobb on any day, and in four months of being partners, I hadn't found a good side.

"How long have you been there?" I asked, wondering how much he'd heard.

"Long enough. Hemlock, huh? So very literary. How easy is it to come by?"

Ziggy crossed her legs again and smiled up at Cobb. "Grows by the side of the road, irrigation ditches, almost anywhere in the U.S. Its roots resemble wild parsnips, and the leaves look like parsley. There are common cases of livestock death because of consumption. A knowledge of chemistry and some time in a lab would be needed to render it in liquid or powder form."

"Our perp takes a day trip to western Pennsylvania and comes back with a loaded weapon," I said.

"Not exactly," Ziggy corrected. "Concentrating it enough to kill someone is—"

"Do you see Balfour as a country day tripper?" Cobb interrupted her. "I think we're making a trip to Harrisburg," he said the Capitol's name like it was a dirty word. "Maybe there's something there on this intern or the senator's team." Cobb turned sideways and jerked his thumb toward the hallway. "Captain wants a briefing on the case."

I stood and rolled the stool back under the counter. "Let me know what else you find after the auto, okay?" I asked Ziggy.

She nodded and gave Cobb a wave, totally oblivious to his glower. Ziggy surveyed my partner's retreating form before turning her grin back to me. "He's just adorable. Oh, and thanks again for the coffee."

We passed our cubicle in Homicide Division, and I followed Cobb's long-legged stride to the captain's office. Walled off from the large anteroom that housed the detective's partitions and tucked into the corner of the building, the office had a single large window obscured by once-white mini blinds. The window rattled as we closed the door behind us.

Captain Dudding sat behind a scarred metal desk. Dudding had been my superior when I worked vice, and he'd never liked me much, so I let Cobb give the case update.

"Our victim was Marcy Jackson, twenty-six, African American woman, a graduate of Villanova, and had worked for Senator Shepherd for eight months. Morgan 'Shep' Shepherd is a respected political darling with designs on the governor's office. Shepherd and Ms. Jackson had been in Philadelphia to view the site of the new casino opening and to meet with the gaming commission. According to Shepherd's office, they'd been in town a couple of days when she fell ill, and yesterday the hotel maid found her dead in her room. Forensics found hemlock in her system. We're waiting on the official autopsy."

"Balfour wouldn't kill someone using hemlock. He'd take them out and shoot them, overdose them, drown them in the river. He's a traditional mob guy," Dudding said.

"Yes, sir. That's what we figured." I spoke for the first time. Dudding's Irish complexion reddened at my words. My mere presence could make his blood pressure rise. Dudding had been one of the few cops to survive a reorganization after his supervisor, Enzo Paradiso, turned over evidence against corruption in the department. Enzo was also my father. During my tenure in vice, I had done nothing to endear Dudding to our family name and pretty much everything to be a pain in the ass. It was a natural inclination on my part.

Cobb forged ahead. "Balfour's front company owns property in North Philly. He has connections in the gaming industry, and that gives him motive. He was also in town at the same time as the intern and the senator—that's opportunity." Cobb looked like he wanted to hit something. The introduction of hemlock as a possible murder weapon was a hitch in our otherwise nicely tied up case against Balfour.

"How long will interviews in Harrisburg take? The brass wants this case wrapped and quick." Dudding rubbed a meaty hand across his eyebrows.

"Not long," I answered. "It could be that Miss Jackson wasn't our intended victim."

"Keep the hemlock news out of the press. And go easy on the senator, Paradiso. I don't want this man's reputation dragged through the mud because of our investigation."

I smiled. "You know me, Captain. Discretion is my middle name."

"Yeah," Dudding scoffed. "More like Hurricane Katrina. Get out of here. You got work to do."

From there it was a pretty ordinary day, lots of reports, interviews, and follow-up phone calls. I signed out of my computer around four and headed to the parking garage. Izzy and Volpi would be waiting for me at Pinkie's bar.

The parking garage under the station is one of the scariest places I've ever encountered. Dark and musty, with the dampness only old concrete can hold for years at a time, it has the atmosphere of a horror movie on steroids. Perfect for Jack Nicolson from The Shining to pop up from behind a concrete pillar. The overhead fluorescents flickered and buzzed as I hurried to my car.

"Hey, Tam," X's ghostly voice came at me from a cold spot. He didn't sound too different from his earthly self, just a trace of echo, a splash of reverb.

"X, it's going, you know. Mondays." I sighed and kept walking, keeping my voice low and sticking to the shadows. Last thing I needed was for a co-worker to see me talking to myself.

"You find anything on the Shepherd case yet?" His non-corporeal self shimmered into view.

"It's the Marcy Jackson case. Shepherd is still very much alive. And don't you have better things, X? You know, harp playing, communing with God, anything like that?"

He looked sad and not a little weary. So I had to give him something. Once a cop, always a cop, even in the afterlife. "Hemlock. She died of hemlock poisoning. You haven't by chance seen her? Like newly departed spirits or something?" I asked.

He snorted. "What am I? The ghost whisperer? They don't pop up and introduce themselves, you know."

"No, I don't know. But that would help, wouldn't it? Solve a lot of cases." I got in my car. X wafted in and appeared in the passenger seat, his bulky figure wavering around before settling. He was dressed in his typical suit, and his tie was badly knotted to the left of his Adam's apple. If his close-cropped head was still flesh and blood it would have grazed the ceiling of my Toyota.

"At least I don't have to worry about putting the seat back." I smiled at him and turned on the ignition. "Looks like I'll have to solve the case the old fashioned way, then."

"It wouldn't matter if I had seen your victim. Once I cross over to this plane of existence, I forget. I wish I could just stay here because the other is just..." He shuddered and changed the subject. "How's it going with Cobb?"

"Eh," I said and pulled out into the street.

"That good, huh?"

"I don't trust him, X. He's a good cop, but I just don't get a good vibe from him."

"So you're not going to tell him about your other job."

"No, of course not. A can of worms I'm not willing to dig up."

"You didn't trust me enough to tell me. So why would I expect you to tell Cobb." His voice held an edge. Great, a petulant ghost.

"It wasn't that I didn't trust you. I trusted you with my life. I was trying to protect you."

"And look how that turned out."

I drove in silence for a while.

"I'm sorry," he said. "That wasn't fair."

"Nope."

"Cops get shot, it happens. And by a human, not anything supernatural. Though me being..." He indicated his ephemeral body. "Like this. That has to be Cruz's grandmother and her blood curse."

When X and I worked the Cynthia Wu murder, we'd run into a perp's grandmother. A Romanian woman from the old country, she put some sort of hex on my partner before sealing the deal by cutting her own throat. X died a day later.

"I will talk to Volpi about the curse, okay? I'm meeting him tonight in fact."

"Good. Not that I mind hanging out, but..." The echo of X's voice faded. "How are they?"

"They're okay," I answered. "I've kept the usual Tuesday night dinners at your house. But it's been hard. Connie is a strong woman. You'd be proud of her, keeping things together."

"I am," he said. "I just wish—"

"I know." I reached for him in an instinctive gesture. X was a family man. Two boys and a baby girl, and his wife and I had been friends even before he and I became partners. If he could visit anyone, it would be them. Unfortunately, I was the only person who could see him in his current form. And I didn't relish going to Connie like some medium to relay messages from her dead husband. So X and I agreed it was better for her not to know. My hand passed through him, feeling nothing but cold air.

"I wish too," I said. Everyone had something they wanted to go back to and do over. Say things they hadn't said, taken back others. Have a last dance, a last kiss, a first kiss. Tell someone they loved them. Thing was, I knew someone who could do that. Someone who had chances to fix things and didn't. I wasn't sure I could forgive Marlowe for having the chance to save X and not taking it.

X heaved a sigh, even without breathing he gave the sign of it. "About Cobb. He could help you a lot. And like you said, he's sharp. He'll know something is up with you, the way you keep skipping out on things. I'm trying to keep you out of trouble."

"Trouble is my middle name," I said.

"And here I thought it was discretion," X snapped back.

Chapter 4

Isabelle

In the basement storeroom of Pinkie's bar, Volpi's feet scuffed the wooden floor as he paced. Close to twenty feet long, the area was fairly large but not extraordinary. Lit by a single hanging bulb on a cord, its narrow shelves against the far wall were packed with bar supplies. Along the floor, a few aluminum kegs edged the wall, and a knee-high stack of flattened liquor boxes lingered in the corner.

The door at the top of the stairs opened, and Tam descended. Lately, she always looked tired, but today even more so. She wore her standard work outfit, white button-down shirt, dark blazer, dark slacks. The only bit of color was a tiny splotch of red at her lapel. Izzy had seen the dime-sized pin up close—a ruby-colored meerkat gazing toward an unseen horizon, a gift from one of X's kids for her birthday.

Izzy tried to be cheerful in her greeting, to force the melancholy out of her sister's expression by infusion. The corners of Tam's mouth tilted up as she nodded at Izzy, but when she turned to Volpi, her smile faded. Angelo was a chameleon. He was a tender, often romantic lover with Izzy, yet with Tam, he became the gruff mentor, focused on the mission of keeping her alive. Izzy let out a sigh as the two launched into conversation about the previous night's hunt.

"So what's the big news?" Tam asked, having run the conversational course with Volpi. "If I'm gonna hang out in a dive bar, it's going to be upstairs where the alcohol is." Still, her gaze swept over to the shelves—to the spot where the portal had appeared.

"Not so big news, warrior. Just news." A disembodied female voice came from a dark corner. Tam reached under her jacket.

Izzy put her hand out toward her and whispered, "It's the gatekeeper."

Tam didn't move her hand. "Show yourself." Gradually the veil faded and a black woman dressed in a gray wide-shouldered business suit came into view. She was round, wide, and short, her gray hair frizzed around her head, and a sticker rested on her ample bosom proclaiming, *Hello, my name is Marva.* "Marva," Tam said. "Wish I could say it was a pleasure."

"Like I care if you're having fun. Ain't nobody here having fun, child. You got your job, I got mine." In spite of her dialect, her voice was that of a much younger woman, and her dark eyes flashed over at Volpi, who in turn gave her an elegant nod of acknowledgment.

"Sensei." He greeted her.

Tam looked at Volpi. "Sensei? What are you a Ninja Turtle now?"

"Michelangelo Volpi." Marva's tone changed. "It's been a while. I see you've managed to survive."

"You *are* a Ninja Turtle," Tam quipped. Volpi's sharp look cut her off before she could say more.

"It's just Angelo now, Sensei. And of course, I have survived. I had a good teacher." He smiled one of his more genuine smiles at the older woman. Neither said anything else, yet Izzy could feel the fondness between them. She guessed the woman was many years his senior, even with his longevity.

Tam's usual impatience got the best of her. "Glad you called me here for the reunion, but—"

Marva rolled her eyes and gestured with a little flick of her hand. "Always yapping 'fore you think. Think now, child."

Tam choked, her hand going to her throat, wheezing as she tried to draw breath. Her eyes blazed as she glared at the old woman.

"What did you do to her?" Izzy asked, turning toward Marva. Marva said nothing, her focus on Tam, who, without making a sound, conveyed her rage eloquently. Izzy felt her own heart ramp up at the struggle between her sister and the gatekeeper. Izzy's eyes implored Angelo to intervene.

"Let's just settle down, before someone gets hurt," Volpi said. He put a gentle hand on Tam's shoulder, who remained still, though her eyes had that dark look of *kill something now* Izzy had become familiar with of late. She shrugged him off, but couldn't move her hands. He sighed and spoke again. "This woman, whom you call Marva, is—was—my teacher. Her name is Maurelle, and she is very old and very powerful. Please be respectful, if not for her, then for me."

Maurelle's hold on Tam was weakening, the strain of it etched across her dark face. Tam however was gaining in strength. She'd quit trying to talk and focused on pulling her gun, her hand moving incrementally toward that end.

The tension between them was palpable. Izzy felt it in her bones—they ached with the psychic hold the woman used on Tam.

She stepped between the two women much like Volpi had. "Stop. Maurelle, let her go. Tam, she's the keeper of the portal, and we need her, so be nice."

Maurelle flicked her hand again, and Tam, released from the hold, doubled over coughing. "What the hell was that?"

"Just a little mind trick," Maurelle said, stepping back and wiping a hand across her brow. "You are surprisingly strong."

Tam coughed again, holding her throat. "I'd love to show—"

Izzy pulled at Tam's arm, still worried that her sister would shoot first and think later.

"I need to get through to the world of ancients again," Izzy said.

The others ignored her words, and she clenched her teeth. Everyone seemed to have forgotten their reason for being in the damp basement to begin with. They were so close. The portal and the gatekeeper were right here, and yet everyone was more interested in either war or introductions.

"Maurelle is of the Tessaerat Clan," Volpi explained. "She is able to transcend through several dimensions. And she's also a powerful practitioner of the art. She is the reason you and I met, Tam."

Tam frowned, looking from Volpi to Maurelle, her expression softening as she remembered. "Ah, the magic business card."

"The magic business card?" Izzy repeated.

"That's why I was in the Italian Market in the first place, way back when." Tam mused. "I found this card with Volpi's name. I'd throw it away, and the next day I'd find it back in my pocket. I'd toss it again and find it on my dresser, in my car—the thing was everywhere. So I finally went to the market and his shop. That was ...ten? Eleven years ago?"

Maurelle shrugged like a decade was a blink of her droopy eyelid. Perhaps it was.

"How did you do that? Freezing me like that?" Tam asked, her previous irritation overcome by curiosity.

Maurelle put her hands on her hips and gave a slight tsk before answering. "Tessaerats move molecules. This dimension, that dimension. Air, skin, muscle—all molecules. Now, why are you here? This is my workspace." Her tone turned grumpy again.

Volpi spoke before Tam could say something rude and restart

the hostility. "We've come about the rift. We need passage to the old world."

Izzy rolled her eyes. Hadn't she just said that? She ignored Angelo and feeling the tension building up in her sister, she leaned toward her, trying to displace some of her angry energy. "Tam, I have a theory about the equation, but I have to go back first. Talk to the ancestors. They have what I need." Izzy said this under her breath, glancing at the older woman in front of them. Maurelle was meticulously picking lint from the front of her outfit in a fabulous show of disinterest.

"You think I'm letting you go back there? Alone? Absolutely not." Tam straightened her shoulders, her expression taking on that resolute look she got whenever Izzy proposed anything outside her research skill set.

Izzy turned to the preoccupied Maurelle. "You know who we are. We are the sword and the charm. You know the legend. This will help us do what we are meant to do. Please help us."

Maurelle didn't answer for a moment. Her jaw twitched and worked from side to side like she was trying to dislodge some bit of food in her teeth. Eventually, she stopped and stared at Volpi.

"Quite a task you've taken upon yourself, *Daigaku insei.*" Her eyes crinkled as she addressed him.

The Japanese term flowed easily from her tongue in spite of her previous mangling of the English language. "Both of them. This one," she pointed to Izzy. "Has learned much in a short time. I can feel her power now. It will not open unless I allow it, child." Maurelle glanced at Izzy. Izzy released the breath she'd been holding. She hadn't realized she'd been trying to open the rift. The desire of it pulling at her insides like a hunger. She took a deep breath and forced her neck muscles to relax.

Tam had taken a step back, her arms folded across her chest, watching the scene. Maurelle swung her gaze from one sister to another and then back to Angelo. "And this one is still the same." She pointed to Tam. "All motion and no thought."

"Hey," Tam protested. "I think about stuff." She ground

one foot into the floor like she was stamping out a cigarette. "Sometimes."

Her full attention on Volpi, Maurelle's words dropped into the sharp cadence of Japanese as the two conversed in the language. Whatever was said it seemed to satisfy the gatekeeper, and she returned to English to speak at Izzy and Tam. "Come back tomorrow night. Moon'll be better then. Now, shoo."

Chapter 5

Tamberlyn

I followed my sister and Volpi back to his loft, just a few blocks from Pinkie's and the mysterious gatekeeper. The last time I'd seen her, she'd been dressed as a cleaning woman, complete with gray uniform and a nameplate. Apparently, she'd upgraded her wardrobe, if not her attitude.

Volpi had taught me, or at least tried to teach me, about various beings in the supernatural world, but I was usually only interested in the ones who could eat me. Even then I really only wanted to know how to kill them.

But if I remembered right, a being who could manipulate molecules was an Elemental. Someone who had particular powers over an element—air, water, fire, etc. They could be wizard, witch, a practitioner of some kind, although more powerful with one or more elements. Volpi's cranky mentor was a hyped-up version of one of those.

"She's fae, isn't she?" Izzy asked as we mounted the outside metal stairs to Volpi's building.

"Let's get inside," Volpi said, holding the door.

In the hallway, he touched the charms embedded in the casing before unlocking the industrial-strength door. There were five symbols, rune-like and carved into the metal. Volpi touched them in a certain order, like a combination lock. Volpi had a lot of weird quirks, maybe even suffered from OCD, but this wasn't a symptom. The symbols created an energy field, a barrier to prevent hostiles from entering.

Just like vampires had to be invited in to someone's home, this was true for almost any supernatural being. Crossing the threshold of an occupied home was breaking an invisible barrier of energy. Not all paranormal beings adhered to the rule of invitation. I'd felt safe and secure behind my locked doors until an ancient creature called a Strigoi Mort—the precursor to vampires—broke into my apartment and tried to kill me. After that, I'd employed some of Volpi's magical security measures on my own front door.

Volpi's place was spacious and airy in comparison to my little apartment. A former printing press warehouse, it was developed into four lofts during the late sixties. Exposed brick and big windows that let in lots of light, if not a spectacular view. The furnishings were decidedly old world and well used.

He headed straight for his kitchen, flicking on the under cabinet lights and placing a kettle on the stove. Except for the occasional beer I bought him or a splash of single malt, tea was pretty much all I'd seen him drink.

Darkness had fallen by the time we arrived, and I could see the faint glow of downtown lights in the night sky. Too urban for stars. Marlowe's comment came back to me that we had truly lost something in the inability to see the magnificence that was the night sky.

Marlowe. I'd told myself I wasn't going to think about him. I promised. The crescent moon had come and gone several times now without the appearance of my time traveling lover. Since I wasn't sure I wanted to see him again, that was fine with me. I searched for stars as I lied to myself.

Truth was I was dying to see him. I missed him. His laugh, his quirky clothes, and over the top gallantry. I missed his poetic lamentation about the lack of stars, his possessiveness about a sword named Grim, his glorious hands and body, and the way they made me feel. I even missed his damned sixteenth-century sense of duty and honor. All of that power and knowledge, and he'd let my partner die, knowing full well it was going to happen. How could I forgive that? But I still missed him.

I turned my back on the sky and asked Volpi where he kept his good stuff. He poured a glass for me and then, after a beat, poured one for himself. We sipped a moment, appreciating the smooth liquor on our palettes.

"So Michelangelo, huh?" I smiled at him.

Volpi scowled, but he cocked his head, explaining. "Mom was a fan. It's been Angelo for decades." He finished his drink. "For years after I realized who I was, or rather what, I searched for someone who could teach me. Which is harder than you'd think." He looked at me pointedly, fishing for some appreciation of his efforts toward my own education. "My mother's people wouldn't have anything to do with me. She'd abandoned them and their lifestyle for my father. So I wandered and fumbled through the craft until I found Maurelle in Paris."

Volpi's mother had been a practitioner, which is another word for witch, sorcerer, conjurer, fortune teller, or all of the above. Like me, he was descended from a line of humans with preternatural abilities, and also like me, he'd nourished and enhanced those gifts.

"She's fae, isn't she?" Izzy asked again, going behind him, taking the kettle off the stove, and pouring two cups of tea. She slid a cup in front of Volpi as he poured me another two fingers of his whiskey.

He acknowledged the tea from Izzy with a warm smile. Volpi was the gruffest guy I'd ever met until he met my sister. "You're right, Maurelle is fae. The Tessaerat are the fringe, a border clan between the upper and lower fae. Because of their abilities, most clans leave them alone. It was Maurelle who intervened for you, Tam." He nodded toward the couch. "Let's sit down."

I settled in on his couch, wondering just how bad this could be if I had to be sitting down to hear it. Izzy sat on the other end, curling her legs under her. Volpi settled in his usual crappy chair opposite us.

"Intervened for what? With who?" I asked. As far as I knew, I hadn't met Maurelle until Izzy decided to investigate portal travel.

"Years ago, Maurelle convinced the council that you were valuable in this world and should be allowed to return. She convinced them that she could alter your memory, just enough so you wouldn't remember the conclave or what led to it."

"Apparently that worked because I have no idea of what you're talking about."

Volpi paused and took a breath. "Mostly the fact that Theo was fae, and it was his idea to bring you into their world." The serious expression on his face hadn't prepared me. Volpi was generally serious and standoffish, but now I sensed a glimmer of sympathy in his tone as he spoke.

Theo. I hadn't heard that name in a long time. It still hadn't been long enough. Before I could react, and thankfully before Izzy could ask a question, Volpi went on. "The upper fae do not interfere with mortals. They consider us beneath them. It's more than law, it's a sacred covenant. So except for a rare occasion with someone like Maurelle, we never see them. The lower fae are different, a lot of them are our hostiles. The griffins, trolls, mages—all part of the lower fae. Even ghouls and wraiths are in some way related to that realm."

"Who is Theo?" Izzy asked.

"Nobody important." I snapped. I'm sure my expression told her otherwise, but Izzy would wait until some unguarded moment before inquiring into my past. She was sneaky like that.

"So if the lower fae can come and go and basically mess with us, why not the upper? And what is a conclave?" Izzy asked.

"A meeting of the clans, usually when something big has to be decided," Volpi answered. "And they don't interfere with humans because the fae have been at war for hundreds of years. It occupies a lot of their time. It's astounding they even know we exist."

"At war with who?" I asked, trying to stay with the current conversation.

"Each other, mostly. Fae live a very long time. They're not immortal, but they may as well be, and they have very, very long memories. When they bond, it's a strong emotional and psychic connection. Imagine living so long, you forget what death is like. Forget how it feels to lose someone." Volpi looked at Izzy as if they had a similar bond and for a second I was envious. Regardless of his proclivity for aging very slowly and her own very human youthfulness, their life seemed rather simple compared to mine and Marlowe's.

Volpi glanced at me, checking that I was still with them and not lost down some fuzzy lane of memory. "When a mate dies, they can't handle it. A highly emotional fae with grief and anger issues is only slightly less dangerous than a street full of wraiths.

"Now imagine such a being falling in love with a mortal who has a life span of eighty-odd years. If that happened again and again, their world and their ways would change dramatically. For their own protection, the Queen of Old declared mortals off limits."

My mind still reeled at the mention of my first love. Tall, dark blond, and handsome—of course, Theo had been of the fae. It made sense now, his exotic looks and his mystery were not of this world.

"What do you remember about that time? Before we met?" Volpi asked me.

I shrugged. "You mean before I showed up in your shop? When I met Theo?"

"Again, who's Theo?" Izzy asked.

"The summer after high school. We had a thing. " I glanced at my sister for a brief moment. "I'd been accepted at Penn State. He was a junior there, and we were going to rent a place together once I got to school. But before fall semester, for some inexplicable reason, we broke up. I spent a lot of time drowning my sorrows in mint chocolate chip, Purple Rain on an endless loop, and taking my rage out on hostiles. I switched my registration to La Salle, told myself it was because it was closer to home. I never saw him again."

Theo North was everything a lonely seventeen-year-old girl could want. He said most of the right things, but not all because that would have been too much. He was gentle and gentlemanly until I didn't want him to be. He told me I was beautiful and smart, and for the first time in my life, I'd truly felt that way. And it was all an elaborate lie. Theo was fae—cunning, beautiful, and deadly.

"Why me?"

Volpi shrugged, and at my obvious frustration, he posited a few options. "Perhaps he was fascinated by your abilities. While the fae are very powerful, time traveling is not one of their gifts. They tend to use portals between realms. It's possible he knew of your potential before you did. Maybe he was just curious about mortals. From what I know, he was a young fae, only a couple hundred years old. He could have simply wanted an adventure."

"Or he could have really liked you, Tam. It's not impossible, you know," Izzy said.

I sipped the whiskey, feeling it burn in my gut. I had a pretty good sense of my own attractiveness. I'm too short for supermodel status, but good bone structure from mom and large dark eyes from dad worked into an okay combination. I considered myself to be sexually open enough to please a man and confident enough to get him if I were interested. But that's now. When I was a gawky high school girl, the nerds at my lunch table barely noticed I was female. Yet for some reason, it never occurred to me that the gorgeous guy I dated would have ulterior motives. Theo had been very convincing.

"Or maybe he liked to live dangerously," I said. "Because if I'd known he was fae, I'd have killed him before the afterglow kicked in."

"Sex with a fae. How was that?" Izzy mused aloud and somewhat dreamily. I sighed and glared at her, mostly because I knew if I said anything it would lead to her sharing. Izzy was a sharer. She empathized, she sympathized, feeling everyone else's feelings, happy or sad thoughts, living on that emotional crap roller coaster ride. Hell, she sat in the front car with her hands up yelling *Wheee!*

I did not. Nor did I want the visuals associated with sexual exploits of her and Volpi. I was resigned to the two of them being together. She was happy—great, but it was like your best friend having sex with the principal.

Before I could deflect her question about fae sexual prowess, there was a knock at the door, or more like a stampede at the door, sharp and desperate. Izzy moved to answer it. Volpi's reaction was faster than my own, and he rose to stand not far from her, his hands at his side, ready. I pulled my Glock from the holster. I guess you could say Volpi didn't get a lot of visitors. Or maybe we were just paranoid as hell.

Except for Izzy of course, who pulled open the door as though she expected there to be a Girl Scout on the other side. It was not a Girl Scout.

What we got was a bloodied, smelly, bedraggled poet, holding a sword in one hand and his side with the other. Christopher Marlowe had come back to me.

Chapter 6

Tamberlyn

"Izzy, help him inside," I said and moved around my sister and Volpi to the doorway. I glanced down the hall and then back at Marlowe. He wore dark clothes, but blood had stained them darker in a large area just above his hip. He must be in pain, but his eyes were clear and the grip on his sword was determined. His breath had evened out now, but he had been running. Volpi left him to Izzy and went to fetch his med kit.

"Two vampires." Marlowe's eyes found mine, his voice tight. "One I dispatched, the other..."

I put my gun away—bullets would do nothing to a vampire— and grabbed the first knife I saw. An oversized, jeweled machete displayed on the wall beside the door. I raced down the stairwell, not trying to be quiet.

Ultra-good-looking, sexy vampires are rare in my world. Usually, they're more animal than human, fast, deadly with both fang and claw, and speaking in monosyllabic threats. Unlike in fantasy books, vampires rarely turned the beautiful girl into a vamp because they've fallen in love. Would you fall in love with a hamburger? We were food, plain and simple.

As an ultimate hunter, their vision was far superior to mine, but once outside, I kept to the shadows nonetheless. I moved quietly, more for me than for them. My night vision is good, but my hearing is better, probably more so than your average human. Volpi and I sometimes trained with blindfolds, just to keep that skill in practice.

After a circle around the parking lot and then the building, there was no sign of the remaining vamp, and I returned to Volpi's. I rapped twice on the door with the butt of the machete.

"It's gone," I said after Izzy opened the door. I rehung the knife back on the wall and turned toward the couch where Volpi stitched up a semi-naked Marlowe.

He watched me approach, flickers of pain reflecting in the dark amber of his eyes. His pale skin was covered in blood, and some had dripped onto the bath towel he was lying on. There was another towel over his hips. Strong thighs and calves were bare, and they stretched over the length of the couch. His clothes were nowhere to be seen.

Volpi, his reading glasses on, bent over Marlowe's flank, an adjustable lamp shining light on his work. Marlowe's blood-stained fingers swept toward me as he kept his breathing steady. I sat on the coffee table beside Volpi and took Marlowe's hand. His fingers were warm and strong.

"How serious?" I asked Volpi, deliberately avoiding Marlowe's eyes.

"Not bad. Deep, but nothing vital." Volpi looked at me over his glasses. "That was a thirteenth-century ceremonial knife you took with you. You didn't get blood on it, did you?"

"Vamp was gone, so no." I rolled my eyes. Marlowe smiled at the gesture.

Volpi turned back to him. "How do you feel? Weak, light-headed? Tell me if you're going to pass out."

"I assure thee, Master Volpi, I am alert to every pass of thine needle. My heart gladdens at the sight of thee. How fortuitous, you are here, dearest Tamberlyn." His glance flickered over me again. "Thine beauty is a balm to my weary heart." A poet's heart, apparently.

I said nothing as Volpi finished up, clipping the sutures and tossing the wads of bloody gauze into a small metal dish. He stood and threw the contents into the fire burning in a tiny antique woodstove. Izzy brought a small pan of warm water and set it in the space Volpi had just vacated. She covered Marlowe's legs with a blanket and looked at me.

"Do you want me to—" She handed me a cloth before I could answer. "There's antibacterial solution, too. I've put your clothes to soak in the tub, Marlowe. I will transfer them to the washer in a bit."

"Much gratitude, Mistress Isabelle. Your kindness is as always a beacon."

I turned my teenage expression of exasperation toward Marlowe as Izzy left us.

"Your kindness is a beacon?" I couldn't help but tease him. He was always so serious when he first got to the modern world. I wiped at his abdomen with the wet face cloth, scrubbing at a spot of dried blood. He didn't gasp, but the muscles tensed under his skin. "Sorry," I said and applied the antiseptic solution. "Let that dry, and I'll cover it with a dressing."

"Thank you," he said, reaching for my hand again. I took it and set about cleaning his bloodied fingers in the warm water.

"When did you get here?" I asked.

"At moon rise. Master Volpi lives a very long way across town. I'd run into our creatures of the night several streets over. I killed the first straight off. The other evaded me until I gave up the search. I'm afraid he picked up my trail not too far from here."

"He probably scented the blood. You were wounded and went after the other one anyway?" I scolded.

"I did not want to bring danger to Angelo's house. To my friends. Or to you."

I looked at him. He was more than handsome, his jawline and cheekbones cutting more angles than his well-known portrait gave him credit for. His dark brown hair was longer, wavy and thick, falling an inch below his trimmed beard. There were light lines around the corners of his eyes—eyes that could change from deep brown to light hazel depending on his mood or the light. The laugh lines were new. He looked pale, but that could be from loss of blood rather than lack of sunlight.

His words burned inside of me, his concern for all of us, obvious. Yet all of us weren't here. My former worry over Marlowe faded against the still-fresh pain of X's death.

"Because God forbid anyone should get hurt because of you. Or die even because of your sense of the bloody fucking timeline." My voice rose with the last words. I hadn't meant it to, but it did.

His eyes closed. "Xavier," he whispered. "It has happened, then."

I heard Volpi behind me. "A drink, Marlowe." He set a tumbler of amber liquid on the coffee table.

I left, taking the bowl of bloody water and antiseptic with me. Izzy was putting Marlowe's clothes in the washer as I dumped the water in the sink. "You could give the guy a break, Tam," she chided.

I stood at the sink, turning toward the washer/dryer unit at the far end of the galley kitchen. "Why are you using that machine?" I asked, indicating the washer.

She frowned at me. "Because his clothes are bloody and filthy."

"But why use the machine? Less work right? It's a tool that makes the task easier, more efficient." I flicked my hand back toward the couch. "He had a tool at his disposal to prevent someone from dying. And he didn't use it. He fucking stood there and didn't use it. Tell Connie and her kids to give him a break." I sighed. Behind me, I could hear the murmur of Volpi and Marlowe's voices, but they'd stopped when I mentioned Connie's name.

I moved closer and pulled the washer knob under Izzy's stilled hand. "I know he isn't directly responsible. It was Munson who shot X. But he knew, Iz. He knew it, and he lied to me, essentially." And that was the rub, wasn't it? I had put my trust in someone who put his duty above trusting me—above me entirely. It was something when I allowed someone to get that close. I didn't trust easily. At seventeen, I'd fallen in love and trusted a man who turned out to be an elf with ulterior motives. Now, I'd done the same with a knightly poet. I was probably angrier with myself than Marlowe, but he was a good representative.

"Come sit down. Hear him out at least." Izzy pulled me back to the sitting area. I didn't sit on the couch, even though Marlowe was sitting up by this time. I pulled an old rocker out from its place against the radiator and placed it equidistant between Marlowe and Volpi's chair.

Izzy lit on the ottoman at Volpi's feet and leaned back between his knees, his hand resting on her shoulder. Marlowe's mouth flickered only a moment, but I could tell he was pleased to see them so close. His eyes shifted wistfully to me. I looked away.

"Do you think vampires are the reason you are here?" Volpi asked.

"Mayhaps," Marlowe replied. He shifted on the couch, tucking the blanket around his hips to cover himself and pulling a second throw over his shoulders, wincing slightly as he did so. "They did not follow me through this time." He looked at me again. He spoke of the ancient creature from his last visit. "When was I here last? What is the date?" he asked, his voice tired but resolute. I knew he didn't want to bring up X again, or what had happened the last time he'd been here, but he needed to know where in the timeline he'd landed.

"Six months," I answered. "It's been six months since your last visit." Half a year since he'd held me, since anyone had held me for that matter. Each time Marlowe arrived we became closer. Our time together felt like a whole life lived in a few days, with long spans of total uncertainty in between.

His expression fell into resignation. I'd thought he looked different because he was in pain as Volpi stitched him up, but it was age. He had aged since I'd seen him last. Been through hell and back was more like it.

"Marlowe, How long has it been? For you?" The date of his death loomed in my mind. The date he refused to hear about. According to history, he'd been barely twenty-nine when he died. My heart skipped around in my chest. He wouldn't want to know—no knowledge of the future, no messing with destiny, the sacred duty must be fulfilled, yada, yada.

I wasn't kidding about the knight thing. Marlowe took his abilities very seriously. He was a damned hero. Smart, strong, noble to the fucking nth degree, all those things one could fall in love with. Except that none of them made for someone who would do anything and everything to be with the one they loved. He loved me. I knew that as surely as my own name. Yet this would not change his view of the world or his destiny. He would make me fall in love with him all over again, we'd laugh, fight, make love, and we'd save people and kill hostiles. Then he would go, taking whatever was left of me with him. And I would be here, just a shell of Tamberlyn Paradiso, stuck in a solitary life.

"A fair amount of time has passed for me. Six years." He sighed, the weariness seeping into his entire body. Traveling takes a lot of energy. Fighting vampires and bleeding out on the sidewalk does too. "It has been a very long journey to get back."

Six years. My heart got in the way of my math skills for a moment—to be without him for six years was unthinkable. I'd waited two years once, and it was hell.

"What year?" I asked, trying to keep my voice steady.

"Year of our Lord, 1593." Came the answer.

I breathed again. May of 1593 was the date etched into my mind. I couldn't stop it. He would do nothing to prevent it. And at most, it was only months away.

"You should rest, my friend. We will talk more in the morning," Volpi said. He looked at me and his unruly brows came together to urge me forward. To get my stubborn butt out of the chair and go to Marlowe. He and Izzy rose from the chair and ottoman as one and left us alone.

I moved to sit on the edge of the couch, careful not to nudge his injured side, and pushed at his shoulder to get him to lie back. He did, and his hand came around my neck to pull me down with him. I leaned forward, our foreheads together.

"I'm still mad at you," I said.

His lips twitched. "I know."

I kissed him, lightly. His full lips were both familiar and strange as they moved under my own. I pulled away before it went further. The magnetic pull of him was the same as if I'd seen him yesterday. Brushing his hair away from his forehead, I sat up and pulled the blanket up over him. There were shadows under his eyes, the fair skin translucent. Long dark lashes closed against it. I touched him again, in that space between neck and shoulder, feeling the corded muscle from long years of sword wielding. He smiled at the touch, relaxed further, and fell into sleep.

Izzy had found some sweat pants and a T-shirt and placed the folded clothes on the coffee table. I got up quietly, thinking of Marlowe walking around naked in Volpi's apartment before he noticed the clothes. Modesty was not a trait in Marlowe's repertoire.

I headed toward the door.

"You're leaving?" Izzy asked.

"I have work in the morning." I avoided my sister's eyes. I also had a vampire to hunt, but I didn't mention that.

"So just like that? He's here and he's hurt and this time …this time we have a real chance. He could stay, for more than just a moon phase. He's what now, twenty-nine? You know he—"

"Don't." I stopped her. If we did our jobs, if we didn't interfere in the timeline, when he left this time—and he would leave, I knew this—I would never see him again.

Izzy stopped, her gray eyes shining and serious. The emotional sympathy poured from her to me like a slog of honey. "We're so close. All of that could be possible now." Her tone changed from empathy to disapproval. "And you have work in the morning."

I smiled. This was our normal. "I'll be back," I said in my really bad Terminator voice.

"Great. You're joking. He's finally back and you—"

I closed the door on her words. The heaviness of it muffled the rest of whatever lesson in compassion I was destined to get. That was me. Closing doors on destiny wherever I could.

Chapter 7

Tamberlyn

A good thing about my cop partner, Cobb, was he never felt the need for inane conversation. The two-hour drive to Harrisburg gave me time to go over how I really felt about seeing Marlowe again. The idea that it had been six years since he'd been here was heartbreaking. Every time Marlowe traveled, the possibility of landing in my city and my timeline was there. Scarce, but a possibility. He only traveled to places he had a connection to—Philadelphia and various places around London. As for Philly? Well, we didn't know what anchored him here. He'd told me once that I was his anchor, even before we met. He was a bit of a romantic that way.

Just when my heart would feel for him, the memory of X's death and Marlowe's secrecy about it came back to me. X was right. Being a cop was a dangerous business. But so was hunting hostiles, and I did both, so why was I still kicking and Hernandez a ghost? Was that just the luck of the draw? Of all the things I believed in, luck wasn't one of them. Fate wasn't either. Our lives were a series of choices, decisions that put us on one path or another. X chose to be a cop. I chose to keep my other life a secret from him.

X had just been in the wrong place at the wrong time—in between a bullet and me, actually. As soon as he died, Izzy knew that it had happened before, just in a different way. She told me that Marlowe had tried to prevent his death, keeping us out of the club where X died the first time. He'd tried to keep X from the warehouse too. But through it all, he'd never told me. Not one word.

Only Marlowe remembered the original time line when we'd first met—for us, it hadn't happened yet. If I had known about Munson, the cop on the take, I'd have taken different steps. Just like if I had known Theo was fae, I wouldn't have fallen so hard for him ...maybe.

One thing I did know for sure, is that I hated being kept in the dark. Volpi said that Maurelle took my memories in order to protect me from the fae. Marlowe kept things from me to protect the timeline and me, so he said. Goddamned fae and time travelers. You couldn't trust anybody these days.

I must have made some kind of derisive noise or said something out loud because Cobb looked over from the driver's seat.

"What the hell has got you in a snit?" he asked.

"Just the case," I lied. Lying about my thoughts was second nature by now. "The more I think about it, the more I think it's not the intern. Ziggy found that the fruit basket had been tainted. I think the poison was meant for the senator. Who wants to kill a young intern with no enemies, no real political ties? She wasn't sleeping with the senator, was she?"

"Not that we know of."

"We have a serious lack of motive, here."

Cobb said nothing. His dark eyes focused on the traffic ahead. In the passing lane since Philly, he drove a good twelve miles over the limit, passing on the right if necessary and with less irritation than I would have had. X had always been an overly cautious driver. I was the road rage cliché. Cobb's driving was academy textbook perfect. We'd be in Harrisburg in a matter of minutes. I leaned over to turn down the radio, some uptown funk playing too loud for my brain. A scent wafted over from him, a heady mix of spice and earth. He smelled really good. I'd been riding shotgun with Cobb for over five months now and had never noticed his scent.

"Are you wearing cologne?" I asked, not bothering to keep the accusing tone out of my voice. At first glance, my partner may look like an oversized drug dealer with his long hair and permanent scowl, but today the locks were pulled back neatly from his face and his button-down shirt and trousers were pristine.

Cobb had been undercover in Pittsburg for four years. He'd lived the life of crack dealers and pimps before breaking a big case and moving to homicide, but he couldn't take Pittsburg anymore and had applied for a transfer to our district.

"Are you seriously asking me that?" His tone was irritated, but I caught a note of something else. Apprehension? Nerves? I looked at him sharply. He faced forward, eyes on the road. It was a bold profile, large nose, strong chin outlined by a goatee.

"Never mind," I said. "Which do you want? The girl's friends or the senator?"

We talked interview strategy for the next couple of exits and he dropped me at our victim's apartment.

I spent the next hour or two talking to roommates, professors, and her former employer at a coffee shop. The picture I got was of a typical, bright college girl who worked hard, wasn't a partyer, and had ambitions of a job on the political scene. Marcy Jackson had wanted to save the world, instead, she'd eaten the wrong piece of fruit, and it killed her.

As I sat at the corner table in Marcy's former place of employment, I compiled my notes on a tablet. It was a similar establishment to where my sister worked back in Philly. Just one of her part-time jobs.

Izzy had wanted to be a teacher—math or science or something. Because of my vocation as a hunter, she'd added romance languages to her already heavy post-grad schedule. She worked part-time slinging coffee in the mornings and draft beer on the weekends. Classes at the university had taken a back seat to lessons with Volpi and working with me. Izzy also wanted to save the world. I had long since given up on the idea. I just wanted to save young impressionable folks like Izzy and Marcy.

I texted my sister to see how things were going. It wasn't about Marlowe, it wasn't. Rather than texting me back like a good sister, she called.

"Hey." Her voice was breathless like she'd been running.

"Where are you?"

"Just getting back to Ange's." Ange? I cringed. He'd always been Volpi to me. I hadn't even known his full first name until our conversation with Maurelle. Only my sister would nickname the dark lord of grumpiness. "I ran out to get some more suitable clothes for Marlowe. He's rather tall, isn't he?" she asked.

It wasn't really a question, because the answer was no, Marlowe was just under six feet, so more average than tall, but compared to Volpi, who was a spare five foot nine, I guessed she would think of him as such. And modern clothes were a necessity. The typical sixteenth-century couture of ballooned pantaloons and flowy shirts would only serve to make him stand out.

I'd been about to mention that I kept clothes in his size in the bottom drawer of my bureau, but I held back. I'd have to hear Izzy's sigh of sweetness at the gesture. "So I, ah—" She paused, and I could hear the rustling of plastic shopping bags and the door to the loft being opened. "Hi," she said, apparently to someone else. "I've got you some clothes and I guess the shirt didn't fit?" From which I surmised two things, one she was talking to Marlowe and two, he was shirtless, or naked. I waited a few minutes more, listening as he thanked her and eventually she came back to our conversation. "You were right." She spoke in an undertone. "He's not into clothes all that much."

I laughed. "Was he wearing any?"

"Boxers," she said, her embarrassment obvious. "Black with hearts. A valentine present for Ange last year."

I pictured Marlowe walking around Volpi's apartment with heart spattered underwear. Imagining all of his pale skin marked with the occasional scar, his broad shoulders, incredible abs, and muscled thighs flexing as he paced. It wasn't a bad picture. Not one that I necessarily wanted my sister to see, but still.

"He's better then?" I asked.

"Yes, he seems to heal fast." She stopped as Volpi said something in the background. "Um, will Marlowe be staying at your place tonight? Apparently, he used up all the hot water this morning."

"We'll see. I'm in Harrisburg at the moment. In fact, I should get back to Cobb. He's probably pissed off everyone in the senator's office by now. I just texted to check in."

"He's fine, Tam. He did wonder where you were this morning. I had to tell him you'd left last night."

I ignored the chiding comment. "I'll see you when I get back, and Iz? Let's not tell him about the portal just yet." I'd still have some time to convince her the risk was too great.

"Too late," she said. "He and Ange have been discussing it all morning. He's anxious to get to work."

A text from Cobb came in before I could protest further. "I got to go. Please don't do anything until I see you tonight. Okay?"

She agreed, and I found myself a cab to head to the senator's office.

∞

Upstairs in the seven-story North Office Building, situated behind the Capitol and overlooking the East Wing, I found Cobb jotting down notes the old fashioned way, in a spiral-bound notepad. He looked up as I opened the door to the anteroom just outside the senator's office.

There were two desks, both of them manned by young whipcord professionals with hipster haircuts and earbuds. The admins talked into space and neither looked at me as I entered. A flat screen on the wall, permanently tuned to CNN was flashing news of the day, including a small inset picture of Marcy Jackson with the accompanying headline: *Senator Shepherd's intern found dead in Philadelphia hotel room.* Several leather chairs sat unoccupied under the TV and there was a fancy coffee machine in one corner.

Cobb's tall frame dominated the large window, obscuring a nice view of the Capitol dome. Not that the two hipsters were listening, but I walked over to him so we could confer in relative privacy.

"You've been waiting all this time?"

"No, I spoke to the senator. Got his statement and a timeline." He tapped his notebook. "You find anything on her?"

I shook my head. "No, pretty normal. Hard-working, well-liked, no boyfriend, too busy with school and work for very much socializing."

"Like we thought. No motive."

"Certainly nothing that would inspire death by hemlock." I glanced around. "You get a take on the staff?"

Cobb deepened the semi-permanent scowl. "Some, nothing noteworthy. Apparently, the senator has ambitions to run for governor and hired a big-shot campaign guy out of New York, name of Locran Theopolis. He handles almost all the contact with the staff and was supposed to go to Philly with the senator, but didn't." He gestured away from his notebook toward the closed door. "He's in with the senator now."

As if on cue at Cobb's words, the door opened, and several people exited the senator's office. Two women with bun hair and iPads walked out ahead of two men in suits and glasses, all talking, some to each other, and some on phones. Cobb spoke up.

"Mr. Theopolis, Philadelphia PD, could we have a word?" Cobb had his badge out, front and center. I turned as he spoke to the taller of the men.

Dark blond, almost brown hair, classic features, strong jawline, and very familiar eyes—dark, piercing and looking at me with a shocked expression. Hidden behind Clark Kent glasses, they were the same. A decade hadn't changed them, or the rest of him all that much. But then what else do you expect of a fae?

Chapter 8

Isabelle

Izzy hung up the phone after Tam's call and was relieved to see Marlowe dressed in the jeans and T-shirt she'd purchased. Except for the occasional item for Angelo, she hadn't shopped for men's clothing since her father died.

For Father's Day, she'd always purchased Dad his favorite Van Heusen shirts, a summer, and a winter—short and long sleeves in white or navy blue. Enzo Paradiso had been a creature of habit. Growing up she remembered him coming home, putting his badge on the table by the door, locking his gun away in the hall closet, and rolling up the cuffs of his dress shirt.

The Father's Day before she passed away, Izzy's mother had driven her to The Toggery, a tiny local department store, and sat in the car while Izzy went in to buy the shirts—the size and type written in her mother's neat handwriting on a crumpled piece of paper. Her mother was thin then, her sparse hair covered by scarves and knit hats. She rarely left the house, except for the doctor and chemo. Izzy had been eleven, and she remembered tears in her father's eyes as he'd opened the present.

Shirts may not have seemed like an awesome gift. Dads of Izzy's friends got golf clubs or fancy ties, but seeing how her dad looked at her mom, with her pale face enveloped in an enormous flowered scarf, Izzy knew it had been the perfect present.

"When your father first made detective, you were only two," Grace Paradiso had said from her usual half-recline in Enzo's recliner. She'd hated being in bed—it was too hard on her back, so she'd taken to sleeping in his chair in the living room. "We had just moved and were broke half the time. So the only present I could afford was a shirt from the thrift shop. A Van Heusen, a pristine white for his first day out of uniform."

Cancer had taken her strong melodic voice and crumpled it to a wavering crackle, but she forged ahead. "What I didn't see was a moth hole in the back. It was summertime, but your father had to keep his jacket on all day so it wouldn't show." The woman's tremulous smile shone through her illness. "He still said it was the best present ever."

Izzy's father placed a hand on his wife's shoulder, giving it a fond squeeze. "It was the hottest June on record that year. And it *was* the best present ever."

Tam had not remembered the holiday, and at the last minute, she'd given their father a Bic lighter and a crime novel she'd picked up at the convenience store.

Years later, Izzy and her grandmother had been the ones to go through Enzo's closet after the funeral and give all those Father's Day shirts to Goodwill. Tam, like usual, had been working a case and totally used it as an excuse not to involve herself. Much like she had with Marlowe the night before.

Izzy glanced at the finally clothed Marlowe, noting the jeans she'd picked out fit a little too well, but at least he had pants. Not that she minded seeing a well-built, half-naked male from time to time, but he was her sister's boyfriend. She winced at the word. Tam would too. Boyfriend was inadequate to explain the relationship between Marlowe and Tam.

For one thing, no one could call Marlowe a boy, not even when they'd first met him and he'd scarcely been older than herself. At twenty-four, Izzy didn't think of herself as full-grown at all. But for someone from 1587, that was well into adulthood. Now, he and Tam were into their late twenties, the odd circumstance of time travel allowing him to catch up with Tam in age.

Izzy had learned enough of her sister's mannerisms and expressions to know she was completely in love with the traveling poet. The relationship was life or death, the man literally crossing the ages for her, and far too intense to ever be called boyfriend and girlfriend. Marlowe was at the windows and out of ear shot.

"Iz?" Angelo spoke with quiet concern. "You okay?"

"Yeah, I'm fine. Just thinking."

He pulled her close to him as he stood in the kitchen. Kissing her temple, he asked what was on her mind. She could never keep secrets from him, and it had been a long while since she'd wanted to.

"You remember the art gallery? When we went to Shawn's showing?" Angelo wasn't a socializer, not at all, but he could be charming when he needed to, occasionally having drinks with her friends. She remembered the first time she'd convinced him to go to an art show downtown. They'd gone and mingled, and Volpi had drunk white wine and told funny stories. He'd looked amazing in his black T-shirt and blazer, and she'd told him so. In fact, they'd flirted with each other until the end of the evening, when he'd followed her into the restroom and had sex with her in one of the stalls. It was the most dangerous thing Izzy had ever done.

"That was an interesting night." His voice low, seductive, and she felt the hair on her arms raise up. He could always do that to her—it had nothing to do with his dark arts abilities. She and Angelo had their own complications, but nothing that wasn't insurmountable. Not like her sister.

"Why haven't you told me about Maurelle before yesterday?" Izzy asked.

He shrugged and poured coffee into a mug that proclaimed *Lizards are awesome,* with a picture of a gecko under it. Except the *L* in lizard had been crossed out and a *W* put in its place. Marlowe approached the counter and took the cup Volpi handed to him. He smiled at the logo and drank gratefully. "It never came up," Volpi said and turned to Marlowe, "Breakfast?" Marlowe, still not fully awake and relishing the exotic taste of breakfast blend, broke into a grin.

The small kitchen had little room for more than one cook, so Izzy came around to sit next to Marlowe as Volpi prepared breakfast. He talked as he fetched eggs from the fridge.

"I was very young, barely twenty." He glanced at the two twenty-somethings before him. "For me, twenty was very young, and I'd gone to a music festival in Paris. Wes Montgomery played, and his songs transformed everything I thought I knew about music. I fell in love with jazz. He was a phenomenal guitarist, completely self-taught."

"I know this term—jazz. It's a jumble of notes, with no apparent order to it at all," Marlowe said. "But it's captivating. It's primal in its way, like a living thing. How extraordinary."

Volpi inclined his head toward Marlowe. "Of course you would describe jazz with a poetic accuracy."

"And Maurelle?" Izzy reminded him.

"Maurelle came later. I met her at a jazz club." He gazed off in memory. "Her appearance was much different back then— young, exotic, captivating. I made a bet with my buddies that I could get her number."

Izzy chuckled. Volpi was charming to a fault, and he loved women, all women. It had always seemed strange that Tam had never felt or known this about him. In fact, their somewhat stilted gruff relationship was an anomaly to Izzy.

"By her number, you mean—" Marlowe held out his mug for

more coffee. Volpi poured.

"I left the club with her. At some point, she told me who she really was—a being of the Tessaerat clan, and demonstrated one of her abilities by levitating coffee cups from her kitchen to the bedroom." He paused. "For the first time in my life, I didn't feel like an outsider."

"Tessaerat clan. I've heard of this before, from Master Gomfrey. Though I did not know they still existed in this world." Marlowe spoke and then looking to the skillet of eggs and ham scramble, his chin gestured outward. "That's fair cooked, my friend." Volpi dished half of the skillet's contents on a plate for Marlowe and offered the balance to Izzy. She declined, saying she'd had her yogurt and granola earlier.

Marlowe looked positively horrified, commenting on her choice of oats and sour milk for breakfast. He dug into his own meal with the relish of a starving artist. His mouth full, he continued. "I have never met such a being. And you apprenticed under one? Are they as powerful as reputed?"

"You may meet her and see for yourself," Volpi answered and after looking at Marlowe's almost empty plate, spooned the balance of the ham and eggs onto it. "We're to go back to Pinkie's tonight to see her. She says the portal will be more conducive to traveling."

"It works on the lunar cycle as well then." Marlowe surmised.

"Yes, and with a little help from Maurelle, we should be able to get to the ancients and back again without much trouble," Izzy said.

"Does Tamberlyn know of this plan?"

Izzy sighed. "Of course, and of course, she's against it. But it's been a long time, and I know so much more now. I can control the situation better. And now with you here, we can put all our work into practice."

Volpi studied her, saying nothing. She'd expected a protest, or at least a lecture about her safety.

"I appreciate thine efforts, my friends. Alas, I cannot allow you to risk your lives for a possible solution to my problem. I've dealt with the unpredictability of my travels thus far and have survived. Mayhap it is best. Tamberlyn's abhorrence for me is obvious." Marlowe pushed his plate away and grabbed a napkin to clean his mouth and beard with rough strokes.

"Tam is angry. But she has missed you." Izzy put a reassuring hand on his arm. "She's been lonely. I know my sister, know when she's hurting. Xavier's death was very difficult to accept. And as you know—" Her lips twitched in a rueful smile. "Tam has this invincibility complex. Knowing that it happened twice and she was unable to prevent it is even more difficult."

"She knows about my recurring visit then?" Marlowe asked.

Izzy cocked her head. "You told us about being here before. The last time." She frowned. "Maybe, I just remember it that way. It's all muddled. I can sometimes feel the differences in the timelines. But often I can't tell what is real and what isn't. And I told Tam that X had died before, the first time you came here. I didn't mean to make things worse, but..."

"Tam's a big girl. She knows the truth," Volpi said. "It's not Marlowe's fault that Hernandez died. Her grief at the loss of not only him, but you, Marlowe, is ruling her thoughts right now. She will come around. Don't forget, it's only been a short time for us—a few months since everything happened."

Marlowe moved with care from the stool and walked to the windows, lifting his face to the sun streaming in. Barefoot and in modern clothes, he looked impossibly young and vulnerable.

A knock at the door interrupted Izzy's notion to comfort him. Angelo let Ziggy into the loft. Dressed in her customary head-to-toe black, she carried a brown leather satchel.

"Tam asked me to check on him." She spoke as she hugged Izzy. Her gaze took in the room, and she gave a brief nod to Volpi before walking toward Marlowe at the windows.

Marlowe turned, sweeping into a bow, with only a slight cringe at the pain in his side.

"Mistress Jane," he said as a smile transformed his face.

Ziggy set the bag on the couch and hugged him gently. She leaned back to see him in the light, and Izzy noted her veiled expression.

"Tam said you were hurt. Let's check on that wound, shall we?" She led the traveler to the couch.

"I assure you, I am quite well. Master Volpi and Isabelle have taken excellent care." He let her guide him to better light and lifted his shirt so she could view his stitches.

"It looks pretty deep, but the wound barely cuts into the muscle. The peritoneum wasn't affected. You heal very fast." She glanced at his face. "That wound looks four or five days old, not just a day."

Marlowe let the shirt down over the bandage. "I have a strong constitution." He smiled at her. "'Tis good to see you again, Mistress—" Ziggy gave him a look. "It's good to see you, Jane." He amended his words.

"Same here, buddy," she said. Ziggy moved to accept a cup of coffee from Volpi. "Nice work on the stitches. Warrior constitution? The healing, I mean."

Volpi shrugged. "Tam does the same thing. She heals maybe twice as fast as most people. It seems to increase with her age strangely enough."

From her place at the counter, Izzy heard the exchange, admiring the casualness of how they talked about Tam's and Marlowe's abilities. As if they were completely normal.

Ziggy was a scientist, yet she took things like wraiths, monsters, and supernatural healing abilities in her stride. Izzy had adjusted to the supernatural, but she was still awed by her sister's abilities and her own emerging ones.

It was like watching a movie and identifying with the main characters, even liking them, and then suddenly finding out they are you. Sometimes, she still had to convince herself it was real. That she and her sister were the descendants of two of the legendary three families.

The Legend with a capital L was like something out of a

Disney movie. The sword and the charm, partners destined to fight evil and put history on the correct path. Ordinary people with genetic traits stemming from ancient family trees.

One trait allowed—or caused in Marlowe's case—them to traverse centuries in the blink of an eye. Another gave them the kinesthetic intelligence to survive and win a fight with something larger, stronger, or faster than they were. Or the mental ability to see when things were just not right. It wasn't precognitive. Izzy wasn't clairvoyant, but she possessed a hyper intuition of wrongness and what to do to fix it.

Tam had the same muscle memory and quickness that Marlowe had, and her speed-healing revealed another similar trait. It was only a matter of time before she started traveling too. The thought only reinforced Izzy's determination to find the last piece of the formula.

"More coffee, Zig?" she asked. Ziggy was well known for her love of the stuff, and soon they were gathered in the living room, coffee in hand as Marlowe relayed tales of his travels. He told them with relish, trying to make them sound adventurous and fun, but to Izzy, it sounded like a lot of dangerous hard work.

She felt the wave of pain and fatigue coming off him and knew he needed less talking and more rest. Volpi was into another question about 1900's London when she put a hand on his arm. He glanced at her, and after a fraction of a second, he realized how much of a toll the conversation was taking on his friend.

"Marlowe, I apologize, but I need to check in at my shop for supplies. Can we table this conversation till later?" Volpi stood, and Izzy and Ziggy moved with him.

"I need to go too," she said. "And you should rest. Tam will be back tonight, and we'll go to the portal."

He protested about not needing rest, but Ziggy pulled the doctor card and agreed with her. They left him on the couch, and once outside the door, they conferred in the hallway.

"That poor man," Ziggy said. "Six years. He looks like he's

aged ten since I've seen him."

"He's been through a lot," Izzy agreed. "And all he wants is to be here with Tam. She's still being pissy about it."

"They're working a big case. It's not like she has a lot of time." Ziggy defended her friend.

"There's always a case. My sister needs to realize how little time Marlowe has here."

"Unless we can fix it," Angelo said, running his hand through his hair.

Chapter 9

Tamberlyn

Theo. My first love was as good-looking as I'd remembered, but every hair on my body stood on high alert. Adrenaline shot through me, and instinct had me pulling the gun from my holster. Fortunately, Cobb reacted, stepping in front of me, his hand forcing mine back down under my jacket.

"What the fuck, Paradiso?" He hissed at me.

"Trust me," I said. Though if I'd shot Theo, which is exactly what I would have done if Cobb had let me, I had no idea how I would explain my actions.

Theo backed up like a giant spider was after him. Which was the opposite reaction of a fae warrior, but it pleased me no end that he was afraid of me.

"Are you armed?" Cobb asked him, getting ready to pull his own gun.

"No." Theo's empty hands raised, his eyes on me as he addressed Cobb. "Please, I can explain, officer."

"Detective Cobb. I'm assuming you know Detective Paradiso." After a glance at me to assure himself no one was getting shot, at least in the next minute, Cobb turned fully toward Theo. "Suppose you explain why my partner wants to shoot you."

"Tam and I knew each other a while ago," he said.

I stepped out from behind Cobb. "I can speak for myself, asshole." I gritted my teeth and glared at Theo, not knowing where all this rage came from, but it was boiling out of me. I felt both strangely attracted, yet murderous at the same time. "What the hell are you doing here?" I asked.

Theo lowered his hands in slow motion. He glanced at Cobb who, now that my gun was holstered, shrugged unhelpfully. "Detective, could you give us a minute?" he asked.

"No. We have questions regarding the murder of Marcy Jackson. If you'd like us to ask them here, we can do that." The hipster receptionists were off their phones and staring at us.

"Let's go to my office." He turned and led us down a short hall to another door. On the way, I tried to find a reason for his sudden cooperation. He may have been startled to see me, but he was of the fae—powerful enough to snap his fingers and break my neck. Or crafty enough to illusion himself out of sight at the appearance of danger, or precog enough to know we would meet. Yet he had done nothing but stand there as I tried to shoot him.

Maybe he thought he deserved it. I was sure he deserved it. I had no actual recall of what he'd done to me, or how we'd broken off our relationship, but I felt betrayed nonetheless. And I remembered all too well how Theo was at the beginning of that summer, if not at the end.

We stepped into his small but elegant office. A walnut desk put his back against the brocade-bordered windows, which gave the room a heavy emerald hue. Two deep-cushioned chairs sat in front of his desk, and we settled in as he moved to sit in the leather office chair on the other side.

I had a million questions, but none really about the case so I nodded to my partner, and he took the lead. Cobb asked the standard questions like how long had he known the victim? Did she have any enemies? Was there any trouble with co-workers? After our rocky start, the interview moved swiftly and professionally, and I was grateful for my partner's expertise.

"Mr. Theopolis, can you tell me who on your staff knew about the senator's trip to Philadelphia?" Cobb leaned forward in the chair, indicating he was almost finished.

Theo's well-formed eyebrows crinkled for a moment. "The senator's secretary, of course. She would have made the travel arrangements. Our publicity coordinator, myself, Marcy Jackson, and I guess all three interns. They all wanted to go, but we picked Marcy because she was the most dedicated." He wrote on a notepad as he spoke, as though he'd be doing some checking on his own. "Do you think Shepherd is in danger?"

"Possibly," I spoke for the first time. "We can't find a motive for anyone wanting to hurt Marcy, but Shepherd has enemies."

"Like any politician. But he is a good man, well-liked, honest. If anyone wanted to stop his policies, wouldn't they be sabotaging his campaign? Murder seems a little extreme."

"Maybe it's you. Did you and Senator Shepherd have an argument, perhaps? Was he going to fire you? Expose you?" My tone snapped back to its previous suspicion.

His confused expression turned to indignation in a heartbeat. "The senator and I have a good rapport. I wasn't even on this trip. And no, he wasn't going to expose me. He has no knowledge of..." He glanced at Cobb. "My former occupation."

"Former?" Cobb asked. "Who did you work for previously?"

"I was in New York, a political consultant for a business group. New York politics is a rough business. The more successful you are, the more enemies you make. Is there anything else?" Theo managed an impatient tone, and his intercom buzzed as if on cue. He pressed the button. "I'll be right there, Mary." He rose from behind the desk. "I have another meeting."

We both rose at the same time, and Cobb snapped his notebook shut. "Don't leave the state. We may have follow-up questions."

"The senator and I plan to be in your area tomorrow anyway. We have some more fundraising to do. Ask Mary to give you my contact info." He looked at me again. "If you want to talk further."

"Cobb, give us a minute, okay?" I asked him, and after a scowl, he left me in the office with Theo.

I stood with my hand on the doorknob. "What are you doing here?"

"I'm here because of Shepherd. He's going to be governor."

"Not in this job, but here. In this world." God, he was so annoying. How did I not remember this?

"Oh." He glanced at the floor, but only a second. He took off his glasses, and his dark eyes pinned me where I stood. I'd forgotten so much about him, and the memories rushed toward me. A speeding train of lust, hope, and innocence. "How did you know? Who I am, or rather, was." His tone was gentle, soft and this created more nostalgia than I wanted to feel. At my frowned silence he went on. "I'm not of the fae anymore." His voice lowered as he rubbed the bridge of his nose. "I haven't been for a long time. I'm of your world now. Believe me, I'm simply making my way."

I pressed him. "Making your way in my world? I thought that was against the rules. I can't help but think you're involved in this murder somehow."

His handsome features twisted and his eyes grew wide with shock. Trouble was, I had no idea if he was faking it or not. I turned toward the door, irritated that I was even listening to his bullshit. His hand came across my arm, trying to keep me from walking away.

"Tam, wait."

I jerked out of his reach and thrust my other hand out, hoping to straight-arm him in the chest. He reacted quickly enough that I missed him, but I breathed easier as he'd stepped out of my space.

"What does that mean? Not of the fae? You must have really pissed your people off."

He jammed his hands into the pockets of his trousers. I suppressed a smile, it was a gesture he'd used often. "You well know what brought me to this fate." His tone was mournful. And serious. When I said nothing, he looked at me as if I'd lost my mind. Maybe I had. "Oberon be damned, you've forgotten. My entire future ruined because of a mortal, and you can't even remember."

"The Tessaerat." As if that explained everything. It would have to because I didn't want to be there any longer. His brows came together, his eyes squinting as if to catch me in a lie. I stood my ground and stared back.

He took a breath. "I was—never mind. I sense that you wouldn't believe me anyway."

This made me curious, but not enough to admit it.

"Hey, I didn't ask you to drag me into your drama. That was all you." I shifted my feet, clenching my hands at my sides. The longer I stayed in his presence, the more the soft and squishy memories invaded my psyche. I had work to do. And Marlowe. I didn't need whatever Locran Theopolis aka Theo North aka fae douchebag was selling. "Cobb will be in touch." I exited the office with as much dignity as I could muster, forcing myself to slow down as I traversed the short hallway back to the entrance.

∞

"You want to tell me what that was all about?" Cobb asked on the way home.

"Not really," I said. He grumbled. Cobb often grumbled, small inconsequential noises that had a variety of meanings I have never discerned. After the first month, I got used to him. "I knew him as Theo—haven't seen him in ten, no, eleven years."

"And you wanted to shoot him? For what? Keeping you out

past curfew?"

"I overreacted okay? Let's just leave it." I turned the radio on, and we rode the rest of the way with the hits of the Seventies filling the car.

I shuffled through the day, typing up the reports of my interviews by rote. All I could think about was the fact that Theo was here. Theo, the ever-loving fae, was back. And I hadn't shot him. Instead, I'd done my job, talking to him like he was just another suspect in a murder case. It was beginning to look like Marcy Jackson was, indeed, an unlucky bystander.

After reading through the full autopsy, viewing more pictures of the scene, and typing up more notes, I gave up and shut down my computer. I could have used someone to talk to. Disappointed that my bestie ghost hadn't shown, I turned the radio on in my car.

I chose to park at Volpi's building and walk around the corner and half a block to Pinkie's bar. I needed answers. The pink neon sign flickered in the evening's low light. Patrons, probably drinking since the bar opened at two, barely glanced at me as I came in.

The bartender, Abraham, a handsome Black man with a shaved head and a diamond stud in his ear looked too polished to be working in such a dive. His white teeth flashed into a smile at me, and I nodded at him as I made my way to the back.

Past the restrooms, the door to the storeroom had a stick-on *Employees Only* sign. *Keeps the riffraff out.* Maurelle's raspy voice came to me so sharply, I stopped, looking around to see if she was behind me. She wasn't, nor was she in her usual spot downstairs. Until last night, the cantankerous woman had never revealed any super powers other than irritating people in a supreme way. I walked back through the bar, stopping to speak to Abraham.

"Paradiso." He smiled again, taking me out of my thoughts long enough to appreciate his looks. Abraham reminded me of Cobb—they were similar in stature, but unlike my partner,

Abraham was cheerful, friendly, and accommodating. Maybe it was the bar-tending job versus police detective, or maybe it was just the lack of hair.

"Hey, Abraham, have you seen Maurelle? I need to speak to her."

He shook his head and drew a beer from the tap, placing it before me. "On the house, and no, I haven't seen her." He nodded across the room, "Got a few waiting for her, though."

I sipped the beer and looked around. Two guys sat at a table against the wall, sipping beer out of bottles. Knit caps and beards, enough flannel to be Canadian, one had a long pronounced jawline that defied human qualities. He laughed at his companion's joke, and I glimpsed rows of pointed inward-facing teeth, like that of a shark.

Under my jacket, I unsnapped the Glock in my shoulder holster as I turned back to Abraham. He raised one eyebrow and then stepped to the side, his hand settling on a large, serrated Ka-bar knife on the back side of the bar. His tapered brown fingers flowed easily over the blade and handle, but he didn't pick it up. He just wanted me to know he was prepared. As I met his eyes again, the dark irises flashed a fiery amber for just a moment. I blinked. Affable Abraham was something other than human.

I took several swallows of the cold beer. "Things okay here?" I asked. "We're coming back later to meet Maurelle."

"We'll be here," he said, his warm brown eyes back to their friendly non-other state. He smiled again. "Gonna be a busy night, come moonrise."

I thanked him for the beer and walked out, glancing at flannel-clad, shark tooth against the wall.

Not all non-humans needed to be extinguished. Often, they were like refugees from a war-torn country. They just wanted somewhere to live and thrive in relative safety. Still, it was difficult to separate the good from the bad. This was something I worked on.

Volpi had finally driven home the point when he told me of his beginnings, and that some would consider him a non-human. Elongated lifespan, the ability to draw energy from his surroundings, his big brain that he so often showed off—all traits that pushed the evolutionary boundary.

And if I took those differences into account as non-human, I had to face the same facts about myself. My ability to see hostiles, my agility, my sensitive hearing, the healing aspect that had just begun to manifest. All of these traits I'd passed off as just getting better at my job. But there are skill sets and then there are preternatural skill sets.

It had taken a while to reconcile that fact with my former mindset. It had been much easier to just make the monsters disappear. Less guilt, less fuss, just saving the human from hostile. But monsters were everywhere—some even in human form. And the humane were everywhere too—compassion, remorse, and honor were traits not limited to the human race.

I knocked on the metal door at Volpi's, and it opened to reveal a freshly showered, jean-clad, T-shirt wearing Marlowe. His devilish smile still made me catch my breath. He pulled me into the apartment and into his arms, holding me tightly for a moment.

"I hath sorely missed thee." He lapsed into his traditional speak. Marlowe had traveled so much into the future that his language skills and mannerisms adapted quickly, and after a few minutes of conversation, he could immolate the natural cadence and contractions of modern English. I'd also heard him converse in Spanish, Italian, and Latin, as well as grasp complex theoretical physics. Marlowe was no dummy.

I stood back and looked at him—all the long, lean, grace of him, with just a bare hint of a slouch to the left where he'd been wounded.

"You're feeling better," I said, shrugging away from him as he tried to take my coat. I pulled it off and hung it on the coat rack by the door. I walked away, needing to put distance between us as well as movement. I meandered a slow pace in front of the windows. The energy of Pinkie's bar was still with me, and the pent-up anger of seeing Theo had returned.

"Jane saw to me," he said. "I'm fine. Could I offer a beverage?" he reverted to a standard politeness.

"No." As an afterthought. "Thanks. Where's Volpi? I need to talk to him."

"He and Miss Isabelle went on an errand. They should return soon. Come sit down." He was by the couch and holding out his hand, waiting. He was so goddamned patient with me it was irritating. Part of me wanted to slap him, the other part wanted to rip his clothes off. I moved toward the couch and then veered off again to continue walking the floor.

"I can't. I need ...never mind. Where did they go? " I pulled out my phone and texted Izzy. And then Volpi. When thirty seconds went by without a response, I called and left terse voicemails.

Patience is not a virtue. Not for me. Not ever. It's a chore, a torture, a device designed to tamp down all of my anger and frustration—a considerable amount—and compact it to an atom bomb waiting to explode. Marlowe was in the blast radius.

"Fear not, they shall be here soon." He moved away from the couch to lean against the sideboard under the windows. His long legs crossed at the ankle, his arms folded across his chest, he watched as I prowled around the loft space. "Is there something I can do to help?"

"No. This has nothing to do with you."

In our past, I had told him of Theo, or rather a boy that had taken my virginity and broken my heart, because, at the time, that's all he'd been to me. Marlowe had made the memory of that fade into nothingness when we were together. I shot a glance at him now. His lips compressed in pain at my words, or his stitched side, I didn't know which.

"Sorry, but it's a case I'm working and it involves something hostile, maybe, I don't really know. And—damn it." I looked at my blank phone again. "And then there's you. I don't suppose you know why you're here? What needs to be fixed? Or who needs to be saved?" I sounded bitter. Rancid-wine-on-a-hot-day bitter.

"Must I apologize again?" His voice held an edge, his patience finally wearing thin. "I am sorry about Master Hernandez. He was a fine man and my friend as well. But he was not the only person I lost." He stepped in front of me, stopping me in my pace around the apartment. "I lost all of you. Volpi, Isabelle, Miss Jane, my friends. And you most of all, I lost you, Tamberlyn. I'd given up hope of ever seeing you again. Or if I did, you would have forgotten me and moved on." He almost choked on the words, but his anger pushed him through it. "Now, here I am, and you won't even look at me. Look at me, Tam."

His hands came around my arms, his fingers pressing in hard enough to keep me still. I looked at him. The amber dark of his eyes expressed desire, passion, and fury all at the same time. I jerked one shoulder away from him, placed a foot behind his, and pulled him to one side. I blocked the other with my shoulder, and he went down.

"Don't," I said. "I'm too angry to do this right now."

He recovered swiftly and rose to stand in front of me again. Challenging. He stepped back two steps and pulled off his socks. Barefoot on the wood floor, he moved on the balls of his feet, grace and power—a boxer's stance.

"Come then." His hands gestured toward me. "Be angry. Let us work this out. For time is not on our side, Tamberlyn, and I will not waste it. Let us be done with this nonsense."

I almost laughed. "What are you doing? You want to fight? Don't be ridiculous." I looked away.

"A friendly sparring is what's called for, methinks. Unless of course, you are not inclined for a beating." A flash of wicked smile.

"Don't be obvious. Goading me won't work. I'm not going to spar with you."

"You do think I will best you. So be it. I will allow that I've had six years to hone my skills whereas you've barely scratched the surface of a street fight. 'Twould be an unfair—"

I hit him. Hard. Right in that forceful chin. It hurt. But it was a good hurt. I threw myself to one side as his laugh and swing at me came at the same time. The punch missed me by a hair. We circled. Both hunched and ready. I lunged. He parried. We came together in a frenzy. My upper cut knocked his teeth together. His roundhouse clipped my ear, and it stung like hell. A cyclone of adrenaline fired through me. I whirled and side kicked at his knee. He moved away but not far enough, and he went down, rolled, and came back up to broad arm me in the chest.

There is a certain rush in traveling across space not of your own accord. The movement is a rush, landing hard on your ass is not. I used the momentum to somersault over one shoulder. It wasn't pretty, but it got me back on my feet. My boots had little traction on the wood floor, and I lost ground against him.

We fell backward over the coffee table and rolled to the floor beside the couch. Breath rushed out of my lungs in a whumpf as he landed on top of me. All I could see were his eyes and marvel at the length and curl of his lashes before his mouth touched mine. More like crashed against mine. And the fight was over, just like that. We were making out. Madly. And just how romance novel cliché is that?

Except I didn't care. My lips, tongue, hands, and other parts of me didn't give a damn how idyllically corny it looked. It felt amazing. He was here and mine, and that's all I cared about.

I peeled off his shirt and ran my hands across his torso, hesitating over the taped bandage on his side.

"Worry not. I am fine," he murmured into my neck, moving my hand away from the gauze to the small of his back. My fingers dipped just under the waistband of his jeans, and he sat up to unfasten them. I pulled him down again, wanting the feel of him on me. His warmth, his weight.

We'd progressed to the couch and half-undressed before any

kind of common sense came back to me. "Wait," I said between kisses. Ignoring me, his mouth burned a trail from my lips to my neck and back again. "We can't do this here. Iz and Volpi will be back."

It took a moment. Marlowe sighed and propped on his elbows above me.

"I suppose it would be considered rude to make use of Angelo's sleeping quarters?"

"Yes. Very rude." I smiled. God, I had missed him. He was the light to my darkness. Everything felt easier when he was here—my job, my life, hunting monsters. He pulled my random focus into what was really important. I felt like I could breathe again.

He sat up, his naked chest calling me to touch him. I did.

"You have your little house, correct? Not far by vehicle as I recall?" he asked.

I moved my legs out from under him and turned to pull my shirt on. "Yes. It's not far." I stood to fasten my pants and he did the same, both of us pulling on socks and boots in haste. He handed me my pink lace bra. I stuffed it into my jacket pocket, and we stopped to kiss again at the door. It was a long kiss, lingering and warm, and much gentler than our former heated exchange. Still, my body throbbed with desire as he pulled away to reach for his cape. He grabbed his sword in its scabbard. Normally carried in an apparatus worn down the middle of his back to conceal it, he rested the entire contraption in the crook of his arm and pulled the door open.

Izzy was there. Reaching up to press in the warded combination of icons in the door frame. She lowered her hand and smiled.

"Oh good, Tam, you're here. We've got to go. Ange is saving our place in line."

Without another word, she turned around and headed back down the hallway to the outside stairwell. I turned to Marlowe. A lifetime of resignation passed through his features. This was familiar too. A glass partition of a troubled world that often slid between us, keeping us apart. So close and yet so far.

Ahead of us, Izzy was rambling on. Pinkie's was packed full of hostiles. A line. Take a number.

I didn't listen. All I could hear was the soft sound of Marlowe's breath, his footsteps beside me as we descended to the parking lot. Izzy passed my car and kept walking and talking, very excited, as she headed on foot toward the bar.

I stopped, letting her continue as I stood by my car, hesitant, tired, the ebb of passion flowing out of me as I sensed the moment slipping away. Marlowe stood with me, a question in his eyes.

I reached for him, one hand just above his hip on the uninjured side. "Every damned time, this happens. We have to—"

"Save the bloody world?" Marlowe's lips twitched into a smile, but only a brief one. He put his hand over mine where it rested on the door handle. I nodded agreement.

But this time, did we really have to save the world? We weren't under attack, no one else's life hung in the balance that we knew of. Not in the next few hours. It may be only the next few hours we had, ever, anyway. I'd already wasted several of them going to work and being angry over, well, never mind, it didn't matter. What mattered was we were here now and may never be here again. Who knew what would happen once we got to Maurelle and her magical gateway. Chances were the gateway would be around a few hours from now, but Marlowe may not be.

"Tam?" Izzy had stopped a hundred feet away when she realized we weren't following her. "What are you doing?" she called.

"I'm not going," I called back. "Neither is Marlowe." I opened the car door, and he grinned at me, getting in the passenger side as I unlocked it. "We'll meet you there in a couple of hours."

I got in and started the car.

"It may be more than a couple of hours," he said.

"God, I hope so."

Chapter 10

Tamberlyn

My bed was a haven from the troubled world. Usually a place of solace and comfort, that evening it was a destination for a party of two. We'd stumbled through my apartment like horny teenagers. Laughing, stripping, and kissing our way to my unmade bed. I reacquainted myself with him, the way he felt, the way he tasted. Hot, slick skin, lightly peppered with coarse hair over his pecs and the softer trail just under his navel. The way he sounded as I moved above him. Moved until I could blot out everything that whirled in my head and I let it go. I'd forgotten how good it felt to be with him. How amazing it was to just be myself. No pretense, no snark, just the white-hot spark between us. Afterward, we lay side by side, catching the breath of reunited lovers.

His northern European pallor contrasted sharply against my olive skin, and I liked the look of my hand against his belly. The bandage compress against his side was rough and dry under my fingers. He pulled at the tape holding it, the skin pulling up as he did.

"The tape pains me more than the stitch. Confounded invention this," he muttered, and the bandage came away. I took it from him, folding it carefully, and put it on my nightstand. I'd burn it later. I knew enough from Volpi that even a drop of blood from someone could be used in nefarious ways with dark magic—his words. We were as careful as a hospital about the disposal of bodily fluids.

The incision was a healthy pink, knitting fast and even. Volpi had a knack.

"You heal fast," I said.

"It's a good thing," he said. "The way you spar, I could have been seriously injured."

"Bullshit." I smiled at him. "You held your own—then as well as now." Our coupling had been vigorous, with a desperation just short of violence. We both needed to burn off the excess energy that sparring had only enhanced.

I curled into his side, my head resting on his chest, and his dark hair tickled my cheek. I kissed him again lightly. "Tell me about this?" I ran a light finger just under one nipple, outlining a semi-circular scar. "Human or hostile?"

He flinched. Marlowe was ticklish. A delightful fun fact I had forgotten.

"Hostile, a griffin on the outskirts of Newkirk. 1800's if I remember."

"How many journeys have you—" I didn't want to continue. It only served to remind me of his time away.

"Since leaving you, you mean? A fair amount." He sighed. "Far too many, maybe twenty? Each and every one I yearned to end up here. I thought I had once, the manner of technology was close. It was 1989 in London."

"You could have called," I chided, though I'd been an infant at the time. And what purpose would it have served? He could have contacted Volpi, but who knew what Volpi had been up to in 1989. A visit from a time traveler named Christopher Marlowe may well have circumvented us meeting at all. "What about your life? I mean aside from traveling?" I didn't want to think about his journeys. "Tell me of your life at home." My question was an obvious one, because according to history, Marlowe didn't die on one of his journeys fighting a hostile. He died in his own timeline, in the town of Deptford, not too far from where he lived and worked.

"You want me to start at the beginning?" His chin pressed against the top of my head. "Truth be told, it does not feel like home anymore, for you are not there. Today, I am home. Yesterday I was elsewhere."

He stopped talking for a moment, adjusting himself into a more comfortable position around me. His fingers played without intent to arouse, as if to memorize the expanse of my skin. "When I was there, I did my best to stay solvent. I wrote, I translated some documents—Italian into Latin, Latin into English, the like. I found a benefactor, a renowned actor named Alleyn who commissioned some plays. He opened his own theater in London, and I had three productions of my work. It was satisfying, but through it all, I missed thee."

He nuzzled at my neck, his hand cupping my breast. Throughout his tale, his hands never stayed still for long. "Alleyn is a greedy fellow, pompous to a fault, and he also acts in Will's pieces, though I think he prefers my words. My kings and noblemen are much more suited to his height and personality."

"Will's? You mean Shakespeare?" I recalled his disdain for the dramatist from our first meeting.

"Indeed." He sighed. "He's a grievous player, his quill much sharper than his skill on the stage. Methinks he should stay within his talents, and I told him so."

"You told William Shakespeare to quit acting and write?"

"I told him the truth, though he was not pleased. Thought himself beyond his measure. He is too slight of build and small of stature to play anything but a knave or a maid. We shall not mention his thin and shrill delivery. Alas, no one would speak thusly to him."

"I think you've done the world a great service." To think that Shakespeare may not have become the prolific writer he was without Marlowe to critique his acting skills. "But I wasn't asking about work."

He pulled away to look at me. As much fun as it was to talk about the bard in terms of being a real person and not just an icon of the English language, I wanted to know of Marlowe. Had he been happy over the last six years? Sad? Lonely? I hoped he'd had moments of laughter, or peace and contentment.

"I see. You fear my affections have strayed."

Okay, not the contentment I had meant, but... "Don't get me wrong. I have no doubt of your affections, as you call them, but six years is a long time to be celibate. There must have been someone, or possibly a few?"

He looked up at the ceiling, clearly uncomfortable. "Yes. You are correct, six years is a long time, and as you know, I've never claimed to be a monk." Lips quirked into a smile. A slight flush bloomed across cheekbones. "As for my dalliances, I assure you, I've taken great care to prevent disease from coming upon me, and while the young maids endeared me of a few glorious moments of release, they were never in my heart." The words came out in a rush to reassure me. I hadn't thought of being stricken with any sort of sixteenth-century malady. "At any crescent moon, I could, in every hope, be back with thee. It would not do to delay our union in order for me to be cured of some vileness garnered from a strumpet."

"Absolutely," I agreed. "No strumpet vile, no delays. Thank you for that."

"In fact—" His brow furrowed. "I've been the object of speculation. Most men of my age are wed and have started families. Even Master Shakespeare, as skint of wealth as he is to support a wife, has married. As I have not shown any interest in so doing, toward any marriageable lady of good birth, there is talk of my sexual proclivities. My occupation as a play maker and therefore in the company of men a good deal of the time only serves to enhance the rumors." A big sigh from him.

"They think you're a homosexual?"

His eyebrows raised at the word. I clarified the term to assure him we were speaking of the same thing.

"It is a strange notion your timeline has, to put a designation on everyone. In my time, it is the act that is named, not the person. It is still forbidden, but unless someone has truly wronged a person, the act may be overlooked."

"Is it overlooked? In your case?" I asked slyly.

I received a sly smile in return. "At Cambridge. In my early years. I have no shame in it. There was naught but lads there, and..."

"Boys will be boys." I smiled at him.

Now, he ducked his head, cheeks pink. "Yes. But my tastes run differently. A prefer a comely maid, fair of face and dark of eyes, with strength of will and lips like sweet berries on the vine." He kissed me. "Waiting to be plucked and savored."

I kissed him back. "Please be careful." I wanted to say more. Tell him that he was treading water in a dangerous sea and it would overcome him soon. "I don't suppose you could just try and stay out of trouble?"

This brought a laugh. "Trouble seeks me, my love. I do not seek it. Sometimes, simple talk is enough if the political winds are right. Unfortunately, I have never been one to stay my words on a topic."

Marlowe's time was fraught with religious and political infighting—clerics and politicians jockeying for power, and if he got caught in the middle of something, the truth rarely mattered and would not save him. That, and I knew him well enough to know that injustice could not go uncorrected in his mind, and he would speak to it, even if his words put him in danger.

"Not to mention your position in the queen's employ. That is still a thing, right?"

Marlowe made a credible spy, traveling around Europe under the guise of playwright and translator. "Yes. Sir Francis hath passed on. But his cousin, Thomas, and Lord Burghley work to keep the information flowing. The funds that paid us have dwindled. The work is not hard, but fair treacherous. A man seeking to hold onto his political power is far more dangerous than the vampires I encountered on my arrival here."

Aside from the dangers of time traveling onto the expressway, or having his throat torn out by a werewolf, wraith, vampire, shape-shifter, skinwalker—not the same thing by the way—trolls, trogs, demon-possessed humans, or just your average meth addict, he had to watch his back lest it be stabbed by members of his own time and species over a grudge or unrealized ambition. Or he could just die of infection from a friggin' paper cut. The life of a traveling hostile hunter is not for the faint of heart.

"Alas, it pays better than writing, and I wish to keep myself in ink and quills. And a full trencher."

I poked at him. "You are thin. Thinner than the last time you were here. Oh, and I got the other vampire last night, by the way." I reassured him. I wanted desperately to keep him here, to feed him whenever he was hungry, to let him rest, to let him write, unencumbered by searching for his next meal or place to stay.

"I've taken to rooming with another writer, Thomas Kyd. But the lad is pious and priggish, with no sense of humor, and it is often bleak." He turned to me, stroking my hair back from my face. "Back there, being put to death for one's beliefs is common, especially if they are the wrong ones. It is most difficult to watch and be still. I veil my notions in clever words, but only the most capable realize my intent. It's a challenging and weary time. A time I merely exist in, Tamberlyn—" He took my hand, kissing the fingertips. "For this—" he brought my hand over my heart, "is where I truly live." My fingers splayed over his pectoral muscle, feeling the strong beat of his heart beneath it.

"At some point, you will have to go back, and I may never see you again. Unless—"

"Do not say it, I beg of thee. It is my duty to serve my queen and destiny to protect humanity for as long as my life continues ...however long that may be. To interfere with that is not only wrong but dangerous, for you as much as I. You know this."

"We mess with it all the time. Every time you travel, the people you save or run into, it changes things. This is what we do, Marlowe."

"But not for selfish gain."

"Is it selfish to have you around more? Correcting mistakes in time, saving damsels in distress?"

"What makes my life more important than another's? All life has value, Tamberlyn. We cannot be the ones who decide. At least not for others."

"But they decide, don't they? Walsingham." I paused for a split second. "Or Munson in X's case."

Marlowe sat up abruptly, and I felt the absence of his warmth with a sharpness I didn't admit. "Are thou vexed with me? Still? What would you have done in my stead?"

I let out a breath, heavily. "I don't know. And I don't want to fight." I pulled him back down to the bed. "I wish we could be more open with each other, that's all."

His lips placed hot kisses along my neck, moving south as I arched under him. He stopped, his eyes a soft amber once again.

"Come, let us speak no more of this. We have but a few hours, nay minutes, and I can think of much better use of them."

∞

I considered it time extremely well-spent, but eventually, the evening found us outside Pinkie's bar, searching for my sister and Volpi. Abraham acted as a doorman, his shaved head gleaming in the pink neon as he tried to control the small crowd. We pushed our way to the front, irritating more than a few non-humans, a fox-like young woman, whom everyone avoided making eye contact with, some Grendels—bi-ped beasts about nine feet tall, covered in reddish-brown hair, and except for deadly halitosis, relatively benign. A werewolf mix of dubious descent—he had the canine eyes of a wolf, but frizzy curly hair like that of a poodle.

"Hey, Abraham." I turned toward Marlowe who stood just behind me, his hand warm on the small of my back. "This is—"

"Kit Marlowe." Abraham's stern face broke into a smile, his white teeth a blinding slash in his dark face. "By the gods, man. It's good to see you." He gripped Marlowe's hand.

"Abraham Puck." Marlowe marveled. "How can this be?" He turned to me. "This fellow is a player."

"I bet," I said with a wink at Abraham. This served to conceal my surprise at their acquaintance. "My sister and Volpi were here earlier. Are they still inside?"

The tall man frowned. "No, I believe they left before seeing Maurelle." He looked out over the crowd, addressing them. "Everyone will get their turn. First one to raise a claw will lose it and his place in the queue." His eyes flashed a fiery bronze. "Now keep it down or this one will have the cops on us in no time." He jerked a thumb at me, and several turned to look.

"Way to endear me to the crowd, Abe, thanks," I grumbled. He grinned and opened the door behind him. We ducked under his arm and entered the packed bar. Marlowe addressed Abraham as he followed us into the noise.

"My friend, how did you come to be in this place? Art thou a traveler also?"

Abraham laughed, clapping him on the back. "No. There are few of your kind, Marlowe. But my kind live a very long time. I've not seen you in more than four hundred years. Come." He led us to the storeroom door and turned to me. "When Volpi and your sister arrive I will bring them."

"Thanks," I said. He and Marlowe clasped hands once again and then he was gone, disappearing back into the crowd. I knew the not-so-innocuous bartender was an "other," but his age was another surprise. He was remarkably well preserved for four hundred plus.

We waited at the top of the steps leading into the basement. From where we were, I could hear the occasional whoosh and swoop of the portal opening, but except for the flash of green light, I couldn't see it.

"I had no idea it would be this crowded," I said.

"Oh yeah." A petite young woman in front of us turned and looked up. "Everyone wants to get to their destinations and back again before the window closes. Because if you go at the end of the cycle, you're stuck until the next crescent. Unless of course, it's a one-way trip." She cocked her head at an angle, the movement slightly avian in nature.

Her slight build, jerky twitches, and watchful eyes reminded me of a bird of prey. Her dark hair was up into a haphazard mass on the top of her head and held with a massive pronged hair clip of neon blue and glittering black. She was dressed for functionality, black tights, tall boots, and a blue and black tunic the size of Marlowe's shirt, edging her mid-thigh. She kept her eyes on us as the line moved down a step.

"Are you on such a journey?" asked Marlowe.

"Round trip for me. I'm Arial," the girl said, hesitating only a second before putting her hand in Marlowe's outstretched one.

"I am most pleased to meet such a lovely creature as you, Arial. I am Marlowe, this is Tamberlyn." I nodded at the girl. Her head bobbed at me in response.

"Where are you hoping to go?" I asked. "Unless that's a personal question. I'm a novice at portal etiquette."

"Home, visit the parents, you know."

Obviously, I did not. "So you live here?" I wondered where home was. Most of the beings wanting to go through the portal were non-humans who'd used the same method to get here in the first place. It was a rare human who knew of its existence. Her head bobbed again, the large comb waving back and forth in the air. A scent of pine trees and honeysuckle tickled my nose.

Looking closer, I realized that the large blue and black clip in her hair was not a hair accessory. It was part of her, made of bone or cartilage or something, it crested the top of her head like plumage. I wondered how she disguised it when she went for coffee.

"I'm a senior at La Salle," she said. "Getting my degree in psychology."

My alma mater—where I'd toiled over core classes and midterms in avoidance of all things and beings at Penn State. "Human psychology?"

She giggled. "I know. Weird huh. But I think they're fascinating. They're so fragile and yet so violent. Both needy and fiercely independent. Humans are such a dichotomy."

I smiled politely as she turned back to her friends. Pretty good observation from a non-human. I wanted to ask what she was, but for once, kept my curiosity under control.

The conversation reminded me of another non-human I'd spoken with today. I turned to Marlowe as we descended another step. "I need to tell you something. Something that happened today." I paused, not sure how to proceed. "Do you remember me telling you about an old boyfriend? The first one? Theo?"

He nodded, his arm coming around me. "Indeed. You were hurt by this mongrel cad, and I had notions of violence on your behalf. But I remember our interlude afterward as well." His eyes darkened with the memory.

I flushed under his gaze. Which was only slightly embarrassing. "Yes. Well, he's back. In this realm." There was silence—that damned patience again. "He's a person of interest in my investigation. And as I found out yesterday, he is also fae—of the upper variety." My glance took in those around us— most of them would be related to the lower fae. "Or maybe his status is a thing of the past. But this is what I need to ask the gatekeeper about."

"How can that be? You mean he's a Pan, a trickster,

disguising himself as human?"

"No, I mean of the *upper fae*. A real honest to hades, forbidden to interact with mortals much less seduce them, upper fae."

"God's teeth," he whispered. "You saw him today? Here?"

"A town not far from here, but yes. He's the campaign manager for the senator. And I want to know what he's doing back in my world." I needed to know what had transpired in mine and Theo's past. "Whatever. It's why I'm here." I swept a hand toward the dingy basement below us. I was relaying all I knew about my past dealings with the upper fae when Volpi and Izzy came down the stairs. They scrunched in behind us in spite of the half-hearted protests of the Grendels looming farther back in the line.

Chapter 11

Isabelle

Izzy had been fully prepared to give her sister grief about taking off with Marlowe. How could she waste precious time like that? Now that she had Marlowe back, Tam was content to live in the moment, while Izzy was trying to fix things for their future together. Angelo had agreed with her to a certain extent, but he also rationalized that her sister might benefit from a little private time with Marlowe. Ange was such a romantic.

When she saw them at Pinkie's, it made Izzy realize just how right he'd been. Tam looked truly happy—a rare occurrence.

They arrived in time to hear Tam's explanation of Theo's— there was that name again—latest persona. This news caused Volpi's expression to darken as he listened.

"I get that fae are dangerous." Izzy shrugged off Angelo's admonition to keep her voice down. "But what exactly happened between you guys? Did he try to kill you? The other way around?" She thought this the more likely. As Izzy said the words, she felt the relaxed energy between Tam and Marlowe. A warmth emanated from both of them, and she smiled to herself. There could be no doubt as to their activities prior to arriving at the bar. Not only did her sister deserve a little happiness, she was much easier to live with when not sexually frustrated.

"If Maurelle hadn't messed with my memory, I'd know that, wouldn't I?" Tam's response was quick, but she softened immediately at Marlowe's touch. "And now, Theo is here, and I want to know exactly what happened at the conclave."

"You didn't ask him?" Izzy asked.

"Would I trust a syllable coming out of his mouth?" Tam shot back. "Hell, no."

They had crept steadily down the basement steps until they clustered one step above the basement floor. Along the back wall of the storeroom, Maurelle stood in front of the shelves. Her suit jacket flapped open, crinkling her nametag as she manipulated the atmosphere beside her.

A slight visual disturbance grew into a sickly green orb, the circumference expanding along the entire wall space. Izzy felt herself drawn toward it. She looked at Tam, her hand inside Marlowe's as they stood on the step together. Tam had barely noticed the portal opening. It was the biggest thing in the room. How could she not feel that? Izzy felt like her insides were boiling. A man beside Maurelle stepped through the opening. As soon as he had, the outer edges caved in until the light faded, and with a swoosh-pop, the gate closed again. Izzy's stomach settled and she relaxed. Everyone moved down a step.

"Abraham got us to the top of the stairs," Tam was saying. "Apparently, he and Marlowe know each other from back in the day."

Volpi looked questioningly at Marlowe.

"He was a player in my time, quite good, and if anyone needed a man of color in their work, he was in demand," Marlowe said.

"Oh, you mean an actor, not a *player*," Tam exclaimed. "I get it now, I thought you meant ...never mind." She smiled up at Marlowe. Izzy kept her focus on the gatekeeper and the latest traveler. Across the narrow space, a petite woman with a vulpine-shaped face had words with Maurelle, and the argument became quite heated. Apparently, she did not have the proper paperwork to be allowed through the portal.

Izzy's mind whirled in sudden panic. Paperwork?

"Angelo, you said nothing about paperwork. Look." She indicated the woman, who was transforming as they watched. Maurelle continued to deny passage. The being seemed to grow in stature, her face becoming more fox-like with beady eyes and a sharp chin.

"Damn it, Vyx," Angelo muttered under his breath. "She's going to cause trouble."

"What is she?" Tam asked from her step above them.

"A Kitsune. If she draws her katana, this will be over in a matter of seconds."

Izzy cast a worried frown at her partner as he conversed with Tam. He had no desire to see her travel back to the ancients, regardless of how important it was. Right now, when things were falling into place, she had hit another roadblock—a lack of documentation and angry vixens.

The argument at the portal escalated into an interspecies altercation. A mealy-mouthed man stepped up beside the Kitsune, and the two were protesting. The line of travelers jostled, someone pushed at the sharp-faced man, but he stepped aside and they hit Vyx. The sword appeared in her hand, and she whirled it overhead with a battle cry.

Volpi, Tam, and Marlowe sped into action, jumping onto the main floor in an effort to stop the violence.

Maurelle had moved back out of the way, creating an invisible bubble of protection around herself and ignoring the entire fray as she consulted her—yes, it was a cell phone she had in her hand.

Izzy scooted aside as Marlowe blocked a flying were-cat from landing on her head. Angelo shouted at her to get Abraham and then ducked under a blow from some hairy-armed thing resembling a green orangutan.

Izzy was half-way up the stairs when Abraham appeared, eyes blazing a red-gold gleam as he leaped over the heads of the crowd into the middle of the brawl. A long seven-foot barbed tail emerged from under his jacket and functioned as a weapon, protecting him from a rear attack as he forged ahead with a short Roman sword.

Weapons had emerged soon after the katana sword appeared in Vyx's hand. Abraham whirled, slashing and thrusting his way toward Maurelle, who was perfectly fine behind her invisible shield. Apparently, this sort of thing happened often.

Still, Izzy was amazed at how many ran into the fight rather than away from it. Only she and the two Grendels were left on the stairs. They cowered behind her, their knees shaking violently.

"Calm down." Her tone was gentle but firm. "You're perfectly safe unless you shake these stairs so much you bring the whole thing down." She turned back to the fight below them. The orangutan thing climbed onto the supply shelf, gaining the necessary height to leap down on its opponents. He hung there, great long arms swatting the fighters, legs bent and ready to spring. Tam ducked a blow from something black and shapeless and rolled toward the shelf within the primate's reach.

Izzy wanted to warn her, but a girl leaped into the air, wings unfolding in beautiful blue-black plumage behind her, and with a screech, she soared around the low ceilinged room. She had human hands but very long claw-like black nails, and they were busy molding an orange light like a snowball. She tossed it down onto the ape. His hair burst into flame, and he fell from his perch, screaming and beating his hands about his head. Tam looked up, and the girl grinned at her from above, giving a taloned thumbs up as she flew by.

Marlowe had come to Tam's side, protecting her flank. Parrying and thrusting, the sword flashed in the single bulb light, which swung back and forth, throwing the battle into both light and shadow. Tam had a mop handle—the mop head broken off and tossed aside—and used the thing as a staff. Tam was usually far more gun-happy, yet she hadn't pulled her service weapon.

"Angelo!" Izzy shouted a warning as a werewolf in full wolf form leaped for his throat. He ducked under, the teeth missing him by inches, turned, and punched the animal in the snout. Wolf spit went flying, splattering Abraham's back and he turned, his short sword whirling around. It caught the wolf just under his jaw. A wolf head rolled across the floor, his canine gums pulled back in a silent snarl.

"Enough." Maurelle had put her phone away, and the protective shield was melting around her. She snapped her fingers at one side of the room, and fighters fell where they stood. "Rules is here for a reason. No beheadings. Messes up my clean floors. And since this one—" she pointed at Tam, "done broke my mop, how am I gonna clean this up?"

Abraham looked chagrined. "My apologies, Maurelle. It was an accident."

Tam looked stunned, holding the mop handle. Angelo approached her with the straggly gray mop head in his hands. The other half of the room stood in scolded silence. Still, it was better than the first half, lying about on a losing battlefield.

The fox who'd started it all, scrambled to the prone form of her partner, as he raised his head and blinked around him. The girl who'd flown around the room landed just under Izzy on the stairs. Her wings settled, folded, and sunk back into her shoulder blades. Her claws became fingernails—though still painted black, as she carefully preened her hair and clothes into order.

"You're a phoenix," Izzy marveled, her voice soft as not to draw Maurelle's attention. The girl turned toward her, a beautiful wide smile across her ebony face. She shrugged her petite frame as if settling more feathers into place. "Thanks for helping my sister out." Izzy nodded toward Tam and the others among the upright. "Did she just kill half these people?" Though

Izzy was quite positive they weren't human, she had no other term for the crowd on the storeroom floor.

"Oh no, they're just asleep. They'll wake up in a few minutes with a massive headache. Maurelle manipulated the serotonin in their bloodstreams."

"Neat trick," Izzy said. She'd have to ask Angelo about that one.

Sure enough, within a few minutes, the fallen stirred and clutched at their heads as Maurelle ordered everyone out. The phoenix girl turned and sighed. "Well, that's it. May as well go home until tomorrow."

"What?" Izzy moved aside as beings filed solemnly past her, holding their heads.

"The portal's shut down. No more jumps tonight," the girl said, picking up her backpack. She slung it over her shoulder and headed up the stairs.

Izzy joined Angelo who assured her he was fine. She touched a darkening bruise along his jawline. The wolves had reverted to human form and were carrying their dead comrade out, Abraham apologizing profusely as he followed them, carrying the severed head. One wolf with poodle-like hair jerked the head out of his arms and growled.

Tam did the oddest thing of all—on her hands and knees, she mopped the floor. Izzy started toward her but Angelo pulled her back.

"She has a reason," he said. Marlowe fetched fresh water in the mop bucket. "She's stalling," Angelo whispered in Izzy's ear. When the blood was cleaned from the floor and the mop put away, only the four of them were left with the surly gatekeeper.

"You go on with yourselves now. Git. I needs my rest." The old woman turned away.

Tam spoke. "Theo's back," she said, simply. Maurelle jerked back to scrutinize Tam. "He's been in New York, but now he's here, and claims to not be of the fae anymore."

Angelo spoke in less accusatory tones. "This is a real

problem, Sensei. If you know about this."

"I do not."

"Is he telling the truth?" Tam asked. "Is he human? Harmless? Well, okay not harmless, but less dangerous than if he were fae? I don't trust him."

"And you should not, child. Fae of the Falchion Clan are known for their ruthless ways." The old woman sighed, and with a crook of her finger, an old wing chair slid itself into the center of the room.

"He tells you true." She lapsed into her fractured English diction. "When he faced the conclave, he, like you, was sentenced to death. I's spoke for you. The mortal world needs their sword." She pointed a gnarled finger at Marlowe. "Didn't know 'bout you, yet." She sat heavily in the chair and settled herself for a moment. "The Vanguard—the one you call Theo, is the Queen of Old's descendant, and much was made of his betrayal to his house for the likes of a human. His punishment for breaking the sacred law had to be severe. So they did worse than death. They took his power and banished him to here. He be mortal, but not quite. He still have the long life. Harder that way, you see? Them fae, they be harsh people. Harsh."

"So he has no power, he can't disappear, move objects, or read minds? No exceptional strength or speed? He's human then," Tam said, taking a deep breath.

"He can die. Just like you, but unless someone kill him, he live a long, long time. Life span of the fae." She frowned. "I said that already, right? He be mortal, but not quite. Listen, child."

Izzy spoke up from where she stood next to Marlowe.

"Ms. Maurelle." She started out as politely as possible. "This, as you know, is Marlowe. He is a hunter like my sister, a traveler. But he has no guide and has been wandering through the timeline without purpose, without a mission." She glanced up at Marlowe and smiled. "He's done well, in spite of this. He is a good and valiant warrior, and I wish to help him. To find a way for him to guide himself. The ancients have that answer."

Marlowe stepped forward into a bow. "Meeting you is my pleasure, madam," he said, his head inclined toward the floor. He rose and stepped back.

Maurelle sat for some time. She looked from one to another before speaking. During the silence, Tam's phone rang and she silenced it, apologizing. Izzy glared at her and she gave a helpless shrug.

The old woman sighed. "That be your mortal world calling child, you best answer. As for you." She pointed at Marlowe. "Come back tomorrow."

"But he may be gone tomorrow. He can't control—" Izzy protested.

"I hear ya." Maurelle cut her off. "No more portal today. I's tired. I'm an old woman now."

Angelo hid a smile as he pulled Izzy back toward him.

Izzy, however, was as stubborn as her sister and then some. "We can't take the chance. If he leaves before I get the answer, we may never see him. He may be..." She trailed off.

"Thank you for your time, Sensei," Angelo said. "You and I both know, your age is but a mask. We shall abide by your wishes and come back tomorrow."

"I did not mean yourself, protégé. Nor the sword. With the disgraced fae here, you may be needed. Just the warrior poet and the guide are needed tomorrow. Now, shoo." She flicked her hands, and all of them were heaved off their feet and backed away several feet. Izzy lost her balance, and Angelo steadied her. Tam and Marlowe remained upright as their feet slid along the floor. Tam's phone buzzed again, and she answered it, heading up the stairs.

The bar had emptied except for a few monsters drowning their sorrows at their canceled travel plans. Izzy and company walked through the sparse crowd to the exit. The night was quiet, hopeful travelers having disappeared back into the woodwork from where they came.

"Tomorrow may be too late," Izzy said.

"Rest assured, Miss Isabelle." Marlowe put a gentle hand on her arm. "I have not felt the signs of imminent travel. I will be here on morrow."

"I'm not letting you go alone," Angelo said. "Maurelle is stubborn, if she says Tam is needed here, then neither of us will be able to get through the portal."

"I shall travel with her, old friend," Marlowe said. "And protect her with my life."

"And Tam?" Angelo asked, nodding to where Tam stood a few feet away talking into her phone.

The three of them lingered in the cool evening air, away from the light and noise of the bar. Only the sound of Tam's murmured phone conversation could be heard. The clear sky was gray-black and sported a few diligent stars.

Marlowe gazed in Tam's direction, a flicker of both sadness and pride in his face.

"She shall have you if she needs assistance. You heard your mentor. The fae may be devious and clever, but so is my lady Tamberlyn. And unlike him, she is not without power."

Tam had hung up her phone and approached them. "Work," she said. "I have to go. There's been another attempt on the senator's life."

"I shall accompany thee." Marlowe's hand found hers.

"No. I'll be home soon. I'm meeting Cobb—my new partner," she explained. "The senator is in the emergency room." She glanced at Izzy and Angelo briefly. "Well, this was an eventful evening."

"Good times," Angelo said. "Watch yourself, Tam."

Tam pulled Marlowe aside to say their goodbyes in relative privacy.

Izzy whispered to Angelo. "So tell me about paperwork for portal travel. Is this a thing? Will Maurelle open the rift for us? For me?"

He put an arm around her shoulder pulling her into him. "I worry about you. You've been training yes, but the ancients ...I know it has to be done, but you should wait until I can go with you." He was warm from fighting, slightly damp where his neck met his shoulder.

She kissed him there, tasting the salty tang of his skin. "But you'll help me anyway, won't you?" They were both silent as Tam pulled away from Marlowe, giving them a little wave before striding off to her car. Marlowe made his way back to where she and Angelo stood under the Pinkie's sign. "Time is not our friend," she said.

Marlowe had a ruminative smile as he spoke. "Miss Isabelle, could I ask for a ride in your vehicle. I will wait at Tamberlyn's for her return."

"Sure," Izzy said, and they turned toward Angelo's loft complex and her car. Marlowe hesitated, looking back at Tam's car as she drove away. Izzy pulled at his arm, "She'll be fine. You'll see her soon."

Marlowe turned to her, his eyes suddenly sad.

"Pray, you speak the truth."

Chapter 12

Tamberlyn

I hate hospitals. Nothing good ever comes of them. They are just germ-infested, antiseptic-smelling places where people say goodbye. I parked in the emergency room parking lot and came in through the automatic doors, striding through the sick and injured to flip my badge at the nurse behind the glass window. She buzzed me in, and I found Cobb talking to a uniformed cop outside a curtain in the ER bay.

"Bout time you got here, Paradiso." He turned away from the uni.

"You just called me." I glanced at the clock over the nurse's station. It was eleven-thirty. Marlowe had been here twenty-six hours, and I was away from him again, working a case. "What happened?"

Cobb thrust his chin at the curtain. "Someone took a shot at Shepherd with a freakin' arrow. His campaign manager knocked him out of the way. Doc's stitching him up now."

Expecting to see the senator, my lack of patience burned me again as I poked my head through the curtain. Theo turned toward me from where he lay on the bed. A young woman was on the other side of him, administering to his shoulder. She glanced up. At the sight of me, her smile for her patient vanished.

"Sorry, Philadelphia PD. I thought the senator was in here." I could feel Cobb's smirk behind me. Very deliberately, I kept my gaze on the doctor, away from the naked torso of her patient. My peripheral vision was better than I anticipated, taking in more than enough of Theo. Every human-looking muscle was defined under the fluorescent light, with a mix of blood and Betadine being carefully sponged up by the intern's gloved hand. He'd turned back toward her, the beginnings of a smile pulling at his mouth. I knew it was his gratitude expression. I'd seen it before.

"The senator went down to x-ray," she said, paying far too much attention to a pectoral. "Just a precaution. This man saved his life." Her teeth disappeared behind tight lips as she turned to me. "We'll be finished in a moment, officer."

I backed up, letting the curtain fall, and my teeth clenched together. Cobb could have told me the senator wasn't in here, but he'd let me barge in. I glared at him and tried to relax my jaw.

"Do you need something for the pain?" Her tone changed to saccharine behind the curtain. I hoped Theo's shoulder hurt like hell. He declined the meds and thanked her. She shot me a dismissive glare as she left, leaving the curtain half open for us. I stepped back through the opening.

"Are you going to shoot me this time?" He winced as he sat up in the bed. Good.

"You giving me a reason?"

"Haven't I already done that?" He smiled. Expression number two that I remembered. The shit-eating grin. Cobb said nothing, merely stood at the edge of the curtained area.

Picking up a hospital smock from the end of the bed, I tossed it at him. As I did, I saw the doc had missed one blood-stained four by four on the tray. I palmed it into my pocket as Theo struggled with the hospital gown. "Tell me what happened." I was determined to be professional, and that was easier to do with him more or less fully clothed.

The smock fell half over his injured arm and shoulder, and he waggled his wrist helplessly. I rolled my eyes, but I leaned across him to help him into the other sleeve. He shrugged his good shoulder into it, leaving it untied in the front. "I don't know. We were heading back for a meeting and parked in the back of the justice building. The senator got out and someone started shooting arrows at us. I caught one in the shoulder."

"Arrows? Plural?"

"Two that I know of." Theo glanced at Cobb.

"I bagged them," Cobb said. "We'll see if we can find any trace evidence on them."

Theo let out a weary sigh. I guessed he wasn't used to getting the pointy end of arrows. He frowned. "Arrows. Who does that?"

My question exactly.

He glanced from Cobb to me and back again. "Detective, would you mind checking on the senator for me? I'm worried about him."

Cobb didn't move, his face impassive. He wasn't the kind of guy one asked favors of, but with a warning glance at me—presumably, to not kill our witness, he left the curtained area.

Theo lowered his voice and I saw expression number three—sincerity. "Bows are not the usual weapon of choice for human assassins, right? Your world is predictable if anything."

"You think this was otherworldly? The lower fae usually have teeth, claws, venom, that sort of thing. If it was a hostile, you're a suspect. Retaliation for being stuck here with us mere mortals."

"I would never hurt the senator." All pretense of charm, sincerity, and gratitude dropped from his expression as he spoke again. "My penance is to be in this world, without power, a mere mortal, as you say, and yet not. If you had consented to be our warrior, I would have been promoted. Instead, here I am."

"A warrior? What the hell, Theo?" I hissed at him. "I was seventeen years old—a kid who thought she was..." I couldn't say the word love, I wouldn't give him that. "I know that doesn't mean much to you, being two hundred and forty whatever, but—"

"Two hundred and fifty-one." He frowned. "For a fae, it's young, maybe even the equivalent of seventeen."

Something flickered behind his eyes—dark brown and so unlike Marlowe's liquid amber color. But the lashes I remembered keenly, long and thick, they closed momentarily as though he regretted what he'd done, and not just because he'd been caught. The memory of our first meeting sparked to life in my brain, unbidden, and unwelcome.

I'd been shy in high school. After the altercation with my first hostile—a vampire in the school library, I became downright reclusive. Until my senior year, I'd been able to avoid prom, homecoming, every single sporting event, and non-required attendance assembly. I belonged to no clubs, societies, or organizations. But Dad and Freya, my grandmother, had insisted I go on the senior trip to New York, just a week or two from graduation. I had done so, under protest, packing a long dagger and several books, all of them defensive weapons in my arsenal.

During intermission of an off-Broadway play, Theo smiled at us from the other side of the room. He was the most beautiful man I'd ever seen. That angelic face, the lean muscles on a tall frame, he had the kind of GQ look that turned heads of every woman in that theater. Including Natalie, one of the more popular and annoying girls in my senior class.

"This is Theo North." Natalie had practically squealed as she introduced him as her brother's friend. He was polite, shaking hands with everyone as their names were given. I'd hung back, on the fringe of the group like usual. The others chattered on about the play, which they hated, and the city, which they loved.

Just as the lights dimmed signaling the start of the second act, he told me he had tickets to another play the following night.

"We're supposed to go to Rockefeller Plaza," I said.

"Rockefeller Plaza is great. This play is better." His hand came close to a casual touch on my arm. I deflected, moving to one side just as casually. "I'll wait outside the theater if you want to come." He'd shrugged as if it didn't matter. "If not, that's fine."

"Lots of other girls would go with you." I made my way to my seat. He was just behind me.

"I didn't ask anyone else." His voice was low and close to my ear. He moved down the aisle to his seat near the stage. I felt the tingle of his words and presence throughout the rest of the play.

The next night I'd ditched my school mates at Rockefeller Plaza and blew the majority of my spending money on a cab. The play was in Tribeca, another Arthur Miller work, and Theo held my hand in the darkened theater.

We'd gone to a late supper afterward, eating pizza and talking about the play. He stroked my fingers, his passionate words leaving little track marks on my brain. He walked me back to the Paramount hotel and helped me sneak past the teachers who had set up in the lobby as vigilantes against their charges sneaking out. Or sneaking in, as I was. I experienced my first real kiss in the fourth-floor stairwell. I'd been kissed before, having a few sporadic dates with Robert of the lunch table crowd, but nothing like this.

His tongue parted my lips with such gentleness I thought I'd break apart. When his mouth finally closed over mine the taste of him was so sweet I couldn't get enough. My heart fluttered against my ribcage as he sucked on my tongue. His large hands were sure and quick under my shirt, the clasp of my bra unhooked to allow him access. Hard nippled and drenched with desire, I would have let him take me there and then, on the grimy back stairs of the three-star hotel. But he didn't.

It felt strange to remember every vivid detail of that meeting, and then to have him sitting in front of me again after all these years. Strange that the beginning of our relationship was so distinct, but the end I couldn't recall.

I found myself moving away from the hospital bed, wanting to put some distance between us. I could study him in the harsh ER lighting. He still had the good looks, the smooth charm, but I knew who he was now.

"You see the guy who shot you?" I asked, my tone professional once again. I heard Cobb's voice as he approached the curtains surrounding the bed. Memories and private conversation changed into the task at hand.

"No. I saw the first one and tried to get the senator back into the car."

Cobb stepped through the open curtain. "The senator's being checked out, but he appears to be fine." He flipped out his notebook. "The first one? So you knew it was an arrow?"

Theo sat up and lied through his perfectly straight teeth. "Had no idea what it was. Saw something come at the car, so I moved. Quite frankly, I was trying to take cover." His glance stayed on Cobb's face. Theo could recognize an arrow coming at him from the next dimension. He may not have fae speed or super-vision anymore, but he had two hundred-odd years of wartime experience, and I suspected the fae waged war with traditional artillery. Cobb grunted.

"Anybody on the motive list an archery expert that you know of?" I asked.

"Now that would be your problem, wouldn't it?" Theo shot back.

"What problem is that?" The senator pulled the curtain aside, moving toward Theo. "Locran, are you okay?" It was odd to hear his given name. I wondered if it was fae given or made up.

"Yes, sir. I'm fine. Just a scratch." He spoke in deferential tones to his boss. This I hadn't remembered. If there was anything Theo had a lack of, it was humility. Perhaps, the fae had sought to remedy this by making him like the rest of us. He even managed to look concerned for the older man. "Are you, okay, sir?"

"Quite fine. Got the all clear." The senator smiled fondly at Theo before turning to us. Cobb introduced me. The senator's eyes switched from Cobb to myself as he spoke. "Have you figured out who is responsible for this?"

"Working on it, Senator," I answered. "To that end, do you know anyone who is both proficient with a bow and would want to kill you?" His eyebrows drew up in surprise before shaking his head.

Cobb let out a short sigh before saying what I'd been thinking. "We believe the poisoning of Ms. Jackson is related. The lab has confirmed the fruit basket was tainted. It was sent to your room, is that correct?

"Yes," Shepherd answered, a tinge of regret in his voice. "I don't do well with citrus fruit, so I'd sent it to Marcy's room. Of course, I'd had no idea of its—"

Cobb interrupted him. "We'd like to put a team on you, to insure your safety until we can solve this."

"Your manager." I indicated Theo, who by this time, had gotten up and pulled on his bloodied shirt. "Gave us a list of names of people who may have motive. We'll check it out. In the meantime, you should stay in the city."

"I've got an apartment that I use when I'm here." He gave us the address and looked at Theo. "Are you okay to leave? Doctor say you can go home?"

"Yes."

"It would be easier if the two of you stayed in the same place." Cobb flipped his notebook back into his pocket. "We're going to go check out the scene. And we'll be in touch."

"Of course," Shepherd said. "My apartment is a two bedroom, plenty of room for both of us." He placed a fatherly hand on Theo's shoulder. A lightness moved across the younger man's features. Genuine affection—a human connection between them. I knew then that Theo was telling the truth. He wasn't the one behind this.

"There'll be a car out front to take you," I said. "A team will stay at the apartment complex. And if you plan on going back to Harrisburg, or anywhere else, please let us know."

"Thank you, detectives." Shepherd inclined his head and turned to Theo. "Let's see if we can't get you checked out of here." He moved past us to the hallway. After a moment of awkwardness, where no one spoke, Cobb moved through the curtains also, leaving us alone.

"Please find out who's doing this," Theo asked, putting his shoes on. "Whatever you think of me, Shepherd doesn't deserve this."

I wanted to quip something snarky back to him, but my memories and his concern for the senator stopped me. I nodded and turned to go.

"May the gods guard your well-being." His voice was soft behind me.

I stopped in my tracks.

We'd been in the stairwell of the New York hotel the first time he'd said it. I barely noticed as I could think of nothing other than how talented his lips were. The second time he used the phrase had been back home in Philly, outside my front door. I'd asked him what it meant. It was not the sort of line a frat boy would use, and he'd made a joke of it at the time.

"It means what it says. I wish you well. Goodbye is an annotated version of that." He'd cracked a smile. "Would you prefer see you later, alligator?"

He explained that his grandfather from the old country used to say it all the time. And he told me the traditional response— after yours. It had become a thing after that—our thing. We'd said it at every parting.

But there wasn't an *us*. And it wasn't our thing any longer. I looked over my shoulder at the man he'd become, not at all sure he wasn't guilty of something, even if it wasn't murder. I merely nodded, pushing my way through the curtains, and went to find

Cobb.

∞

Cobb and I drove separately to the justice building where they'd cordoned off the parking space and the town car used by Theo and Shepherd. Cobb was walking around the space by the time I parked my car.

"So Shepherd wasn't expected in town until tomorrow or rather this morning?" I noted it was after midnight now. Marlowe would be waiting for me, and I wanted to be done with this and get back to him. Memories of Theo stirred up a windstorm of emotions, and I needed Marlowe's calm.

"Senator said it was a last-minute decision. Theopolis offered to drive them in early, the rest of the team would come in later. Why?"

"Well, the last time things had changed too. Theo ...polis—" I hurriedly tacked on the rest of his name, "was supposed to be on that trip when Marcy Jackson died, but he wasn't. Could this be an inside job? Someone inside the campaign. Someone on the team who knows when the schedule changes."

"Which points to the guy with a shoulder wound."

"Yes."

Cobb looked at me. "But you don't think it's him. Earlier, you were ready to shoot him on sight. What changed?"

I thought for a moment. That afternoon I had been angry. Seeing Theo had been a shock. Now, I knew more about what had happened years ago. The fact that I'd resolved things with Marlowe probably also had something to do with my compliant mood. Life was just better. I could see Theo as he was now instead of my broken memory of him. But of course, I couldn't tell Cobb this stuff.

"Pretty elaborate set up to get yourself shot with a crossbow just to shift the blame. And how he acted with the senator. He admires the man. You can see it." We walked around the car, looking at angles of trajectory from the chalk marks made by the forensics team. I glanced at the building across the way. "A team check things out up there?" I pointed.

"I was going to but wanted to catch the senator at the hospital first. Let's go check it out." We crossed the street, entered the building, and climbed five flights of stairs to the roof before he spoke again. "How did you know it was a crossbow?" he asked.

I knew because Volpi had me training with a variety of weapons since I was eighteen. Crossbows, compounds, and the traditional bow were just a few of them. I was better with a gun and favored them, but I could bullseye a target at seventy-five yards with a bow if I needed to. Eyeballing the distance, I lied to Cobb.

"This had to be a high-powered crossbow at this distance. You can shoot farther, well over a couple of hundred yards but it loses accuracy. Someone would have to get height on the shot and hitting a target at that distance is difficult. I mean, I'm no expert, but..." I trailed off as Cobb walked the roofline, his flashlight searching for evidence.

He stopped, and the flashlight wavered toward me. "You sound pretty informed to be no expert." His tone was suspicious, and I was grateful for the darkness and distance between us.

"I dated a guy who did competitive archery." I realized how close to the truth my words were as Cobb grunted and resumed his search. "A very long time ago."

Chapter 13

Isabelle

Izzy's apartment was in the neighborhood of Covington. Not far from the university, it was an old neighborhood of oak trees and retirees living in pillbox houses with flowers in the window boxes. Izzy rented the downstairs one bedroom of Mrs. Van Devander's blue house on the corner.

She'd moved from her old apartment the year before to be closer to both Volpi's and Tam's places. There was nothing in her price range in the warehouse district of Volpi's, and she couldn't bear living in Tam's broken down neighborhood. Covington was equidistant and west of both of them. In fact, if you drew lines on a map between the residences, you'd form a triangle. As soon as Izzy saw Mrs. Van Devander's sign in the window, she knew she had to live there.

In the center of the triangle was a small broken down park with old trees and some badly trimmed pathways. No playground equipment, nor pond, nor benches or monuments, it was just a spot of green in an otherwise sea of pavement and housing. But the park held a cross-section of ley lines. The only other cross-section of such lines in Philadelphia was Pinkie's bar.

She parked her car on the street and walked the narrow path that led to her stairs at the back. It was a clear night, and she looked up at the still crescent moon, calculating both the time of night—about half past midnight—and the hours remaining before the gravity pull would change and Marlowe would be gone—fifty-two.

Neither Tam nor Marlowe had calculated his journeys to such a degree, but Izzy had scoured his journals, making a spreadsheet of hours, locations, days of the calendar, and coordinated them with celestial events. She had never relayed this information to her sister, but her research had allowed her to pinpoint almost the exact number of hours Marlowe would stay in one place at a given time of year.

The telling of time by the moon and sun was a skill she'd picked up from living with the ancients and a helpful one as timekeeping devices never worked around her. The digital clock on her stove read a constant 00:00. Even the clock on her phone blinked on and off, showing random yet inaccurate times.

She let herself into the apartment. It was tiny and dark, with two windows opposite the entryway, a small kitchen with a narrow table separating it from the green shag carpet of the living room. A bathroom the size of a closet, but no actual closet, her clothes hung on a rack inside her bedroom. It was more cramped and dark than her last place, but she convinced her sister and Angelo that it was perfect, and the rent was two hundred less a month.

She was tired but forced herself to crawl into the tiny stall of a shower before pulling on her favorite flannel pajamas—pink with blue llamas dressed as unicorns.

She had felt the strong pull of the portal tonight at Pinkie's, and it drained her. It was like an itch she couldn't scratch, and the energy of it sapped her strength. *Because you resisted.*

The words came to her clearly, and she knew they were true. Before, she'd been able to open the portal on her own, without Maurelle. Then the ancients—her ancestors—had helped from the other side. She wasn't at all sure she could do it again. But she wouldn't need to, would she? She would show up tomorrow, and Maurelle would send her through. Easy as pie.

Izzy took deep breaths as she lay down, trying to shut off her brain using the exercises that Angelo had taught her. Soon, she slept. And dreamed.

She was in the loft and it smelled of Christmas—pine boughs, apple pie, peppermint, roast chicken. Her grandmother, Freya, had been cooking in Ange's galley kitchen and had never made the traditional turkey and dressing for holidays. Snow pelted the windows as Izzy walked by them and re-started the turntable. Cracking strains of Wes Montgomery's guitar wafted through the house, mingling with the low pleasant timbre of Ange's voice as he talked to her sister.

Izzy walked over to him and sat in her usual spot on the worn ottoman in front of his chair, leaning back into him between his legs. The whole atmosphere was Hallmark perfect—a fire in the woodstove, a Douglas Fir twinkling with colorful lights. Her sister sat crossed-legged in one corner of the couch, a glass of wine sloshing slightly as she gestured to make a point.

Izzy couldn't really hear what she said and dismissed it. The feeling was what was important. She had a euphoric sense of well-being as she sat there taking it all in. Tam looked back toward the kitchen. Marlowe, dressed in completely modern clothes came into view.

A happy, gurgling infant bounced in his arms as he came around the couch. The baby was a beautiful child with dark curls and chubby cheeks. Izzy's heart melted as she saw Tam hold her arms out to take the child. She was positive this was how life was supposed to be.

The awareness part of her started to niggle at her brain, just an itch of conflict, of doubt that she tried to bury as she listened and felt her surroundings. *Go away, you're not real* she told the voice. This is real. *Ain't gonna happen.*

The vision wavered, and as she turned to ask Angelo, he'd disappeared and she was alone on the ottoman. The couch was barren, her sister and Marlowe and their baby gone. Freya, who'd been puttering in the kitchen was no longer there. A fog crept up from the floor. She ran through the house, looking for them. She found Tam on the floor of the kitchen, a pool of blood seeping out from under her. Izzy touched her and the blood stained her fingers, morphing into a red line scrolling and turning its way up her arm, swirling back and forth upon itself in a complicated burgundy tattoo.

Marlowe appeared, staggering into the room. Blood everywhere, he was gaunt, half-starved, and held his midsection together with both hands. His cry of anguish echoed her own.

Now she wanted the voice to sound. It's just a dream. This isn't real.

But it could be.

Izzy sat up in bed and unwound the sheets from her legs. Her hand searched for Ange beside her, but he wasn't there. Oh, why had she come home?

Because the visions and the energy of the portal had pulled at her. She needed the calm and control she felt in her little place. Her mind went over the dream. It had been so perfect—all of them, together, happy, safe. She wanted it to be a vision of their future. Maybe the second half of the dream was an anomaly. Maybe it was just her nerves at traveling back to the ancients that caused it. Flinging the covers back, she got out of bed and dressed hastily. Dream or vision, she couldn't wait. It would be less than fifty hours now—barely over two days until Marlowe was gone again, very possibly for the last time. She couldn't wait for Maurelle. She had to act.

Hopping on one foot, she pulled at her shoe and grabbed for her keys. Going through the rift alone was not her first choice, but she could do it. She could be back in a day. Time in the world of the ancients was different. Time moved slower there—weeks there could be but a day in the modern world. She would live the life of the old ones, living in a cave, tending fires, and dressing in animal skins. The time had been cold, harsh, and brutal. It was also amazing. The people there had believed in magic. And because of that belief, she'd experienced it for herself.

Ange could do lots of things, moving energy, an illusionary veil, subterfuge, but the ancestors could do things she'd never seen before. She wanted to bring that knowledge back.

Izzy locked her house and ran to her car parked on the street. She opened the car door and slid behind the wheel, but let out a small shriek when she saw a figure to her right.

The man in her passenger seat blinked in the light. Marlowe sat up, adjusted the seat after a moment, and rubbed his yet untrimmed beard.

"What are you doing here?" Izzy turned to face him, wondering how he got into her locked car.

"Waiting for you. It is about time, as they say." His smile was as all-knowing as her sister's. Tam always knew when she'd tried something stupid as a kid. "I have become accustomed to the stubborn determination that is the Paradiso sisters. "It was only a matter of time until you would take matters of your own accord. I shall attend thee."

"Thanks, Marlowe but—" He put a hand on her arm to stop her.

"You know thy sister. If I knew thy plans and let you go into such danger alone, she would flay me alive."

"How do you know my plans?"

"You plan to travel through the rift, do you not?" His eyebrow quirked.

"I'm not your responsibility." But she let him stay as she put the car into gear, carefully pulling out into nonexistent traffic. At one in the morning, her neighborhood was quiet. Still, she looked both ways and checked her blind spot.

"I assure you, Isabelle. I believe you quite a capable young woman. I am merely going as, what does Tamberlyn say? Backup, yes, that's it—to watch your six. And the light is green, I believe." He nodded at the traffic light.

She drove on.

"I don't think we should tell Angelo," she said, trying for confidence she didn't feel. "He'd just stop me." If Marlowe insisted on going, then Volpi was best left at home to help Tam.

"Do you think he could stop you? For I do not."

They approached Pinkie's, and Izzy parked her car some distance down the street and killed the lights. The bar lights were still on, and she needed to wait until Abraham left. If she could confront Maurelle on her own, she could convince her to open the portal.

"What has happened?" Marlowe asked.

"What do you mean?" Izzy fidgeted with her keys until he finally took them from her hand and placed them on the dashboard. She didn't want to tell him. The dream, or vision, or whatever it was still reverberating in her brain. Suddenly warm inside the car, she swiped her hair off her forehead. "It wasn't a vision, it was just a dream."

"Dreams are of the greatest import. It is the universe speaking to us as we slumber. If you've no wish to speak of it, I will not force you. Alas, I think you should, for if it comes to pass as your visions of Tamberlyn often do, I would be amiss if I did not protect her." He chuckled softly and shook his head. "I still feel that need, though I know her strength. She is my better in some ways. Yet, I doubt the urge to protect will ever go away."

"You are a good man. My sister and all of us are lucky to have you." She turned and smiled at him. "My dream was good. Or it started out that way. Of family and home and safety. But things changed and there was a tattoo, like runes, covering my hand and arm. I have no idea what it means." They heard the door slam as Abraham emerged from the bar. They both hunched down into the seat of her tiny car and waited in the dark for him to leave. "Did you see him, in the fight earlier? What is he?" Izzy asked.

"I've not seen such as Abraham. I thought him a mere man, until finding him in this time. But my own alchemist, Master Gomfrey, has told me of the Lyncus. Hast thou learned of the Greeks? Ovid's Metamorphoses?"

"Sure." Izzy tapped her fingers on the steering wheel. "The goddess Demeter commands Triptolemus to travel the world. He arrives at the court of King Lyncus, who is jealous and wants the goddess's favor. He plots to kill Triptolemus in his sleep and is turned into a Lynx."

"Very good. That which is myth is used to explain what cannot be—a man with the tail and features of a cat, long-lived, and can see into your very soul. I believe our Abraham is a Lyncus who can change his appearance at will."

"The world is a strange and wonderful place," Izzy said.

"Indeed. Shall we go?" His hand rested on the door handle. At her nod, they got out and slunk toward the door of the closed-up bar.

Marlowe demonstrated a surprising knack for lock-picking, and once inside, they made their way to the supply room door. After her surprise at their ease of entry, Izzy concentrated on what her words would be to Maurelle.

Marlowe stood at the door to the basement storeroom when she held up a finger. Taking a napkin from behind the bar, she wrote a hasty note to Angelo. She pulled out her cell phone and waved it at Marlowe with a small smile. "No cell service where we're going." She put the phone on the bar. "If we disappeared without a trace," she said. "Tam and Ange would do nothing else but look for us."

Marlowe pulled a key from his pocket and signet ring off his finger. He left both items beside the phone. "Tamberlyn will keep it safe for me." He looked at it a moment, before striding to the door of the storeroom.

Izzy needn't have worried about what to say to Maurelle for she wasn't there. They called out politely as they searched for invisible barriers or cloaks that may hide her appearance. After a few minutes with no magic unveiled, Marlowe looked at her in question.

The portal opening, though invisible, still called to her. She felt the energy of it in her bones, vibrating through her like static electricity. Closing her eyes, she blocked out the idea of finding Maurelle, of leaving Ange and her sister behind, of their anger and worry, even leaving Marlowe out of her current mindset. He no longer existed in the room with her. Her mind searched out for the key, the odd combination of words and gestures that would bring the orb of light and energy into the room.

She stood completely still, facing the wooden shelf along the wall. Stocked with toilet paper, jars of maraschino cherries, and cocktail onions, it appeared quite ordinary, dusty even.

With a single word and gesture from Izzy, the wall shimmered into a glowing mass. A tiny circle appeared between a box of plastic stir sticks and a jar of pimento-stuffed olives. It manifested into a heptogram about the size of a man's head. Izzy pulled a stick of colored chalk off the shelf and just underneath the wavering shape, its seven-pointed angles and planes expanding and contracting, she wrote a quick mathematical formula.

Absent both the ancestors' and Maurelle's help, she was on her own. She used her knowledge of the mortal physical world and the power to manipulate energy to create a doorway where none had been.

The polyhedron breathed to life under the complex formula. Izzy stepped back, repeating a phrase from her time with the ancients—a conversation with the elements, with time itself.

At the last syllable, the shelf disappeared from view and in its place was the great shimmering green light of the portal. It had seemed much less imposing earlier in the evening, an illusion of smoke and light. A trick of the mind into which beings disappeared. Now, it was a presence.

Izzy turned to Marlowe. "You realize that if we survive this, my sister will kill us."

Marlowe smiled and held out his hand to her. "Fortune favors the foolhardy."

She took his hand, and they jumped.

Chapter 14

Tamberlyn

It was almost three a.m. when I pulled into my parking space in front of my building. Not a designated space, but it was the place I always parked—the one just in front of my apartment. It wasn't the closest to the door, but I could keep an eye on my car.

After leaving the crime scene, my first instinct had been to contact Volpi and see what kind of hostile could bullseye a moving target with an arrow at two hundred yards. But the idea of Marlowe waiting for me changed my mind. I jogged to the apartment door, cursing as I dropped my keys before finally jamming them into the lock and fumbling through the door. "Christopher Marlowe, be prepared to be ravished." I called out as I entered, pulling off my boots and storing my gun in the hall table drawer. I stripped off my clothes on the way into my bedroom. My apartment is not large, so I got as far as my shirt and bra.

My bed sat in the same state we'd left it—rumpled and

empty. No Marlowe. He'd said he'd wait for me here. I'd given him my extra key, told him the combination of wards to press. Maybe he'd stayed with Volpi? I found my phone. Now, I had no qualms about getting Volpi up.

"Is Marlowe there?" I rushed over Volpi's groggy hello when he answered on the fourth ring.

"No, Izzy took him to your place. She's staying at hers tonight." There was a tiny pause. "What's happened? Is Marlowe—has he gone back?"

That had been my first thought, but I'd pushed it away, not wanting to even entertain the idea. We'd spent only a few hours together.

"Tam?" he asked. "Did you try Izzy's phone?" He paused, and I knew he was texting her.

Isabelle. She was the last to have seen him. She would know. My heart skipped. "She wouldn't have gone back to the bar, would she? Not after Maurelle said to come back later."

"She's your sister, what do you think?"

"Damn it, Izzy."

"I'll meet you at Pinkie's." The phone clicked off.

Sure enough, Izzy's car was parked not far from the bar. Volpi was waiting for me as I drove up.

"Her car was unlocked and the keys were on the dashboard." His voice was tense.

The front door lock had been picked, and the place felt empty and dark. Downstairs was just as vacant—no one hiding in the shadows waiting to pop out at us. Maurelle seemed to be out wherever fringe fae go at three in the morning.

"She's done it," Volpi said, his hands in front of him as if he were trying to catch a basketball. "There's residual energy. She's gone through the portal, damn it all."

"And Marlowe with her." I choked back a wave of emotion and paced the room. "Maurelle! Where the hell are you?"

Volpi put a hand on my arm. "This wasn't Maurelle's fault. Izzy did this on her own. She's done it before."

"God dammit, Izzy." I rubbed my temples with some force. Everyone had always known Izzy to be the good one. She was polite to her elders, got good grades in school, and even went to church with the family. All things opposite of me. But we did share a stubborn streak, and when she wanted to do something, nothing short of the zombie apocalypse could stop her. And then she'd probably do it anyway, Louisville slugger in hand.

Volpi waited beside me, a worried look on his face. "Even if you could go after them, it may be messier than if you'd stayed out of it."

"How is it that you're okay with this?" I asked him. "She was supposed to wait."

Back upstairs, I helped myself to the scotch Abraham kept behind the bar—the good stuff. Volpi took a stool on the other side, facing me. I poured him a glass too. The man's face was wan, and he looked shaken.

"Have you known your sister to wait? For anything?" His empty glass rapped sharply on the bar. I poured him another. He was used to being the one left behind. This was how we worked. Volpi stayed behind and researched, I went out in the field.

But this was Izzy out there, not me. Now, Volpi and I were on the same side—staying at home, not knowing. The knowledge sank into me with every sip of scotch. Marlowe was gone. In his timeline, it was very close to the date of his death. Those scant hours we'd spent together may well be the last I ever see of him. And my sister had taken him into a world where human sacrifices were the norm.

"Will Marlowe—what if he travels while he's there? Can she work the formula from there? If they even find it. Can—"

Volpi put a hand up to stop my frantic stream of consciousness.

"You know your sister. If the solution is there, she won't stop till she finds it. As for Marlowe, he only travels forward, never before his own birthdate, so..." He trailed off, not wanting to finish.

"So what happens when he is forced back in time? Like going through the portal?"

"I don't know."

I noticed a cell phone at the end of the bar and went toward it. It was Izzy's. Locked. I handed it to Volpi, and he unlocked it with a wave of his hand. I looked at him. "Remind me not to keep secrets from you."

He scrolled through the phone. "There's nothing. No text messages, emails, or reminders."

I turned back to the bar. Catching a glint of gold behind an empty beer glass, I moved it aside. Marlowe's signet ring was there, telling me all of its stories of the past. My breath caught in my throat as I picked it up. A flat front with a simple M inscribed against a dark background. The sides had intricate swirls in bas-relief. I slipped it on my first finger and rolled it around.

"This is Marlowe's," I said, surprised that my voice didn't crack at all. On the bar, there was a cocktail napkin with a scribbled note.

Don't worry. Be back soon.

It was signed with a heart and the initial I. As if she were going to the friggin' grocery store or something. My house key was under the napkin, and I shoved it into my jeans pocket. "I've lost Marlowe. I can't lose Izzy, I just can't."

I felt Volpi's hand on my shoulder. "Let's go to the loft," he said.

∞

After three more glasses of Volpi's good whiskey and a few hours sleep on his couch, I woke up to the sound of a teapot whistle. Volpi was at his tiny three-burner stove wearing only loose-fitting black jeans.

Even from the couch, I could see a vicious scar on his back, about five inches in length midline along his spinal column. It was too ugly and irregular to be surgical. Maybe Volpi hadn't always been the one left behind. He turned before I could study it further, the dark blue of his eyes squinting in the dimness of the room. The light of the day hadn't breached his windows yet.

"You want some tea?" he asked. "Marlowe drank up all my coffee."

"Anything with caffeine," I answered and sat up.

There was a steaming mug on the counter for me when I came out of his bathroom. His tiny bathroom had been redecorated in pure Isabelle style. A pink flamingo throw rug and heart-shaped soap dish. "I can't believe my sister has domesticated you already. Pink flamingos? What's next? Little kids running around in rompers?"

Volpi chuckled. "Definitely not rompers."

The idea of curly-haired rug rats with my sister's gray eyes cooking up potions in their play yards left me stunned. "You ever have kids?" Strange, in all the years I knew Volpi, I'd never asked. He'd always told stories of stuff in his youth, events, people he'd met, things he'd done. But he stayed carefully away from the personal. And I, not being all that intuitive or even interested when it came to people, hadn't asked.

He studied me for a moment before answering. When he did, it was only to fish a wallet out of his back pocket and pull a faded black and white photo from it. It was small, passport photo size, of a dark-haired woman and small child on her lap. The child had lighter hair and curly, like Volpi's. I guessed it to be a boy of about two.

"They both died—car accident. Anthony was four at the time." He took the picture back from me, rubbing a thumb over the face of it before replacing it in his wallet.

"How long ago? Does Izzy know?" I deliberately left out the usual sympathetic mention. Both Volpi and I had lost enough people for it to be felt without saying. In fact, saying it would have felt like a platitude.

"A lifetime ago," he said. "And yes, your sister knows."

Of course, she would know. Izzy could get confessions

out of a gay priest in the Vatican. Not that Volpi's words were a big confession or anything, but it was deeply personal stuff for my gruff, reserved mentor. The fact that my sister had not only redecorated his bathroom but redecorated his psyche was startling. Where had I been that I hadn't noticed how close they'd become?

"What about the fae?" He interrupted my thoughts, probably intentionally. We had an understanding, Volpi and I. A silent mutual agreement to never fall into the sappy sweetness of a buddy movie. "He still alive? And here?" Work the problem. That had always been our thing.

I nodded. "He's under protective custody, believe it or not. The attempt on the senator's life last night could not have been executed by Theo. He was with him at the time. Threw himself in front of, get this, an arrow." I hesitated just a moment, unable to believe my own words. "I don't think he's the one after Shepherd. He seems genuinely concerned about the man. We're monitoring them. Cobb and I will probably check in with the unit on duty in a couple of hours. See what else we can dig up."

"An arrow?"

"Yeah. From across the street, over a couple hundred plus yards. Quite the shot actually, St. Valentine would be ecstatic," I said.

"Come with me." He pointed up, and I followed him upstairs. In the years I'd known him, I'd never been to his loft workshop. In fact, prior to meeting Marlowe for the first time, my meetings with Volpi were conducted in his shop in the Italian Market.

The room was spare and not sizeable, with a large table in the center. The tabletop was bare except for an old fashioned set of scales in the center. One side held a fist-sized purple crystal, the other a long gray feather. I was tempted to mess with it, but fearing I'd upset the balance of the universe or something, I left it alone.

One entire wall was covered with whiteboard material in three sections, various mathematical formulas across the top.

Another side held a map of the city, with red and green lines crisscrossed over it. Two circles were drawn in black around intersecting points. In one circle was Pinkie's bar—the portal. The other circle was some blocks away. Three points surrounded the circle—Volpi's loft, my apartment, and Izzy's.

"What's this?" I asked.

Volpi looked up. "Ley line crossings. Alignments of mystical energy or they connect sacred sites, ancient monuments."

I glared at him and tapped the map where our addresses were marked.

"When Izzy rented her place, it completed a triangle, a way to harness the ley line crossing's energy, I suspect. She doesn't talk about it, but it was a smart move as I think it helps her to focus." His eyes softened toward me. "She probably doesn't say much, but the visions are becoming more frequent."

"Did you tell her to do that?"

He shook his head. "Izzy's intellect is often at war with her instinct, but sometimes instinct is stronger and it works out. She had a feeling about the place."

"I remember she went on and on about how cute it was—the little garden, the tiny kitchen. It's a fucking shoebox, but whatever."

"I think it was more the location than the amenities."

I turned away from the map toward the end wall covered in corkboard. Heavy stick pins holding various things related to Marlowe and time travel were scattered across it.

"We put this up right after you both came back from the ancient world, and have steadily added to it ever since. She was serious about us being close to solving the problem."

"I guess." I marveled at the detail of all the information they'd gathered. A list drew my attention, written in Marlowe's flourishing handwriting.

Behead a ghoul

Take Tamberlyn to hospital

Meet Hernandez and Connie

Follow T and H to night club. H dies.

Chase Strigoi Mort through the sewers and kill it.

This was not how I remembered Marlowe's last visit, but traveling was tricky. It was Volpi who'd beheaded the ghoul in the timeline I remembered; the previous one where Marlowe rescued me had faded from everyone's memory. Only Marlowe would have lived through both timelines.

"Izzy remembered this too, right? Like in a vision?" I asked.

Volpi pulled an oversized book off a shelf. "It's still scattered, but she's beginning to recognize timeline differences in her visions. They're not just a portent of the future, but where the past has deviated from its original."

This is what the ancient legend portrayed. The charm, or the guide knew where and when to correct history. The sword, or the warrior was the fixer. They worked in tandem. Marlowe's problem was he was without his guide, wandering aimlessly through time, trying his best to fix things he had no idea were wrong. Marlowe lived in dangerous times, and his own guide probably died before his abilities kicked in.

Volpi flipped through pages of the ancient-looking book. "Here." He pointed to a page. I peered over his shoulder at the sketch of a long-limbed human-like figure, but overlarge eyes and ears. Instead of being grotesque, the being commanded a certain beauty. "A Toxeute is elf-like but heavier. They're known to hold grudges for hundreds of years, and revenge is kind of their thing."

"Okay. He's kind of cute, in an odd sort of way."

"Now you sound like Izzy. Make no mistake, Toxeutes are deadly." Volpi studied me.

"You think that's what could be going after the senator?'

"They're rare. Like I said, I've never seen one. But I'll ask around."

Who does he ask about this stuff? I wondered. I waved back at the board. "What's all this?"

He looked up. "Yes, Marlowe knew we were working on

it. And he wrote this down for us yesterday, hoping the other timeline would shake some memory loose," he said, rubbing at his temple.

"All his talk about not meddling in the space-time continuum. I knew he was worried that I would start to travel soon."

Volpi chuckled. "That's Doc Brown, not Marlowe. This is your DeLorean, Marty McFly." He tapped the board. "Or it will be if Izzy gets what she needs."

"Let's go back to Pinkie's." I nodded toward the stairway. "Maybe Abraham or Maurelle are back now. I can't just sit here and wait."

"Go to work, Tam. I'll go to Pinkie's. You need to keep an eye on Theo. If he's working with a Toxeute, we, or you rather, need to stop him."

"Speaking of." I pulled the blood-stained four by four gauze out of my pocket and gave it to him. "I swiped this from the hospital last night. Maybe it will come in handy if we need it."

Volpi took it from me by the corner, not touching the blood.

"Theo's?" he asked. "Are you needing a poison or tracking spell?"

"Neither. At least not now. You never know when the blood of a former fae might be useful."

Chapter 15

Tamberlyn

Cobb was already at the station when I got there. Seated at his small desk and grousing into the phone—never one to make with the social niceties, he wanted others to get to the point as well. And when they didn't, he tended to be less than pleasant. He hung up as I tossed my satchel into my bottom desk drawer and kicked it shut.

Grabbing my coffee mug off my desk, I nodded at his empty one. "You want a refill?"

Instead of handing me his cup, he rose and headed toward the tiny break room with me. It was an alcove really, with a prefab counter that held a microwave old enough to leak radiation and restaurant-style coffee maker that made the best sludge this side of Pittsburg. After pouring our cups, we stood with our backs to the coffeepot so we could view the expanse of the homicide division workspace.

Our division took up about half the third floor of the building.

A room divided by cheap partitions stacked at angles to each other like a house of cards. Each cubicle housed two small metal desks and squeaky chairs.

Mine and Cobb's workspace was in the farthest corner from Captain Dudding's office. I figured that was intentional. It was also a change from the spot where I'd worked with X, which was good. I hadn't relished looking across my old desk and seeing someone else there.

"I checked into your old friend's background," Cobb said. "Theopolis." His tone was normal, not overly loud or secretive, but there was a reason he'd followed me into the break room. In our flimsy cubicles, anyone could eavesdrop. Normally, this is not a big deal, as everyone there was a cop and had enough cases of their own to worry about. But a high-profile case involving a senator had everyone on edge, and we'd had more than one co-worker stop by to chat about it. "How long did you say you've known him? Because prior to 2005, he doesn't exist."

I shrugged. "I was a kid, just out of high school. He was a lying bastard. For all I know, he could be in witness protection."

"I checked with the Federal Marshall's office, he's not. It's like the guy came from Mars or something." He wasn't that far off. Maybe X was right, and I should level with Cobb. "Look." He spoke behind his coffee cup. "I know you trust your gut a lot of the time, but Theopolis looks pretty suspicious. I'd like to bring him in." He paused. "But the blowback, if we're wrong, would be epic, so..."

"You want me to talk to him? Off the record? It's not gonna work. We didn't exactly start off on the right foot."

"And whose fault is that? I'm sure the guy won't hold it against you that you tried to shoot him." His mouth twitched behind his goatee. In that second, I realized he wasn't angry, but amused. As though I'd done something he'd finally approved of.

"So we keep an eye on him. Let's go to Shepherd's place, just to check on his welfare." I smiled at my partner.

"I just called the team watching him. Nothing happening.

He's fine."

I swallowed the last of my coffee and turned to rinse out my mug. "You know, we could stand to be more diligent. Concerned officers of the law and all that."

Surprisingly, he flashed something of a smile back. "Okay, I'll drive."

Shepherd's Philadelphia apartment was forty-five minutes away, and we got there in forty thanks to Cobb's aggressively efficient driving.

Center City had some plush high rises, and Shepherd kept a two-bedroom unit in one of the plushest—a thirty-story number with a marble-floored lobby and valet parking. Which Cobb adamantly refused to use, so we parked half a block down and walked. Even after flashing our badges, the doorman insisted on calling the senator's place to let him know we were coming.

Heading to the twenty-seventh floor, Cobb murmured, "This is the best damn safe house I've ever seen."

"I wanna live in WITSEC if it's all like this." I agreed.

The elevator doors opened, and our guys were seated outside in the foyer, playing rummy on a marble-topped table. I recognized Sanderson. A slightly pudgy fellow I'd worked with in vice. "Hey, Sandy," I nodded at him. "Any excitement?"

"Nah. Fancy digs, but dull as a door-mouse." Sandy always did mix his metaphors. "Pretty boy came out and gave us an itinerary for today." He waved a piece of paper at me. Night shift said there's some big whoop-tee-do tonight. But you know, Moretti's wife is about to pop, so..." He looked across to his rummy partner, a young Italian, nice-looking, clean cut, and fresh out of the patrol units.

"We'll take tonight," Cobb said and knocked on the door. I looked at him but didn't say anything. If my sister and Marlowe weren't back by tonight, I'd planned to go looking for them, not attend some posh fundraiser to babysit a senator. I wondered yet again if Cobb even had a life outside the job. He was in the office before me, often left after I did, and never talked about his personal life.

The door opened, and Theo stood there, his hands still buttoning a dress shirt—dark blue that set off his darker eyes. He blinked at Cobb, the crease in his forehead smoothing out when he saw me, and he turned to the side to let us in. He smelled good as I passed under his gaze. Theo had always smelled good. Fresh pine forest smells: trees, grass, even wet earth, but always new, never old and mildewy. Now his scent was different, more urban and manufactured, some expensive cologne. Surprised at the memory, I shoved it to the back of my mind.

Shepherd was on the phone as we came in and we waited politely, trying not to gawk at the elegant furnishings and artwork. I looked at my work-worn boots from Payless on the polished hardwood floor. At least I wasn't standing on the three-inch-thick carpet that lay under the coffee table and a soft leather couch. Delicate French chairs that dared you to place your polyestered butt in them were opposite the sofa. Across the room, a baby grand was angled for full effect on people who walked in the door. It worked exceptionally well.

"Jesus," Cobb muttered under his breath.

Shepherd waved from where he stood at the windows as he finished up his call. Theo had disappeared and reappeared, shirt appropriately buttoned as he held a white coffee cup on a saucer.

"Would either of you like some coffee?" he asked politely.

"Yes, that would be great, thank you." My partner was just as polite. I stared at him as if he were enchanted or something. He shrugged. "I only had two cups at the station."

"Detectives." Senator Shepherd approached us, indicating we should sit. The carpet gave under my feet like a down pillow, and I sat gingerly on one of the curvy-legged chairs. Cobb selected the opposite one—Papa Bear in Goldilock's living room, and I waited for it to crack under his weight.

Theo reappeared with a tray that held china cups and a French press coffee pot. He set it on the marble coffee table and busied himself with the preparation. It smelled heavenly. Real coffee, not overcooked bitters like our sludge maker produced. Enchanted or not, I was glad Cobb had said yes to coffee. I took the proffered cup and sipped daintily. Without asking, Theo had added just the right amount of cream to mine. The stuff tasted as good as it smelled.

"Senator," Cobb began and was told to call him, Shep. "Okay, Shep. We looked at the vantage point from where the shooter was last night. It's some distance away, about two hundred yards. Had to be a marksman with a very good compound or high-powered crossbow. Do you know anyone like that? Someone training for the Olympics or something?"

"Really?" Shepherd asked.

"Yes, sir," I answered. "It's a difficult shot to make at that distance." At this, Theo snorted, making an unimpressed sound though his Romanesque nose. I turned toward him. "People can shoot that far, yes. But to hit a target? And a moving one at that? Extremely difficult. It's almost an inhuman shot to make."

I narrowed my eyes at the snorter and sipped more coffee.

"But he didn't hit his target, Ms. Paradiso." Theo spoke in his well-modulated baritone. "He missed the senator."

"Which brings us to our next question. Is there anyone who would have motive to hurt you, Mr. Theopolis?" Cobb's eyes zeroed in on Theo. I almost felt sorry for him.

"You were supposed to be on the first trip to Philly, were you not? When Ms. Jackson was killed?" I asked as casually as possible, leaning forward to place my cup and saucer on the table. He'd basically told me he'd pissed off his entire nation, so I couldn't imagine Theo not making a few enemies in New York. A fae could easily make a shot across that distance, and might even use a hemlock-laced fruit basket as a weapon.

He managed a smile as he answered. "I have my share of enemies. Being a campaign manager for the mayor of New York does come with its challenges. I worked with, and consequently, had a few altercations with lots of people on the campaign trail." Theo's expression was calm and matter of fact.

Shepherd looked concerned. "So this could be about Locran?" he asked.

"If that were true, why not go after me in New York? Why wait until I moved here?" Theo asked.

I shrugged. "I don't know. These are all just theories. We are going through the list of possibilities from last night. We've compiled a short list from the original list you gave us. We'd like you to go over it, if you will, and give us some additional details."

He nodded, still frowning.

"I'm sorry, sir." Theo addressed the senator. "If this is about me, I've put you in danger."

"Nonsense," the older man said. "We're both here, and safe, thanks to the good works of these detectives. This will be over soon."

It sounded like platitudes and office politics, but again, I noticed the close relationship between them. The fatherly concern of the senator and Theo's unusual humility made me reconsider my earlier suspicion of him.

Cobb's cup rattled in his saucer as he finished his coffee. "Mr. Theopolis, if you would give my partner a list of those people from New York, the ones with a possible motive, I'd like to chat some more with the senator."

His meaning was clear—separate the witnesses. I cringed inwardly. This was standard procedure. Cobb wasn't throwing me to the wolves or anything. It was just the job.

"Of course." Theo set his cup down and waited for me to rise. He held out his arm, indicating we should go across the room toward the dining room table, a round glass affair surrounded by six maroon leather chairs, but we bypassed it for a breakfast nook instead. A small table and two chairs in a windowed alcove. Privacy with a view.

I dropped into a chair, noting it was far more comfortable than the fancy one in the living room and pulled out my tablet. The view out the window wasn't spectacular—high rises and office buildings. The sun hung over the city, shining on the red brick building to our left. It looked warm and inviting—a beautiful day. Theo sat opposite me and waited patiently. Neither of us spoke for a while. I busied myself with the tablet and tried not to notice the heady scent of him again.

As if reading my mind, he spoke. "You smell different."

"Pardon me?"

"You smell different. Not bad, mind you, just different. You used to have this scent about you like cotton sheets and honeysuckle. Now it's more graphite and gun oil."

"Sorry," I said it in the least apologetic way I could muster. "Could we quit talking about how I smell and get on with the list? Who would want you dead?"

"Besides, you, you mean?"

I clenched my teeth and moved my lips into a brief smile. He laughed and started with some names, mostly New Yorkers. I dutifully plugged them into my tablet. After a few minutes, I asked. "What do you know about a Toxeute?"

His heavy eyebrows arched in a surprised look. I was pleased to have caught him off guard.

"Where did you hear that word?"

"Don't be naïve, Theo. This is my job, remember? One of the reasons you wanted me all those years ago. I have learned a great deal since then."

"Has your memory of events returned?" His dark eyes were almost hopeful.

"No. I spoke with the gatekeeper. She told me you were banished as punishment, which considering the danger you put me in, is rather lenient for my money. But no matter, answer my question. Is it possible that a Toxeute would be after you? And put the senator in danger as well?"

He leaned back in his chair, crossing his legs, gazing at a spot just over my head. He flicked his eyes down to rest on mine for a lengthy few seconds before answering. I figured he was thinking up an elaborate lie, and it was a while before I realized he was listening for the senator's voice. When he heard it and was reassured no one was listening to us, he answered.

"We are forbidden to speak to an outsider about such things. But since I am now an outsider, I suppose it has no bearing. My people are at war, have been for hundreds of years. We have many factions in our forces, aerial assault, ground warriors, illusionists, code breakers. Toxeutes are the contingency of archers."

He had a believable way of speaking, painting a mural that revealed itself in front of his listener. I pictured a war with thousands of armor-clad warriors marching, fighting hand to hand for an unknown reason.

There were lots of wars like that, including human ones, fighting over religion or politics or land or all three. I don't know why it surprised me that the fae would do the same. And they'd thought themselves superior. Across from me, Theo's eyes grew soft as he remembered who he had been.

"I was a vanguard, one of three. It was our job to scout out the enemy, recruit new warriors for specific tasks, and to strategize. It's not unlike managing a political campaign." A smile flickered and then disappeared. "Prior to becoming a vanguard, I commanded several different units, including the archers, and you are correct—a Toxeute could make that shot easily. But if he or she were aiming for me, they would have hit their mark."

"They did." I reminded him. "How's the shoulder?"

"Healing. Not as fast as you would, but it is healing." How did he know of my recent ability? And what else did he know about me? "Does this mean you no longer want to kill me?" he asked.

"That depends. You could still be a suspect in the murder of Ms. Jackson. And a threat to the senator."

"You don't believe that." He said it casually as if it were a simple truth.

"No, I don't. But—"

"You still want revenge or justice? For bringing you to my world? I did what I was ordered to do. I am a soldier. I was to recruit others to help us win the war."

"I am not an *other*." I pointed to myself. "Human. We're out of it, remember? Your job wasn't to seduce and kidnap an innocent girl for your war."

"No kidnapping. You came of your own accord." A wicked grin flashed across his unlined face. "Several times, if I recall correctly."

"Don't be crass," I snapped at him.

"You liked it when I was crass." He snapped back. I got up. He grabbed my forearm to keep me there. I jerked, and he let go. "I'm sorry," he apologized. "You have a way of bringing out the worst in me."

"I get that a lot," I said still standing at the table. I glanced over and saw Cobb watching us from over the senator's shoulder. I sat back down. "Let's try and keep to business, okay? Who among the Toxeute would still harbor a grudge? You've been sentenced to live among the lesser—the mortal world. Isn't that bad enough?"

"Bad enough. It is demoralizing. For whatever wrong you think was done to you, I assure you, my punishment is of the cruelest sort. At the time, I'd begged for death instead." He looked around him. "But I've become acclimated."

"I can see that. So, not so awful after all?"

"Making a living was the hardest concept to grasp. Money is such an odd notion. We have no need of it, you see." He had relaxed again, and it came to me that when I moved suddenly, he did also. It was a battlefield reflex. One hand extended, and he tapped a finger near my tablet. "So you spoke with the gatekeeper?"

I resisted the urge to withdraw my hand away from his proximity. He was trying to be up front about things. I may as well return the favor. At this point, it didn't look like he'd be out of my sight any time soon.

"Do you know of Marva, I mean, Maurelle? She's a Tessaerat."

He pursed his lips in amusement. "You do get around, Tam. Guardians of the Fringe. The no man's land between upper and lower clans. She must have been at the conclave."

I nodded, though I had no memory of it. "She's the one who kept me from being executed by your people for knowing too much. No thanks to you. In order to save me, she altered my memories. Flashes are coming back."

As soon as I realized my mind had been screwed with, it set about repairing itself. Memories of walking in the woods with Theo, late one evening, and him telling me he needed to talk, taking my hand and pulling me into a circle of light. A portal. But not the one at Pinkie's.

I shook my head and blew out a breath, trying to stay on task. "Would there be an archer angry enough to hold a grudge? To come into the mortal world to kill you?"

"No one in particular." He brushed it off. "What do you remember? About the conclave or before?" His tone tread lightly on my memories, as though hunting through a forest.

Before I could answer, Cobb appeared with the senator behind him.

"Paradiso, we've got to go." His voice was urgent.

I asked why, but I was moving. I'd worked with Cobb enough to know that if he said move, he had a reason. When I rose, Theo didn't hesitate. He grabbed the senator's arm and pulled him with us toward the door. As we passed through the living room, a gray mist had started forming along the floor, rolling out the air ducts and across the high-end carpet like a toxic cloud. My eyes watered at the sting of it and we stumbled out into the hall, gasping. Cobb slammed the door, shrugged out of his jacket, and jammed it in the space under the door. His shoulders tensed under his white dress shirt as he called the station. Sanderson and his partner bounded out of their chairs, scattering the deck of cards on the marble floor.

"This is Cobb, I'm at number ten Rittenhouse with Senator

Shepherd. Get a hazmat team up to 2704 ASAP." He nodded toward the elevator, and I punched the button.

"What's going on?" Shepherd asked.

The elevator doors opened, and we all got in. Cobb looked at me from across the small space. "The reason the senator stayed at the hotel last week was this place was being painted. Someone planted something here. I thought it was a bomb."

"Apparently, something a little more subtle," I answered. "Poison gas? But why set it to go off now. They've been here all night."

"Maybe they were waiting for something," Cobb answered. "Like the arrival of two detectives on the case."

Chapter 16

Isabelle

The green light faded behind them, leaving a shimmer in the air as the portal closed. Izzy lay on the stony ground, panting from the exertion of both the travel and activating the rift. She adjusted her body around a protruding rock as she gazed at the sky.

They'd left in the darkness of early morning hours and had arrived in the late afternoon. She knew this as sure as she knew they had transcended not mere hours, but eons of years. Remembering she did not travel alone, she lifted her head to look for her companion. Sudden guilt flooded her. She'd given no thought of how dangerous portal travel might be to Marlowe, thinking that he, like her sister, would suffer no ill effects. "Marlowe?" She called out. A groan some yards away relieved her worry. At least he wasn't dead.

Marlowe had landed on a sparse patch of grassy earth. He scrambled to a standing position, holding his head briefly at the movement. "At your service, Mistress Isabelle," he said, shaking ice crystals off his hair and staggering toward her.

The rift was prone to extreme shifts in temperature, as well as playing havoc with the inner ear. The last time had caused Izzy severe vertigo.

"Let us find your artifact and be gone from this place. Have thee fared well?" He bent toward her, looking a trifle green around the gills.

Izzy was surprised he was upright at all. "I'm fine, I think." She waited a moment to get her bearings before taking his hand.

They were in the lowlands. Rolling hills dipped and stretched to mountains in the distance. The slight smell of fish in the air told her the sea was to her left and home would be in the opposite direction. Not her modern-day basement apartment, but an ancient origin. The knowledge was a memory, much like a childhood one, distant and faded, but definitely there. She noted the slight lines etched on Marlowe's face as he looked about. With all of Marlowe's travels, Izzy figured he'd be used to his brain being stirred and shaken

"This was most disconcerting. Not at all like my travels."

"No?" She breathed deeply to steady the reeling in her head and take in their surroundings. It was not the dead of winter that she'd experienced before, but the crisp air and senescence of plant life told her it soon would be. "Tam told me your journeys were like being struck by lightning. That she'd felt it once."

"True. She attempted to travel with me. I thought it most foolhardy at the time." He let her take the heading as they walked across the spare and rocky ground, surrounded by only the occasional bit of dormant foliage. "That was before I knew her ancestry was like my own. As well is yours. You could be a traveler also, Isabelle."

"No." She shook her head. "I am the charm, the guide. Much less glamorous than the warrior like yourself. I am more comfortable doing the research."

"And yet, here you are, traveling into the unknown." He

smiled.

"Yes, well, this is me, pretending it's research and trying not to be petrified."

"You comport thyself well, Isabelle." He stopped and studied the sky, his head tilted up as though sniffing the air. "We must hasten, a storm is coming."

She picked up her pace as clouds rolled toward them. "If we hurry, we can get to the outpost before nightfall. Most of the people live near the sea, where they make their living, but they go to the foothills to worship and for ceremonies. We'll head to the temple, and see what we can find."

"Pray tell, what is it exactly that we seek? A talisman?"

"Perhaps," Izzy replied. "But my theory is that it is also a series of words or sounds."

"How will you know when you find it?"

They trudged uphill and a strong breeze picked up, blowing her hair across her face. She pulled strands out of her mouth and studied her companion. His cape whipped and billowed in the wind, creating large bird of prey shadows on the ground. Marlowe kept his eyes on the horizon, occasionally scanning to their left and right, wary of other travelers.

To their backs, the sun slid from behind a cloud, throwing his face deeper into shadow, and she could no longer see the fine lines around his eyes, the hollow of his cheeks, or the set of his mouth. In this light, his expression reminded her of her sister. Tam often seemed to slide into a melancholy state.

Marlowe and Tam were very alike in their personalities—more dark than light, more formidable than approachable. Marlowe, with his old-world manners, often put aside this darkness to put his companions at ease. Tam rarely made the effort.

"The short answer is I just have to go with my gut." Izzy smiled at him.

"Interesting turn of phrase," Marlowe said. He shortened his stride to match hers, even though they traveled at a fast enough pace to leave her slightly breathless.

"Coming here is like coming back to a childhood home, everything is familiar, yet changed. I know it, and yet I don't. There's a sense of belonging for me here. Something I haven't really admitted until now." She paused, catching her breath. "When we were here before—Tam and I—all she wanted to do was leave. She hated everything about it, and you know how she gets."

Marlowe chuckled beside her.

"Maybe her attitude was evident to the others, because, after her arrival, the situation changed, became more dangerous, like we were no longer wanted. It was like I belonged and Tam did not. The ancients don't take to strangers."

"You are wary of me causing the same reaction?" He moved ahead of her as their path inclined.

She did her best to keep up and talk at the same time. "Yes. Even if you don't intend to. We may have to leave in a hurry, but I'm telling you right now, I'm not leaving here without the rest of the formula. Whatever it is we need—artifact, talisman, or poem—I will have it before I leave."

Marlowe stopped on a small rise. Izzy stood next to him, her hands on her hips as she sucked in air, yet Marlowe was barely winded. She made a mental note to start working out more when she got home.

Both looked back toward where the portal had spilled them out onto the ground. The gate had closed, leaving no trace of where they'd come from, or could return. Izzy turned to Marlowe and smiled. "Remember where we parked. You may have to get back here without me."

Marlowe gazed back over the terrain as if mentally marking the location of the portal and then turned toward her. "You have always seemed the quiet, amiable sister, yet you have your sister's resolve and stubbornness. Rest assured, dear Isabelle, I will make every attempt to complete our mission. However, I will not be traversing the gate without you. Not if I can help it."

With that statement, he sighed, and they resumed walking. "I've no idea how my particular talent for traveling will surface here. I assume they have the same moon in this world as in ours. A younger moon, perhaps, but still the same, with its ill effects on my person. I may only a have a few days here."

The ground had evened out and the walking was easier. Now that they were closer, Izzy felt the anxiety leave her body. She noticed the air held a sweetness to it, a velvet feel of florals and grass, even in the dead of autumn, such as the modern world had never experienced. She felt at home here, the pull of the place nagging at her insides. Could she stay here, in this time, if she had to? If for some reason their way home was blocked, could she survive? Yes, of course, this place could easily be home.

But not for Marlowe. His place was in the future, in his world, or in modern-day Philly with Tam. But out of concern for Izzy, he was here, forfeiting whatever time he had left with her sister.

The sight of the tiny temple outpost ahead lifted Izzy out of her guilt, and they quickened the pace, making it to the gate just as the sky opened and cold sleet filled the air, stinging their hands and cheeks.

Hardly more than a smattering of wood and stone structures, the small grouping of huts nestled behind the gate. Not really a gate at all, the entrance to the outpost was delineated by two twenty foot-posts connected by a crossbeam. The crossbeam was several feet above their heads and decorated with carvings of dragons and fire.

"This is different than I remember. But I've never approached the temple from this side before. It's open. Anyone could walk through." Izzy's stride slowed to a hesitant walk in spite of the cold rain.

"Look up, that outcropping on the hillside to the right. A guard watches. They've been watching us approach for a mile now." He'd opened his gigantic cape to encircle her shoulders, protecting her from the sleet. "And behind them are the mountains, difficult for an army to traverse, at least in quiet and dead of night. They have no need for barriers or walls. I suggest we don't alarm these people."

Silence greeted them as they passed through the constructed archway. Marlowe called out as they passed the first hut. Isolated from the rest of the outpost, it was cut into a hillside and sported a low turf-covered roof with a round chimney of stone. Gray wisps of smoke wound their tendrils through the sleet. After a moment without an answer, they moved on.

Izzy's felt someone tug at her hand, and she stepped outside the warmth of Marlowe's cape. A young girl of about ten, her blonde braids turning dark in the freezing rain, pulled Izzy sharply away from Marlowe. She seemed frightened, in need of help. Izzy called out to Marlowe who'd moved onto the next hut. Men dressed in dark leather strode out of a long building and headed toward them.

Marlowe turned to face them. To his credit, he did not draw his sword, but his stance was alert and ready.

"*Comst du. Comst du!*" The girl was frantic now, pulling Izzy toward the hut's doorway.

Marlowe turned back to Izzy, his hand waving her into the hut. The young girl and shelter seemed the safer option, but Izzy didn't want to leave him.

"Marlowe." She barely got his name out before another hand, stronger, more insistent, pulled her into the darkness of the hut. Stumbling, she fell onto her hands and knees in the dirt. Izzy took her time getting up, letting her eyes adjust to the darkness. The hut smelled of earth and hair, but it was an oddly clean scent. The balsam wood fire filled the small place with woodsy warmth.

Ignoring the draw of the fire and the hut's occupants, Izzy ran toward the single tiny window cut into the thick wood. Through the opening, she glimpsed Marlowe being hauled away by two of the guardsmen. Their backs turned, she recognized the etched dragon symbols on the thick leather coverings. Temple guards.

She turned back to the interior of the hut. "Please, I need to help my friend." She indicated outside.

The woman who'd pulled her into the house stood in front of the fire, her hands on her hips, fingertips close to the knife hanging from her belt. Izzy raised her hands to show them free of weapons.

"My..." She'd forgotten the ancient word for friend. "*Brudr.*" Close enough. If Tam could ever marry anyone, it would be Marlowe, and then he'd be a brother.

The woman shrugged as if Marlowe's fate was sealed. She spoke to the girl in a string of words that Izzy struggled to translate. The heat from the fire felt good on her shoulders. Her skin prickled inside her modern jacket. Izzy used two of the ancient words she remembered for fire—*aldrnari* and *bruni.* She tentatively held her hands toward the hearth. At the girl's urging, the woman moved aside, giving Izzy access to the fire.

After she'd warmed up, Izzy gleaned bits and pieces of the conversation between mother and daughter. The girl's name was Klacka, and she hadn't finished her chores—care and feeding of *de hœns.* Izzy hadn't seen any sort of fowl when she arrived so they must be sheltered elsewhere. The girl's expression reminded Izzy of Tam whenever Freya asked about homework, but she bundled up and went outside.

Once, they were alone, Izzy introduced herself, using the old world pronunciation of her name—*Isobel,* and gave what she hoped was a plausible explanation of her strange modern clothes.

The woman seemed to understand her, nodding, and indicating a small stool. Izzy lowered herself to the seat and studied her surroundings as the woman ladled some broth out of the small pot hung over the fire. She handed the wooden bowl to Izzy and pulled a proper chair from the table to sit near her at the hearth.

She tapped her chest and spoke a name: Flótjr Fugl.

Fleeing bird, Izzy translated, and then chastised herself for remembering unhelpful words like bird, but not the word for friend. She sipped at her broth, pleased by its spicy flavor, and let its warmth seep into her.

The woman asked about the man traveling with her. Izzy caught the word warrior, which was not a designation she would have given Marlowe. Thinking about a stranger's view of him, though, with his broad sword, his battle-ready stance, and ever watchful concentration—warrior was not a bad description. Izzy explained with both words and gestures that they were traveling to see family, and the sea voyage had gone awry. Travel by sea was commonplace here, but also dangerous—the coastline littered with sharp rocks and rough surf. The ancients were formidable sailors, their range of exploration far exceeding that of the better known and much later explorers, the Vikings.

As they conversed, Klacka returned and scrutinized Izzy with barely subdued interest. Izzy smiled to reassure her, and asked Flótjr about her home life, thinking of the woman as Flo.

"I am a widow," Flo said. "Only stayed near the temple because of Klacka." She nodded at her daughter across the room. "She'll be in service to the temple in a couple of years, and I shall do my work from the village." She held up a small knife and a long arrow shaft, deftly making a notch in one end. Beside her, Izzy noted a small bowl of points. Arrowheads knapped from stones.

"You are a *Vapn smiŏa*. Weapon builder." The words came to Izzy as if she had always had them. The more language she heard, the easier it was to understand. It wasn't like taking Spanish in college, which she struggled with—conjugating verbs for the sake of a decent grade. This language seemed a part of her, much like her visions or her memories.

Flo nodded as she secured the point to the shaft with thin leather strands. Izzy, drawn in by the intricate work, was fascinated by the process. Putting her mission and her worry about Marlowe aside, she asked a question about the craftsmanship of arrow making. The strands of leather had been soaked in water and animal tallow to make them pliable. Once dried, the leather would shrink, holding the arrowhead secure and with little wind resistance when fired.

"Most of the men are away on a hunt before the winter storms come. Your brother can fight, yes?"

Izzy nodded.

"Then he'll not be harmed, but he'll work for the guard or the Earl King." Flo kept to her work, her head down so Izzy could not see her face. The firelight flickered across her features for a brief moment as she focused. Along one side, between the outer edge of her eye and her hairline, a vicious red scar ran the length of her face—temple to chin. It pulled the skin of her mouth into a droop, making for a permanent frown. The scar was thick and mottled, not made by a blade, but a brand. Izzy let out a sympathetic murmur before she realized it. Flo caught her gaze.

"I used to be beautiful," she said, her mouth curving up on the uninjured side. "My mother thought I should dedicate myself to the temple, to be a priestess, but I fell in love with a soldier." She shrugged lightly, her thin shoulders moving under the rough fabric of her shift. "I wanted to stay with Ren and not dedicate myself to the gods. In order to do so, I allowed myself to be marked. It's a warning to others not to take the vows lightly."

"I'm so sorry," Izzy said, reminded of her easy life in the modern world.

"I am not." Flo smiled. "Ren and I had many happy years together before he sailed on the great voyage. And I have Klacka, who is a joy to me in my age."

Izzy noted the woman could not be more than thirty-five, and those many happy years might have only been ten or fifteen in number.

"The scar reminds me of my sacrifice. Before I renounced the ways of the priestess, I'd learned some of the secret rites. This is strictly forbidden." Flo seemed to take it for granted that disfiguring someone over changing their mind was a small thing. Perhaps in a world where people barely lived to their forties, often lost limbs and lives to wars, accidents, and infection, it was a small thing.

"Do you know the priestesses?" Izzy asked, trying to sound casual. "I mean, since you..." Her words faded. There was a short silence where they only heard the crackling fire and Klacka's murmurs as she played nearby. "Stjarna. Have you heard of her?" Izzy immediately felt bad that she may have brought up a painful time for Flo. The last thing she wanted was to make Flo feel bad about her decision.

Stjarna had been Izzy's first friend when she'd come here before. The young girl had been only fifteen or so but was very powerful and second in line to the Exalted Priestess. Stjarna had taught Izzy much about the ways of the ancients. If she remembered Izzy, then getting what she needed would be a simple matter of asking.

"Stjarna was one of the most powerful priestesses of the temple. It's no wonder you've heard of her. Her good works and kindness are legendary." Flo took on a dreamy look. "I wish I'd known her."

Izzy held her breath, dreading the answer to her question, yet knowing it as surely as one of her visions. "So Stjarna is gone then?"

Flo looked suspicious. "Of course. She was before I came to the temple as a young girl. I was fourteen then, and she'd just taken the great voyage. But her reign was long, and our people prospered. Now, it is not so easy of times. The villagers from the sea have made several raids on us in the mountains. The Earl King forbids travel to the sea, and our settlement is poor. We cannot worship the gods as we have in the past. The temple is closed to all now, except for the elders."

Izzy's breath caught in her throat as she listened. Stjarna had risen to the rank of Exalted Priestess, as Izzy had anticipated, but at least thirty or forty years earlier. Her formula had been off.

They had arrived too late. She remembered Stjarna's world. It was a harsh environment, but the people flourished, celebrating with harvest rituals and spring festivals, rites of passage, and abundance. This time seemed bleak and dark in comparison.

"Flo, is there anyone in the temple who would remember her? Back when she reigned or before?"

"Only the *Móðir*," Flo said. "The mother." She bent her head to her work and said nothing further as night fell quick and silent outside.

Flo had found her a pliable deerskin and heavy furs for a pallet, and Izzy lay awake for some time. Her wrong equation had brought them to this harsh world, without allies, and she'd already lost track of Marlowe. She'd taken Tam's chance to be with him, possibly for the final time, in order to fix things, but their odds of survival, let alone success, felt tenuous and puny. Izzy felt much the same as she fell into a fitful sleep on the floor beside the fire.

Chapter 17

Tamberlyn

In spite of his apartment being gassed in another attempt on his life, Senator Shepherd insisted on attending his event that night.

The fundraiser, or whoop-tee-do as Sandy had called it, was held in the Palomar Hotel's ballroom. Just a block from the senator's apartment complex in Center City, the boutique hotel was up and coming to be on par with the Ritz Carlton and the Logan. It was a four-hundred-dollar a plate dinner, complete with a live orchestra, and the senator would be the keynote speaker.

I almost ducked out of the whole affair, but Volpi had texted me that no one had shown at the portal. Izzy and Marlowe were still gone, and Maurelle was in a foul mood when she learned that my sister had once again manipulated her gateway. I may as well work—he'd notify me as soon as they showed up, which would be soon—anytime now.

Damn Izzy and her impulsiveness. But as much as I wished Marlowe was here, I was glad he was with her. The time of the ancients was a dangerous place to be alone.

Not that the here and now was all that safe. Each attempt on the senator's life had escalated, and the last one almost included two homicide detectives. I had a feeling this was more than just one pissed off guy. I'd killed enough hostiles to warrant someone putting a price on my head. And Theo pretty much pissed off everyone who knew him, in both worlds. If my gut was right, the poisoners and the Toxeute were two separate assassins focused on a single target, which told me that there was another fae behind it all.

At the fundraiser, Cobb had stationed himself near the back of the room—standing near the table farthest from the dais. His long locks held back neatly with a black cord that was almost invisible in the mass of hair. The rental tux was of blue-black merino wool, but he looked as comfortable as if he were in casual wear.

"You clean up nice, Cobb." I came to stand beside him. He glowered over at me and snorted.

"Damn pants were too short," he said. "Had to wear my own pair. I should get a discount on the rental since it's only the shirt and jacket. You got your earpiece?" I tapped my ear where my hair covered the flesh-colored earbud. Cobb had a similar one. Much better than the ones I used in vice back in the day, these were voice-activated and almost undetectable. "I put you at Shepherd's table. You can play nice with the VIP's," he said.

"Play nice? Have you met me?"

"Like *I'm* going to do it?" he asked.

He had a point. Neither of us were good at this sort of thing, but Cobb tended to put people off just by looking at them. I, at least, had to open my mouth first. I shrugged and made my way to a table close to the stage.

The round tables seated twelve comfortably, and the room held maybe twenty tables. It wasn't a huge event, but big enough to cause havoc if there was an assassination attempt.

My name card was placed between Theo and Shepherd, who was bringing his daughter. The senator had his own security contingent, and they lined the wall close to our table. Ignoring their stoic frowns, I saluted them with my water glass and surveyed the room, finding the quickest path to the nearest exit.

Narrowing my focus to those at my table, I looked into the eyes of Gianni Balfour, noted mobster and all-around snake. Every strand of his dark expensively cut hair was full of product to keep curls in check. His skin tone was darker than mine, but I doubted he spent more time in the sun—he was a night owl— also like me. He was small-statured and slim, and he moved with a mean-natured grace as if every lift of his hand was meant to be an attack but thought better of it.

He said nothing. Probably spotted me as I crossed the room, so he hadn't been caught off guard. Smiling with his little snake smile, he held out his own water glass in a toast. Artificially white teeth gleamed at me. I gritted my teeth and looked away, murmuring into my shoulder.

"You could have warned me he was here," I spoke to Cobb, not having to mention names. His chuckle crackled in my ear.

"The only fun I'm going to have at this thing is watching you trying *not* to shoot Gianni Balfour. But seriously, if he were to try anything, it wouldn't be while sitting at the same table. Keep your enemies close, right, Paradiso?"

My Sun Tsu quoting partner was right. He usually was, and I was thankful for his practical thinking—and for the wide expanse of the table and the chatter of dinner guests. The generous span of the white table topped with a floral centerpiece made it difficult to converse with the people on the other side. All of these things protected me from doing something that would ruin my career and put me in jail. Also, it's considered bad form to shoot your dinner companions.

Yes, I had a gun. Not my Glock, as my dress, a slinky number from ages ago, did not work well with shoulder holsters, but there was a Sig Sauer strapped just above my knee. It was tiny but could do some damage.

The senator came in with more of his security team and daughter, making the rounds and shaking everyone's hands. He and Gianni exchanged simple polite pleasantries. After a nod to his men, he made his way toward his seat.

"You look lovely, Detective, and thank you for being here."

"It's my job, Senator, the being here part, anyway. Why is Balfour here?"

Shepherd looked across the table. Balfour had turned toward his date for the evening, saying something into her ear. Her smile and laughter were as fake as her silicone implants.

"He wants to contribute to the campaign," Shepherd said. "And significantly more than just this dinner. I didn't invite him."

"If you give him an inch, Senator, you may lose more than a mile with Balfour."

He looked thoughtful for a moment and introduced me to his daughter, a lovely college co-ed named JoAnne. We chatted some about her studies until her eyes widened and tracked someone from across the room, her face aglow with an oncoming blush.

I turned to see Theo making long elegant strides toward us, stopping at a couple of tables to shake hands with guests. His tux was no rental and cut perfectly on his frame, emphasizing the broad and the narrow of him. The beard stubble managed to make him look rugged rather than unkempt, and he and Balfour must use the same barber, only much less product and curl for Theo.

He shook hands with Shepherd and smiled at JoAnne, who'd babbled something inane. He pulled out his chair to sit, grimacing at his name card before tossing it on its end as if it offended by seating him next to me.

I turned from a blushing JoAnne to study Theo, who had pointedly ignored me so far. He looked relaxed as he chatted with others, but there was tension in his shoulders, a vigilance in the way he scanned the room. He was on alert as much as I was.

Eventually, the mayor introduced another dignitary to sing Shep Shepherd's praises. I didn't recognize her name, but she was entertaining, and while I pretended to listen during the salad course, I found myself caught up in her tales of Shepherd during the old days. He was a Philly native, not far from my old neighborhood of Roxborough.

The senator was a good guy. And a politician through and through, laughing good-naturedly at her comments and managing to include everyone at the table even over the noise and chatter. The interaction between him and Balfour was cordial but professional. All's fair in the business of politics and crime.

Cobb's voice bristled in my ear. "Maybe Balfour will be so bored of this shit, he'll confess to all crimes just to get out of here."

I chuckled as the waiter removed my empty salad plate. Theo sat back in his seat, allowing the waiter access. His smile was brief as he spoke. "Your laugh is the same as I remember."

I met his eyes. "Don't act like I was more than a blip on your radar back then. It's insulting."

His smile didn't fade, but he focused on the table, picking up his wine glass. He sipped. His voice was modulated so only I could hear. "Couldn't have that. You might start to dislike me."

"Dislike is far too mild a word for it. Admit it, all you cared about was the mission. A new recruit for your cause." I couldn't help it. Every interaction with him threw me back into the past. I tried to keep my voice at the same confidential level but wasn't quite as successful.

"That was true. In the beginning at least." He said nothing more. I was grateful he didn't fall into the cliché of saying he'd fallen madly in love with me, and it changed him forever. Except for that brief answer, he'd given no indication that he'd felt anything at all. And why did I care, anyway?

"Let's just get through tonight without incident, okay?" I tried to change the subject—present over past. I'd pretty much take that any day.

He wasn't having it at all. "Remember that night we went to the animal park? You laughed a lot then."

"We call it a zoo."

"Yes. A bizarre custom—locking up animals, especially while the lethal ones still roam about freely." His dark eyes shifted to look at Balfour, who was busy smirking at his dinner companion. So he knew of Balfour's less than stellar reputation. Of course, as campaign manager, it was Theo's job to protect his client's reputation. Apparently, he didn't approve. And yet, here Balfour was, at the head table for all the world to see.

The senator leaned toward me. "She's a hard act to follow." His chin tipped toward his predecessor on the podium. "Wish me luck." He winked. It wasn't a salacious, leering kind of wink, more like a friendly conspirator. Like I said, a true politician. Dinner had been served just before he'd been introduced and the room was quiet as they tucked in. There were two choices—prime rib and salmon. I'd picked the prime rib, rare of course, with a baked potato.

I barely listened to the senator's speech. Instead, I surveyed everyone else. On my right, I noticed Theo was doing the same. Neither of us spoke again. In fact, aside from the slight noise of forks on plates, the place was quiet, attention held in the words of the impassioned politician.

I ate mechanically, trying to stay vigilant, but in spite of me wanting to keep things strictly business, my mind had other ideas. As usual.

The event Theo spoke of had been a concert, blues musicians and beer tents, and one of the few times the zoo opened at night. Theo and I had seen each other a few times since I'd met him in New York, and every encounter had left me breathless and needy. All I could think about was being with him, not realizing how lonely I'd been. I'd graduated high school the week before and was summer job hunting. Theo had a summer internship at a law firm in Philly. At least, that's what he'd told me. I didn't much care why he was in my city, only that it meant he was closer.

"It's supposed to be a great concert," he'd said and handed me a beer. Somehow he'd gotten me a paper ID bracelet that declared me old enough to drink at the event. He was ageless—he could have been thirty-two or nineteen depending on how the moonlight shone on his features. More than a decade later, he still looked the same.

He'd walked with his arm around me, occasionally leaning down to pull me closer and murmur in my ear. I didn't remember his words, only the tingle of my earlobe where his lips touched it.

We'd strolled along the wide pathways past the lion's enclosure and toward the orangutan climbing towers, finding a nearby bench to sit and enjoy the cold, dark beer. We ate pretzels and watched people. Theo had an uncanny knack for mimicking tourists. I remembered laughing a lot.

We'd made plans for me to stay at his place that night. I'd regressed into a romantic at some point and had purchased a sheer red baby doll number from a downtown store—an overdone affair in lace and satin bows. It was the most garish thing I'd ever owned. I'd also purchased a box of condoms because as young and innocent as I was, I was also practical. That and Freya would have killed me if I'd ended up pregnant at seventeen. Both Dad and Izzy had been away from home, so that night was the perfect opportunity to lose one's virginity. And Theo had been the perfect man.

When the concert was over and most people were making their way to the exits, Theo had left me, saying he'd wanted a souvenir. Near the reptile building, the park had become shadowed and quiet as people left. Rustling sounds in the trees and bushes had me jittery. I avoided the zoo personnel, wanting to wait for Theo, sure that he'd find me any second. He didn't.

Instead, the rustling noises came closer and I discovered the source. A very large snake slithered toward me, its black tongue flicking out, tasting my fear in the air. Very large was a misnomer. The snake was the size of a small train, like the kiddie ones at malls and theme parks, and it zigzagged along the abandoned pathway.

Like Kaa from the Jungle Book, it hissed out words with triple S's. Succulent. Slurp. Tasty. It didn't take a whole lot of conversation for me to run.

It stopped to lift a small antelope out of its fenced enclosure and gulp it down. Its jaws unhinged to accommodate the animal's flailing legs, the bulge moving down its body as the snake reared its head ten feet in the air. It weaved back and forth, searching the darkness, the ever-moving tongue flicking about.

I ran deeper into the park, past the lion's den, the animals inside and safe now, and headed toward the great ape building, pushing on the heavy glass doors. They were locked, closed for the night. I ran on. Past the pachyderm's area where I found myself in an open space, devoid of trees or buildings or cover. From my vantage point, I couldn't see my pursuer, but I could hear it, hissing its strange words and knocking over small trees and trash cans in its pursuit.

At the far edge of the clearing, a construction fence surrounded the beginnings of a concrete foundation. Heavy equipment scattered around mounds of dirt and brush. I flopped over the fence and ducked behind a truck. As the snake moved closer, I moved too, from one machine to another, hiding behind portable bathrooms and large tires. It didn't need to see me, it could smell me, sense my movement and body heat along the ground. I needed other sources of heat and noise and vibration.

Climbing up into the cab of a back-hoe, settled myself in the seat and started pressing levers and switches. Nothing happened. The silence in the park was eerie, and except for my own heavy breathing, I heard nothing. And then the long slow hiss and thump of the snake as it slithered its way toward me.

I ran to the next machine, a bulldozer with an enclosed cab. The door was unlocked and I pulled it closed behind me. For a moment, I felt safe in the enclosure and five feet off the ground.

The creature wound its way past the dozer, looking for me, and I counted ten seconds before the thing was completely gone from my view. I guessed it to be around thirty feet long—about ten mini-train cars.

I was stuck. I could try and sneak out, get past the equipment, and make a run for it through the park, but how could I leave it there? It was clear its appetite ran toward humans rather than animals. Except for the handy snack of antelope, it had moved past other animals to find me. Between its size and the ability to slither out words in English, I gathered this was not exactly part of the reptile exhibit. This thing fit right into my supernatural wheelhouse.

I was completely unprepared. Being with Theo for the last couple of weeks had made me soft and feeling like my life was normal. A thirty-foot talking python with a head the size of a love seat brought my reality back to me with a vengeance.

The only weapon I had was a three-inch knife in my boot—something I'd carried for the last year, and I doubted it would even penetrate the snake's skin. My knee banged against the dash of the bulldozer as I turned to catch sight of my prey—I had to start thinking of it as prey and not predator or I'd never make it out of there.

I rubbed at my sore knee. My hand ran across wires dangling from below the dash. This thing had been hot-wired once before and the wires had been repaired with electrician's tape. I stripped off the tape, sparked the bare wires to the ground connector and the machine rumbled to life. But it wasn't like driving a car. I couldn't get the thing to move, no matter what lever I pulled or gearshift I moved.

Leaving it running, I jumped from the cab and ran for the farthest piece of heavy equipment, a front-end loader.

I remembered my great uncle had borrowed one of these machines from his construction company and had moved a lot of dirt in my Grandmother Freya's yard one summer.

I had more luck with the loader and was able to hotwire and shift it into gear. I raised the bucket and the wheels rolled toward the rumbling bulldozer and the snake.

I had to catch it unawares. If the snake raised its head, the bucket would be of no use. I hit the brakes and tilted the bucket blade down, ready to strike. I waited. If the snake came from the other side, I'd have to make a run for it, and the loader wasn't all that fast.

The creature approached from the correct side and I dropped the bucket just past its head. Its body writhed viciously on the ground, twisting around. I raised the bucket and dropped it twice more before the head detached, leaving the body still twitching. A river of blood rushed out onto the dirt.

A round of applause broke my memories. The senator beamed and returned to our table. My formerly delicious prime rib juice gathered blood red on my plate. It reminded me too much of other bloody things, and I felt like a flesh-eating monster. I looked over at Theo's plate. Vegetarian lasagna.

"You're a vegetarian?" Suddenly it made sense as I recalled Volpi's incessant lessons. As vicious and bloodthirsty as the fae were with each other, they revered the animal kingdom of their world, so things like zoos and eating meat would be abominations to them.

Theo turned to me after shaking the senator's hand and congratulating him on a fine speech. "You would think that after all these years, I would have changed, and I have, but not my diet. Where were your thoughts just now? You were far away from here." His voice was low and I remembered the earpiece and Cobb on the other end of it. I pulled it out of my ear, closing my hand around the mic portion.

"You knew, didn't you? At the zoo, the Ba shé."

The Ba shé—an elephant eating python that according to Chinese lore, digested its prey over three years and could be tracked by its disgorging huge bones on its way to another meal. They were legend and never seen in the modern world, yet somehow, the Ba shé had been let loose into the Philadelphia Zoo on the exact night I was there.

His eyebrows rose a fraction. "It was a test. Not my idea, by the way, but my superior wanted to see you in action. You were quick thinking, innovative, and fearless. Much like us."

"You asshole," I hissed, sounding very much like the creature in my memory. "I could have been killed." After the dead snake had bled out, I drove the loader some distance away, siphoned its fuel, and set fire to the serpent's body. I couldn't leave a huge thing like that out in the open. Unfortunately, the bulldozer went up in the fire as well.

Fire trucks arrived at the zoo as I'd found Theo just inside the gates. We helped each other over the wall onto the street and ran for his car.

"I knew you took my explanation for the blood too easily," I told him. I'd made up some story of finding a dead dog and trying to help it.

"Dead dogs don't bleed." Theo gave me that smile again. "But we both had our secrets, didn't we? We were more alike than you want to admit. Both of us feel the rush of battle, of victory over something invincible. You were the huntress that night, a true warrior." He leaned toward me, "I don't think you've ever been more beautiful than you were then. It was very attractive." The look on his face told me he remembered the rest of the evening as well as I did.

Back at his apartment, he'd stepped into the shower with me, and I immediately forgot the horrors at the zoo. Later, we'd been too preoccupied to think about the red lingerie in my overnight bag.

My teeth clenched for a moment, and I let out a breath. No use being angry or embarrassed about it now. The past was past. I turned back to my cold prime rib, looking up in time to see Cobb's dark scowl as he strode through the crowd toward our table.

Chapter 18

Isabelle

The next day, the low-hanging sun edged its way up the mountain, its rays warming the ground, the air, and the burbling brooks. Izzy woke stiff and cold from her place on the floor. It was even colder outside, but her bladder was insistent, and she gathered chunks of wood from the pile on her way back in. Knowing she was an extra mouth to feed, the least she could do was help.

In her time here before, she'd been assigned as a handmaiden to the priestesses and lived in the temple. Magic was abundant, and she'd learned to manipulate energy so the daily chore of feeding and clothing seemed simple and easy. She'd tried to focus that energy last night, but nothing came of it, and she wondered if she'd lost the ability that had come to her so easily before.

"Will you be moving on?" Flo asked as she prepared breakfast for Klacka. A gruel-like substance bubbled in a pot on the hearth. She stirred it occasionally as she called to her daughter.

"Yes, but first I will find Marlowe. I will ask at the temple. And to see Móðir as well." Izzy replied, straightening her shift under the belt Flo had given her. She wore leather shoes that slipped on her feet and secured with a drawstring around her ankle. Izzy had several inches on Flo, and the dress came to her mid-thigh. For modesty and warmth, she wore leggings of loose-fitting pants underneath it.

Flo shook her head but shoved a bowl of gruel into Izzy's hands. "The temple guard will likely turn him over to the Earl King's men. The temple is no place for a young woman," she said. "Eat."

Izzy was confused. There had been many young women at the temple before, and she wondered what had transpired in the years hence. But she ate her breakfast and did not let the older woman's foreboding dampen her mood.

The temple was a short walk through the camp, but wishing not to draw attention to herself, Izzy took the long way behind the small huts. Besides, it was a warm day for early fall, and a walk along the edge of the woods would be a good thing.

Wildflowers opened themselves to the sun, and the faded grasses made for soft trails under her feet. Maple and oak trees fluttered hints of orange in the light breeze, and to her left Izzy heard the greetings of the camp workers, *hœnsa* clucking for breakfast, and the peal of the blacksmith's hammer. To her right, the muted sound of water trickling through the damp wood calmed her jangly nerves. Her worries from the night before dissipated in the morning sun, and she felt more comfortable and familiar. The tiny village near the temple was called *Fotr Tíívar,* Foot of the Gods, and held only those few who served the temple in some way, or people like Flo, who wished their daughters to become temple maidens. Situated some distance away from and at the far end of the camp, the building was built into Mount Afi, and there were a few back entrances accessed through a series of tunnels and caves. Isabelle knew of those from her previous visit.

The temple itself was constructed of wood and fieldstone, the centerpiece of which was two massive doors—oak planks bound together by crisscrossed iron. A half-circle of iron decorated one door and met its matching half on the other side, the circle interlocking when the doors were closed as they were now. The building was flanked by wooded glens on both sides with a large open space in front used for gatherings during festivals.

Izzy stood at the edge of this open space for a moment, uncertain of how to approach. This wasn't like someone's house. You couldn't just walk up and knock on the door. She was searching for the ancient words for *good morning, may I speak with the Mother,* when a guard came into view from around the side of the building.

The man was an average height for the era, and Izzy guessed him to be well under six feet, but he was broad, heavy through the shoulders and neck. His arms were bare except for tattoos of dark slashes across his biceps. He wore the typical fur boots and trousers, the belt surrounding his leather tunic strained around his middle. A small ax thumped his leg as he walked. He held a not so small spear. His head was shaved in front so at first glance he appeared bald, but he turned revealing dark blond hair braided down his back. Another tattoo marked his face, along one temple and up into the shaved area. Pacing the steps of the entrance, he yawned, and Izzy suppressed a smile. Temple guards were the older warriors, still strong and viable, but their warring days were over. This guard appeared much younger than the ones Izzy remembered. It had been her job to offer them hot mulled wine on cold days.

Izzy was about to approach him when another man hailed him, calling out the word for brother. He was a massive individual and towered over the guard, clapping him on the back. Both men turned as Izzy stepped into the clearing.

"What is your business here, woman?" The guard asked, his

question tainted with disapproval. She should have waited until the other man had left to approach him. But it was too late now.

"I've come to ask the Móŏir a question," she said and realized she should have brought flowers or salted fish—an offering.

The larger man laughed and said something to his brother she could not hear. She took a step forward. Another mistake, as the first guard man leaped off the steps to run toward her, coming to a stop with his spear pointed at her chest. Izzy gave a startled cry and put her hands up in alarm. "Wait! Please, I need to speak to—" She got no further. The guard stepped back, withdrawing the spear, spinning it, and bringing the staff down on her shoulder with a crack.

A shockwave of numbing pain traveled from her shoulder to hand, the nerves tingling in her fingertips, rendering her arm limp and useless. Stunned, she dropped to her knees, her eyes squeezed shut against the pain. She heard his spew of angry words as she held up her good arm to protect herself. The movement garnered her a sharp kick to her ribs. Apparently, her defensive posture was considered aggressive.

She rolled to her side, onto her injured shoulder and her cry of pain sounded as though someone else had made it. She tried to think of the defensive moves Tam had taught her. Her sister would still be on her feet, able to flee or fight, but Izzy could think of nothing but the pain. The guard grabbed her hair, wrenching her head around to face him. She drew her knees up and squeezed her eyes shut, not wanting to see what came next. She heard his brother's laughter behind him, egging the man on. His breath stank of ale and bitter herbs as he raged at her. Her fears and worries from the night before were valid. She would die here.

"*Aet, Aet,*" The shrill sound of Klacka's voice invaded her pain. The girl's hands grabbed at her arms and pulled at her gently. "Auntie," Klacka addressed her. "Come with me. I will take you home." Klacka, wise beyond her youth, did not speak to the guard, her focus on Izzy.

The guard grunted and let go of Izzy's hair with a jerk, dropping her to the ground with such force her teeth rattled. Her cheek scraped along the graveled ground. She stumbled up with Klacka's help.

"Keeping the gods safe from women and children, brother?" The big man's mocking tone took the guard's focus from her, and she glanced toward the temple steps as she and Klacka retreated. The big, dumb brute stood with his hands on his hips as he mocked the smaller guard. To Izzy's eye, he was seven feet tall, three hundred pounds, with knuckles dragging the ground. Not really, but he was big and hulking.

"Shut up, Mael," the smaller guard said, but his voice was deferential, almost fond as he spoke.

Izzy would remember the name, but in her mind, he would always be Brute.

It hurt to breathe, and the walk back to Flo's hut was slow and torturous. The nerves in her shoulder awakened once again, screaming with pain at the jostling in her arm. She feared a broken collarbone or broken ribs, and she did not have Tam's enhanced healing ability. Why should she? She was the guide— what harm should come to her? Paper cuts from the books? Dust allergies from the scrolls she studied?

She lay on the simple cot in Flo's house and felt sorry for herself.

"I should have warned you not to go to the temple." Flo spoke as she bathed Izzy's scrapes and bruises. "I don't think the arm is broken, but I will wrap it to keep it stable. Your flank will have to heal on its own."

"I just asked a question. It was Mael who encouraged him. If he hadn't been there, the guard would have let me pass," Izzy muttered.

"Mael?" Flo turned to Klacka. "Mael did this to her? He was guarding the temple?"

"No, Mama. His brother is the guard. Mael was there. I don't know why."

Flo turned back to Izzy. "Do not go near him. Mael is known for his ruthlessness. If not for him bringing much wealth from raids, he would be charged for many crimes in the village. He takes what he wants and hurts those that get in his way."

"I didn't intend to go near him today," Izzy replied.

Flo clucked her tongue. "Krig is the guard. They are half-brothers. I'm sure Krig wanted to impress his big brother."

Nothing gives you street cred like beating up a woman. Tam's voice sounded in Izzy's head. Every society had one of those guys. From elementary school to the workplace to politicians. That one guy who was big and blustery on the outside and a ball of insecurity on the inside. Tam had a way of dealing with bullies that Izzy had always admired. She could have used her help today.

"How can I speak with Móðir if I cannot get into the temple?" The people gathered at the temple every full moon to pay homage to the gods and ask for favor. "When is the next moon?"

Flo gave another shake of her head. "We do not gather at high moon. The Earl King forbids it. And the Móðir stays within temple walls. You will see her at the next celebration. There will be a temple gathering on Messa."

Fall Equinox, late September. They should be close. It was cold here, the leaves turning. "When?" Izzy groaned.

"Just over two moon cycles," Flo said. Izzy turned her head so Flo wouldn't see her sudden tears. Marlowe would definitely travel before the month was out. If he survived. If they both survived.

Isabelle gradually recovered from her injuries. After three days, Flo demanded she rise and start earning her keep. Not that the keep was much. Flo and Klacka had little to share, but Izzy was grateful for a place to sleep and good broth.

Her muscles screamed, and she longed for ibuprofen while shuffling around the sparse hut. She fashioned a broom out of heavy straw and a willow branch and swept out the critters from the corners. She tried again to manifest some magic, but all she managed was a pounding headache.

As she worked about the house, cleaning, gathering wood, tending the fire, she practiced her language skills, the memory of words, and phrases coming back to her. Klacka helped with this, as the girl was a chatterbox. Izzy felt if she could remember the right intonation, her power would come back. Having the ability to veil herself, or manifest change in simple objects would go a long way toward getting her back to the temple. Her mind drifted back to her time spent with the temple priestesses.

"Use your senses, Ice." Stjarna had taken Izzy under her wing.

Izzy smiled at her friend's nickname for her, but at Stjarna's fierce look, she sobered and concentrated on her surroundings. The walls of the cave dwelling, the cold stone covered with furs for warmth, the high ceiling with tiny air holes that allowed the fire smoke to escape, and the smell of sweat and blood and roasting meat all mixing together. Izzy closed her eyes, her mind seeking, feeling her surroundings.

"Now," Stjarna's voice came to her through her dream-like haze. "Pull energy in. Feel the stone, the air, the fire, and the water. Shape the power into what you need. A cooking pot, a loom, a cloak. And when you're ready, *leœ liõa*—release." Her last word was sharp and loud against the walls, startling Izzy. But it worked. Izzy jumped and a burst of energy leaped from her like a burp of air. The flame of the fire jumped six feet in the air.

"Yes!" Stjarna clapped her hands, delighted in her pupil's progress. "Keep practicing for we will go to Maj's light ceremony soon. As a virgin, you can attend with me."

Izzy startled at Stjarna's mistake. She was twenty-two, and there had been two boyfriend's in college—Brad, with the soulful eyes and awkward manner—they'd fumbled their way out of virgin territory together. After he transferred out, Ryan had come along. It was odd that she couldn't remember what caused them to call it quits, but they had.

"Why only virgins?" she'd asked.

"One must be pure of heart to attend the light ceremony, so as not to disrupt the energy flow."

"And what happens if someone is not pure?" Izzy had tried to sound casual.

Stjarna shrugged and bid her to practice her energy work again. Izzy had attended the ceremony with no ill effects and thought the virgin requirement might have been metaphorical rather than physical.

Izzy's mind wandered from her friend's words in the past to Angelo, and the passionate nights they spent in his loft. She hoped the purity of her heart was intact enough not to disrupt the energy of the upcoming Messa ceremony. She also missed her lover's reassuring presence at her side.

"Isobel," Flo's voice boomed through her reverie. "Are you deaf? I've been calling. Come help me with this deer carcass. Wolves got to it, poor thing, but I can use some of the intact hide."

Izzy shuddered but rose to follow Flo to the back of the house, wishing her capable but stubborn sister would appear. Or that her priestess friend, Stjarna was still alive. Or that she could relieve the ripped and mauled carcass of its skin with her powers instead of the dull blade Flo gave her.

Izzy occupied herself by helping Flo, playing with Klacka, and staying out of Mael's way. When her shoulder healed sufficiently, Flo taught Izzy how to use the flat knife to scrape the hides to a thin pliable cloth. She tried to teach her flint knapping, but Izzy's edges fell blunt and broken, and after a few tries, Flo took the stones from her and gave her the rawhide strips to work.

One morning, she accompanied Klacka to the village center where they could fetch water from the well and barter for goods. As a well-fed stream ran behind Flo's hut, they did not use the well often, but Flo needed salt and equipped Klacka with goods for trade.

"What's that building?" Izzy asked as they passed a long low hut with few windows.

"The Long House," Klacka replied, her voice low. She guided Izzy toward the opposite side of the pathway. "The temple guards sleep there, and it houses the king's guard when they come for festivals. Behind it, is the earl's meeting room."

Izzy spied the rooftop of the residence rising behind the long building. She stopped directly in front of the barracks. "Would my brother be kept there?"

Klacka pulled at her sleeve. "The king's guard has gone, probably to the sea or over the mountains. They will not return until Messa."

"*Undarligr,* move along." The rough voice sounded from behind them. Turning, Izzy craned her neck to see Mael's leer looming above her. "Unless you wish to be of some service to the temple guard? Yes. I can arrange that."

His smell hit her like a garbage truck and she reeled back, reaching for Klacka. He grabbed her sore shoulder and wrenched her to him, his foul breath hot over her face. Searing pain burned through her healing tendons, and she held her breath in an effort not to cry out. Mael's slobbery lips roved over her cheek as she wrenched her head away from him. His hands roamed over her breasts before he chuckled and pushed her aside.

"You are too skinny and flat for my taste." He spat on the ground.

A part of her wanted to protest his assessment, but the majority of common sense made her grateful he found her unappealing, even if the look in his eyes belied his words.

"Come, Auntie." Klacka to her rescue again, ignoring the big man, she pulled Izzy away. As they hurried toward the central well and the safety of people, Izzy saw Mael's scowl toward a shadow in the doorway of the Long House.

Chapter 19

Tamberlyn

"**P**ut your goddamn com-line in." Cobb swore at me as he approached our table. He turned to the senator. "There's a disturbance on the third floor. I think we should get you out of here."

Theo rose as Cobb approached, his hands clenched at his sides. I bent my head, shoving the earbud back in place, chagrined that I'd forgotten all about it.

Shepherd's security contingent showed up at the table. For the same reason or because Cobb's approach had alarmed them, I didn't know. But they looked as dismayed as I felt in our mutual dereliction of duty. Senator Shepherd interrupted his conversation to speak to my partner.

"Detective, do you really think that's necessary? We're ten floors above it."

"I think it may be a diversion, sir. We have a team checking it out."

"Senator," I piped up, ignoring the withering look from Cobb. So he was angry, okay, I got it. I screwed up. "We don't want to panic these people or to put them in danger. If something should happen up here..." Shepherd glanced at me, and I could tell he was remembering the gas at his apartment. He nodded.

"Okay, but let's be discrete about leaving early." He signaled the mayor who was looking our way. The two men conferred, and the mayor went back to his table. On the dais, another speaker was entertaining the crowd.

"Lock," Shepherd used a shortened version of Locran. "Take JoAnne, would you? I want her out of danger. I'll be along shortly." Theo started to protest, but I interrupted.

"We'll stay with him. Meet you in the back of the building where the limo is."

He nodded somewhat grimly and took JoAnne's arm to lead her out of the ballroom.

After a minute or two, the senator and I moved toward the nearest exit. His team met us outside the ballroom doors, along with Cobb.

"You should work out your personal problems with the ex on your own time, Paradiso. I tried to get your attention for five minutes." Cobb muttered under his breath.

"I know," I said, irritated with myself. "What's on the third floor?"

He spoke to the security team ahead of us. "Take the stairs. I don't want to get trapped in the elevator."

They looked miserable, but they did it. Cobb turned to me as we went through the door to the stairwell. "Domestic disturbance."

"A couple's fight on three, and you think it's a ruse? That's a stretch, isn't it?"

"We were hit with poisoned gas this morning. I'm not taking any chances. Besides, it was hinky."

Hinky was Cobb's word for weird, and since most things in my life were hinky, I had no real frame of reference. Sometimes, he just used the word to explain the unexplainable or a gut feeling. I understood those. I relied on my gut feelings to get me out of jams more than once, so I'd go with Cobb's gut on this one. "Room service heard a disturbance and found two males throwing furniture at each other. They closed the door to the room and called security, which is protocol. But when security arrived, the men were gone, the room empty—trashed, but empty. Room service guy swears he never left the hallway and no one came past him."

"They go out the window?"

"If so, they had a three-story drop."

We'd descended as far as the sixth floor when the stairwell went black. A few seconds later the emergency lights kicked on. We sped up, and the senator kept up, remarking that it was as good a workout as a game of tennis. I admired his calm acceptance of the situation. I'd done lots of protection duty over the years, politicians, some celebrities, one organized crime accountant, and most get cranky. So far, Shep Shepherd had been the easiest and most compliant.

We got to the bottom of the stairs. Cobb and I both cautioning his team to wait. But the two men pulled open the door and rushed into the hallway. Speed ahead of caution.

The blast's concussion blew the senator back into Cobb, the hot air searing the stairwell around us. We could hear people screaming from the lobby as we got to our feet. The stairwell door hung on one hinge, wedged against the frame. It wouldn't budge. The two-man security team was gone, blown deeper into the hallway. Peering through the dust and debris, I could see them lying on the floor.

"Explosion on the main floor near the stairwell," Cobb's face had turned toward his shoulder as he spoke into the comlink. He helped the senator up. "We're—"

"We're heading out the front." I interrupted him and then pulled my earbud out and held it like I had in the ballroom. "They knew we were coming." I spoke in low tones to both men, moving in front to peer under the broken door. Smoke and dust filled the stairwell, and the scent of blood mixed with plaster hit my nose. Cobb pulled his comlink out and dropped it into the pocket of his jacket. His jaw tensed, his eyes narrowed.

"You think this is an inside job?" He asked me. I shrugged. Neither of us wanted that to be true, but we weren't taking any chances either.

"Are Bob and Jim okay?" The senator asked. I glanced up at Cobb.

"I don't know, sir. But our first concern is you. Let's go," Cobb said.

"We'll go to the basement. Come out in the parking garage and go around. Theo and your daughter are meeting us outside," I said, heading down another flight of stairs.

We didn't speak further until we got to the doorway. Cobb handed me a flashlight, and not taking any chances, I opened the door a fraction, aiming the light along the outer edge, looking for tripwires.

"Okay, everybody keep their head down." I stepped out into the garage. I hiked my silk dress up and pulled the Sig Sauer from its holster.

The emergency lighting in the garage was spotty at best, but our entrance was well lit. I wasn't sure that was a good thing. Anybody waiting on us would have a clear view as we came through the door, but we couldn't stay in the stairwell. Skirting the wall of the garage, we kept to the shadows and made our way outside on the side of the building.

A rustling sound to my right made me stop, and the senator almost ran over me. Cobb grabbed him by the back of his jacket and kept him upright. Three cars over I heard a painful grunt followed by the sound of flesh punching into flesh. Another grunt. And a crash. I headed toward the sound as Cobb hung back, covering the senator. I called out that we were police.

A tuxedoed man lay on his back between the cars. His attacker turned and ran as I approached—a short, broad man in a bellman's uniform.

The man on the ground was Gianni Balfour. His lip was bleeding, and his eye already swelling shut, he tried to smile and it came out a wince. Blood dripped onto his white tuxedo shirt.

"Friend of yours?" I helped him to his feet and jerked my head in the direction of his assailant.

"Never saw him before."

"What are you doing here?"

"The way you left with the senator, I knew something was up." He answered. "I came here to—"

I interrupted him. "Please don't tell me you came down here to help."

He wiped the blood from his face with a white silk pocket square. "Not at all," he said smoothly. "I have enough trouble of my own without getting into yours, Detective. I wanted to make sure my dinner guest was out of danger."

"The plastic surgery model you brought?"

"Careful, your feminine side is showing." He groaned as he moved. "We were heading to the car when this guy came out of nowhere. My driver got Talia to the car and safety. He'll circle around and pick me up."

I squinted at him, prepared to reject every word he said. But the blood and bruises didn't lie. And I had seen the man wailing on him. He coughed, wincing from the pain and his hand came away with blood.

"You need a hospital."

Cobb joined us, glancing at Balfour before he spoke. "Everyone okay? Let's get the senator some place safe."

All of us, including Balfour, made our way to the exit. Theo and JoAnne came out of the back exit, and JoAnne ran to her dad as soon as she saw him.

"The senator's limo is gone." Theo looked at me. "It took off as we got outside."

"The stairwell door was rigged. We lost the security team." I glanced back at the senator, his arm around his daughter. I spoke under my breath to Theo. "This was a coordinated effort."

He leaned toward me and spoke in a lower tone. "Redcaps." The bellman's uniform made sense now.

Redcaps were sprites with attitude. They looked like diminutive old men with long hair and grizzled cheeks, but during a battle, or a feeding as they called it, their dark eyes became blood red, and claws extended from gnarled fingers. Traditionally they wore hats that in the old days were soaked in the blood of their victims, dying the cloth red, hence the name.

I'd only seen one once, years ago and he did wear a hat, a baseball cap for the Washington Nationals team. He also escaped my pursuit by running into a wall and disappearing like it was a Kings Cross platform in Harry Potter.

I glanced at Balfour who stood some distance away from the senator and Cobb. He leaned to one side, holding his ribs. He was lucky to be alive if he'd tangled with a Redcap.

"Wait. Redcaps? As in plural, more than one? They're here after you, not the senator." My tone was accusatory. "What did you do to piss off some Redcaps?" I held my hand up. "Never mind. It doesn't matter. We need to get out of the open."

The limo had been taken for a reason, eliminating a means of escape. "We need a car, and mine's back in the garage." I nodded toward the others. I didn't want any of them exposed to this mess.

Theo agreed. Fortunately, Balfour's black windowed SUV pulled up, and the driver jumped out to help Balfour into the back seat. The crime boss declined, saying the senator and his daughter should get in first.

I glared at Balfour. No way could I trust him with the senator. He looked back at me with a wry expression. There was little choice. Smoke and chaos were pouring from the hotel. In the distance, sirens signaled paramedics and more police. Cobb looked at me. "You take the senator and JoAnne. Balfour needs a hospital, but all of you need to get out of here."

"Where are you going?"

"To see what the hell is going on here."

After a glance at Theo, I pulled Cobb aside. "Look, let me deal with the mess here. You know the bomb squad and all kinds of brass will be out front, and you hate that shit. Someone has to go with the senator. We can't leave him with Balfour. Get him to the safe house, and I'll clear the building. Come back and get me, and we can deal with the crime scene techs."

After a few seconds and a thoughtful glance at Theo over my shoulder, he agreed.

"Watch your back," he advised.

The car sped away with my partner, the politician, and the crime boss as we ducked back into the shadows of the garage. Theo never looked at me, his eyes scanning the dim interior.

"I know where they hide, how they hunt. This way." He started off. I grabbed his arm.

"In your world, you're right. But this is my world you're in, remember?" I said.

After a moment of eye contact he relented, and I led him to my car. The hotel insisted on valet parking, but I'd already located my beat-up Toyota. It was parked between a huge Escalade and a Porsche. I found the hide-a-key under the wheel rim, wrenching the plastic container open to find an old rusted key, but it worked, and I popped the trunk. Inside was my go-bag with an assortment of weapons, a first aid kit, and flashlights. I handed a flashlight to Theo, who held his other hand out.

Our eyes locked for a moment. I still had my Sig Sauer, but I wanted a larger caliber weapon. Redcaps could be stopped with a bullet, at least temporarily, or a good old-fashioned beheading would eliminate them. But that didn't mean I wanted to hand Theo a gun.

Seeing my hesitation, Theo's jaw twitched. My head tilted slightly, but neither of us looked away. He took a breath. "How much do you know about Redcaps?"

"I know how to kill them, what else is there?"

"As Vanguard, I recruited them. Redcaps follow a clan

hierarchy, the leader being the strongest and most ruthless. During one particularly bloody skirmish, I recruited the second in command as a spy. One I could not trust and ultimately had to eliminate. It was poor judgment on my part, developing him as an asset in the first place."

"You have more than a few lapses in judgment." I grimaced at him, clenching my fingers around the gun.

"Turns out, my ...elimination of the problem set off a chain reaction in the clan, including a change in leadership that was not welcome. There was considerable unhappiness with my actions."

I laughed, shaking my head. "Pissing people off seems like one of your more prevalent talents."

"One of many." He smiled again. "As you well know." The smile faded and for a moment, in the shadows of the dim garage, I could see him. The young Theo from so long ago, in those moments when he thought I wasn't looking. "Redcaps have long memories. There may even be a bounty. They'll favor capture over killing. You could leave. They would find me eventually, and your revenge would be complete." He pressed his lips together, but his eyes didn't stray from mine.

Back in the day, I'd always been the first to look away when he did that, not wanting to reveal more of myself than I was comfortable with. Now I met his gaze.

"Or you could help. But that would require trust." His eyes softened.

"You're not trustworthy," I said, shuffling weapons and bottles of water around in the bag. Finally, I lifted the heavy bag half out of the trunk. I should take the whole thing.

"I was fae," he said by way of explanation. "I am no longer."

I pulled a machete from the bag, flipping and catching it by the backside of the blade. I gave it to him hilt first. "How familiar are you with guns?"

He set the machete aside, pulled a Glock from the open satchel, checked the sight, pulled the magazine back to chamber a round, and clicked the safety off. I ignored his superior glance and slung the bag on my shoulder, indicating that he should lead.

We skirted our way along the outside wall before heading up the ramp to the second floor. I spoke to his back. "Just because you're no longer fae—which I don't believe for a second by the way—doesn't mean you're automatically trustworthy."

"Being worthy of your trust is not a goal. Surviving the night is." He prowled along the wall, walking in a semi-crouch to make himself less of a target. I followed, occasionally checking our six. "Check the high ground, the Toxeute may be here as well."

I'd almost forgotten the archer, but we were in a low ceilinged garage. There really wasn't much of a high ground. We had climbed the ramp to the second floor of the garage now, away from valet parking and any sign of bystanders. My guess was that Balfour had somehow gotten in the Redcap's way, but unlike most people, Balfour had fought back, which is why he survived. That and we had come along at just the right time. "Is Balfour involved in this, in any way?" I asked.

Theo stopped by a low wall, using it for cover. He looked at me. "With the Redcaps? Or the campaign? First of all, Redcaps are violent by nature, I'm sure Balfour was collateral damage. Second, regardless of Gianni's money and connections, we don't want him involved. His association with Shepherd does more harm than good." He shook his head at me. "You really think I'd risk losing the election to gain some campaign money? You don't know me at all."

"No, I don't." My voice was sharp as we moved on. "That's my point. How do I know you're not the same asshole that you were eleven years ago?"

He stopped again, by the entrance to the building. Facing me, he took my gun hand and pointed the Glock at his chest. "If this is what will give you peace, pull the trigger. Save the Redcaps the trouble." He looked tired, and not just a little worried. "I'm sorry I hurt you. That wasn't the intent." His lips compressed for a few seconds. I moved the gun aside.

"There was enormous pressure for success in my world, especially in my position. You might not ever truly understand. But for the purposes of both of us surviving this night, and vanquishing the Redcaps who are now loose in this city, perhaps you can forgo the recriminations of the past and work with me."

"You broke my heart," I said. The words came out before I could stop them.

He placed a hand along my cheek, leaving it there for a moment. His eyes were just as mysterious and dark as I remembered, and he stepped closer.

I heard it before I saw it. Theo reacted a half-second before I did, throwing both of us to the ground. The arrow struck the door above us with a thwock and a twang. We scrambled backward behind a pillar.

I felt his warmth as he hunched in close. We slowed our breathing, and I peered in the direction of the shooter. The ground floor of the parking garage had some openings for natural light along both sides of the building. The arrow had come from a window in the building across the street, through the opening, over several rows of cars to strike the far door, exactly where we'd been standing. If we'd been in the open, we'd never have heard it coming, but in the garage, sound bounced off concrete walls, cars, and the low ceiling. "Well, we found the Toxeute," I said.

Chapter 20

Tamberlyn

We ran, Theo pulling me along like an errant child. Hunched over, we used SUV's and trucks for cover as we made our way to the outer edge of the garage. Side by side, we sat with our backs to the low wall.

"Did you see where?" he asked.

"Building across the street, second story, I believe the third window from the right." I unclasped my fingers from his and pulled my go-bag to settle it between us. I turned to him in time to catch a wide-eyed blink. "What?" I asked, irritated.

"You seem pretty sure of yourself." Could he not just go with it? Just for a moment?

"I'm not. What did you see?"

"Second story, third window from the right."

I chuckled as I pulled a weapon from the bag. "That was your surprised expression. Haven't seen that before." I handed Theo an infrared, long-range scope and stock, wrapped tightly in a chamois cloth. I pulled the barrel out of the bag, and taking the stock, I screwed the barrel in. Flipping the bipod down, the little feet held the gun level as I pulled a clip from the bag. "I've maybe done this a time or two since you left, you know."

"I hope you're good with that thing. It's likely we'll only get one or two shots before he moves. Once that happens, we'll lose him."

"I'm okay," I said.

Theo looked nervous. "Okay? Great, a mediocre marksman. I suppose you want me to draw him out while you take a few practice shots?"

"I didn't say I was mediocre. I said I was okay." This was less than true. Most of my combat practice was up close and personal. I was much better with handguns than rifles, not having the luxury of stalking my prey from afar. "We don't even know if he's still there."

Theo took his pocket square out and tossed it up and to the side of us. Before it could float back down, an arrow pierced it, carrying it through the garage and embedding itself in the side of a car.

"Shit, he's good," I acknowledged.

"And yet, you are just okay. Mind if I try?"

"Since when do you have—" He took the rifle from me, and like he had with the Glock earlier, he pulled the bolt action back, checked the magazine, and clicked the safety off. This time he also added a silencer and sighted in the scope. From his sitting position on the floor, he placed the bipod on my bag, hunched over, his eye to the scope. The bullet pinged an exit sign at the far end of the garage. I looked through a spotter's scope. There was a hole in the intersection of the letter X in the sign.

"Good sight. It pulls to the left, but not bad," he said.

"Show off." I turned to the wall behind us, the urge to look for the Toxeute was strong, but the need to keep my head in one piece was stronger. "Okay, I'll draw him out."

"With what? Your head? I'll need a sighting first." He

pointed to a pillar not far from us, with a trash receptacle next to it. "I'll be there, give him a target so I can spot him." I frowned. He smirked at me. "Not a body part, just throw something up, doesn't matter what."

He moved then, belly crawling until he could get to his position. He angled the gun toward the building, aiming upward over the cement wall. I waited as he scanned the building across from us. Crawling on the cement, my bare knees stinging from tiny bits of gravel, I traveled along the wall until an upright section of concrete gave me enough cover to stand. I edged up, careful to keep any part of me away from the sightline of our shooter. Openings to both my left and right looked out onto the street.

Without raising his eye from the scope or his finger off the trigger, he spoke. "Now, Tam."

Pulling the longest knife I had out of the bag, I draped the chamois cloth over the end and waved it toward the opening. Another arrow came through, inches from where I was flattened against the concrete.

"I see him," Theo said. "But I don't have a clear shot. He'll move into range when he draws on us again."

"Again?" I asked, trying not to be too rattled about the possibility. I stuck the knife blade out toward the open air. Everything happened at once. The gun went off. A roar of laughter. A blur of Redcap slammed into me, knocking the weapon out of my hand. My head thunked against the cement divider as claws scraped toward my eyes. I grabbed his thick wrist and twisted, the action deflecting the blow to my face, but he was too strong to push away. If I could get him over the wall, he'd fall thirty feet to the ground. The fall probably wouldn't kill him, but it would solve my immediate problem.

Turns out, I didn't need much strength. His hat tilted during the scuffle, revealing a bare head of patchy silver hair. I'd pushed him toward the open window space and felt a rush of air against my hand. Suddenly there was a shaft protruding from both his hat and his oversized ear, the fletching of sleek black feathers still quivering from the impact. His eyes widened. His grip loosened and I let him go. His body toppled to the cement floor. I ducked back behind the cement cover as Theo's rifle rang out again.

"Got him." Theo raised his head from the rifle sight. Seeing the dying Redcap at my feet, he furrowed his brow at me. "Are you sure you're of the mortal realm? You fight like the fae."

The Redcap closed his eyes, breathing his last breath. I touched the arrow sticking out of his head. As I did, the body disintegrated into ash, leaving the arrow on the ground.

"Nice shot," I said. "For both of you."

Theo slung the rifle over his shoulder and moved toward me, looking around. "Come. The other is probably nearby."

I let him take the bag from me and followed him back to the stairwell door. The place should be crawling with cops by now. Fortunately, most of them would be concentrated in the lobby area where the bomb exploded.

"Since when do Redcaps and Toxeutes work together?" I asked.

"Since they have a common enemy," he said and opened the door, indicating I should go ahead. He had also disassembled the rifle and placed it back in the duffle. He held the Glock by his side. We stepped into the darkened stairwell.

"You've really got to work on your people skills," I commented, heading upward.

His deep chuckle sounded behind me as we moved up the stairs. "These aren't people, are they? They are lower fae, and most are enemies of long standing."

"Why go after you now, after all these years?"

It took some moments before he answered. "A dozen or so mortal years is not a long time for us. And this is not their first attempt. But it's the first time they've gone after someone I care about. I suppose before the strategy hadn't occurred to them."

"Why not?"

"I'm sure the thought hadn't occurred to them that I would."

"That you would care about us? Mere mortals?" I stopped on the landing and turned. Standing two steps up from him, I could see level into his eyes. The deep brown of them stared back. Into my own eyes at first, and then lower, taking in my silk dress, the bodice ripped by claws, the skirt filthy from plaster dust and greasy cement floors.

I resisted the urge to smooth out the material or to look down at myself to make sure I was adequately covered. His tuxedo had seen better moments. The bow tie was gone, and the top button of his shirt unfastened. The pristine white front had dark smudges along the collar. Plaster dust coated the shoulders of his jacket. A little blood spatter here and there and we'd be perfect for prom in a Stephen King novel.

"Senator Shepherd has become..." He fumbled for the words.

"Like a father? Do you even know what that means?"

He took a step up, and I turned away, moving up the next set of stairs.

"You act as though we're aliens." He spoke to my back once more. "That we have no love or compassion."

"You are. Completely alien. Devious to a fault and a menace to society. At least our society."

"We are also fiercely loyal and form bonds to those of our choosing. Do you know what my great sin was? At the conclave, when the fae decided my fate—our fate. The most grievous error I committed was not that I brought you to our realm. My superiors had witnessed your success at defeating the Ba shé, and they too, thought you'd make an excellent asset.

"No, my error was in allowing you to choose. To come to us of your own free will and fight by our side—my side. According to them, I should have coerced you, indoctrinated you to our ways, to our life and our war. Erase all memory of your origins, and to use your abilities and strengths for as long as we could."

I stopped on another landing and turned to face him again.

"But I couldn't. Your strength comes not from your abilities as a hunter, but your free will and choices as a human. I refused to change you, to condition you to be like me—a soldier following orders, with no thought to the morality of them." He brushed by me to take the lead. I said nothing. What could I say? I'd no idea that he'd gone against his superiors in any way. Not for me.

After a moment, he spoke again. "I had come to this world to recruit and develop an asset to our cause. You changed me instead." He sighed and cleared his throat. "I paid the price for it." He paused on the step, and I moved to catch up with him.

"Theo," I started, but he left me standing on the stairs. After a moment, I followed him up.

At seventeen, I'd been a directionless, somewhat apathetic teenager. But more so, I had no convictions about anything. I didn't care about fashion or music or politics. I had no naïve notions of saving the world on a grand scale, no concerns about the planet or crimes against humanity as some of my peers did.

I'd wandered through life, killing monsters and keeping that part of my life a secret. This made me reckless and callous about almost everything. By the time I met Theo, the ability to see hostiles had been with me for a couple of years. Because of that focus, I'd missed out on other life skills, like how to deal with people, or how to form relationships. Strong-willed, yes, about some things, but in other ways, I was completely malleable and unsure. How could I have ever influenced a battle-hardened warrior of the fae? *We form bonds to those of our choosing.* My throat felt tight, and I stopped mid-step.

"Will they forgive you? Ever, I mean. Will you ever be allowed to go home?"

His profile swung toward me, his lips compressed. "At this point, I'd be happy if they'd just quit trying to kill me. Let's just focus on getting out of here, alive." We climbed the rest of the way in silence.

People are so complicated. They're battlefields littered with emotional landmines. You have to be careful where you step all the time. Most have no idea why they feel the way they do, but

God forbid you call them on it. I'd poured all my rage and grief out over X onto Marlowe. Even my own anger and confusion about Theo had rained on Marlowe. A far more emotionally mature human than I, Marlowe had accepted my irrational self.

Though he loved me, and I'd been hurt, it wouldn't change how he acted in the future. Because he believed he was right in keeping the future under wraps, even from himself. And maybe he was right. The future is not meant to be known. Because our human nature makes us want to change it to suit ourselves.

In many ways, I was still that apathetic teen, selfishly protecting myself from pain. Marlowe knew what sacrifice was. So did Theo for that matter. I was the only one who hadn't learned.

Theo came to the wrecked stairwell door where Shepherd's team had been lost. The door had been cleared away, and we stepped through the ragged opening.

In the hallway, crime scene investigators were clad in paper suits and booties, crawling over the rubble. I'd managed to hang onto my ID and badge and showed it to the officer in charge. The paramedics had come and gone, taking the injured away. The place was maudlin quiet, only the sound of digital cameras and lowered voices echoed through the room.

We found a small space by the back wall, out of the way. Theo left and returned with two bottles of water. I drank, greedy in my need, and wiped the excess from my mouth before I looked at him. "Thanks," I said.

He finished his water before he responded. "For what? The water? Shooting the Toxeute?"

"For everything," I said. I was going to say more, but behind us, down a short hallway to the entrance of the pool, the rumbling of a laugh—rich, nerve-jangling, and utterly without conscience—reverberated through the door. I looked at Theo. The craggy slash of one eyebrow arched higher on his forehead. In unison, we turned away from the destruction of the hallway and headed toward the closed glass doors at the other end.

Chapter 21

Isabelle

The morning was significantly colder, with frost forming on the brown blades of grass and a thin sheet of ice over the barrel of water outside the hut. After a quick visit to the nearby trees where she relieved herself, Izzy hurried back to the hut she now called home. Breaking through the ice, she ladled water into a kettle before entering the house.

Her job was to stir the coals in the hearth and get the fire going in the mornings. Often, Flo would work late into the night, stringing bows, fashioning arrows, adding to her collection of weaponry. Mornings had become Izzy's domain.

The festival would be soon upon them, and it was a good time for Flo to trade her weaponry. Hunters would be back from their fall hunts and would want to replenish their supply.

As she put another log on the bed of coals, she wondered if Marlowe was still in this world. If so, he'd stayed far longer than his usual journeys. She hoped he was still alive. The dread she'd been pushing back flooded through her—thoughts that if he'd been alive, he'd have made an effort to contact her. Get a message to her, or something.

Yet, on the frigid morning of her forty-sixth day here, she still had not seen the poet warrior. Since her run in with Mael, she had stayed far from the guards and even the temple itself. In fact, she rarely left the sight of their little hut, except on occasion when she'd accompanied Flo and Klacka to the village center to trade for grain or tallow.

"Morning." She smiled at the blonde head of the sleepy girl who rose and came to sit by the fire. Wrapped in a fur, the girl huddled on a hearthrug and told Izzy of a dream.

"The man was tall, but not big like Mael." Klacka's eyes were wide as she spoke. "He rode a black horse and spoke in a different way."

Izzy had often listened to the girl's fanciful stories and dreams. A dreamer herself, she and Klacka had bonded. Klacka had few playmates in *Fotr Tñvar,* so Izzy made time for her, playing games, trading songs. The girl had taught her catchy nursery rhymes, and Izzy taught Klacka the words to "Maxwell Silverhammer."

Izzy listened as she worked, but at the mention of a man who spoke differently, she looked up from her cooking pot.

"Differently how?"

Klacka shrugged. "He sounded different."

"Are you sure this was a dream? That you didn't see this man in the village perhaps?"

Klacka hugged her knees closer. "Do you think it's your brother? The one who came with you?"

Izzy tried to keep her expression impassive, but the girl was perceptive. "I know you miss him," Klacka said quietly. "Will you leave when he comes back?"

Izzy smiled at the girl. "You know I have to leave sometime. But not today. It won't be today. Come, help me cut some meat for breakfast. We have a busy day."

∞

Three days before festival, Izzy stood outside the hut, as she was most days, working on the furs. Her job was to clean the pelts, scraping them free of meat and sinew, and using some of the material to cut long thin strips for Flo's arrows. The rest of the pelt would be used as clothing or tent material, and when the pelt was perfectly clean, she would tie it to a small frame, stretching so it wouldn't curl while it cured.

"They're coming. They're coming," Klacka exclaimed as she ran in from the stream, water sloshing in the bucket she carried.

"Who's coming?" Izzy asked without looking up. She was in the middle of slicing a long strand of boar skin, concentrating on making it as thin and even as possible.

"The Earl King," Klacka explained not so patiently. The Earl King had figured prominently in the girl's stories as the festival date approached. Apparently, this great and foreboding leader came to the temple to signal the time of Equinox.

"We shall have the great feast now. And *Mání-boõ* ceremony," Klacka said.

Klacka squinted at her again, her blue eyes almost disappearing in her broad apple cheeks. Klacka's eyebrows were so pale and fine they blended with the pale skin of her forehead, but the sunlight caught them now, and they glistened, giving her a fairy-like appearance. Indeed, with her light curls fanning around her face and elfin smile, she looked like a sprite ready to do mischief.

"Harvest moon ceremony," Izzy repeated Klacka's words, the translation coming easily now. Equinox. The soon to be winter sun was already at the horizon. She got no further in her questions as the thunder of approaching horse hooves and clanking of metal against wood drowned out words.

Looking past the gateway entrance, she could see nothing but dust rising up against the fading sun. At last, she saw them, horses and the men atop them, hairy, smelly, and fur-clad, though the day was unseasonably warm. The men's voices pelted the air, rough and guttural as they taunted each other.

Flo came rushing out of the hut, her arms full of arrows, quivers, and spear points. "Quick, clear the table, and help me." Izzy moved her skinning tools and pelts to the ground and helped Flo place her wares along the makeshift table—a long plank of wood balanced across a tree stump and a large boulder.

At first, there were the village hunters, and these few would stop to peruse Flo's craft before moving on. Then the king's guard—massive soldiers clad in leather with bits of burnished silver buckles and glints of brass plates across their chests. They would be followed by the Earl King and his queen, and lastly, the villagers from the town by the sea would come single- and double-file up the narrow path behind the procession. Most would be on foot, some pulling carts that bore gifts for the gods and food for the feast that night.

Izzy shrank back against the house as the horses and men passed, a few of them commenting on the quality of the weapons from atop their steeds. They did not stop, however, and Flo let out a sigh of disappointment.

Klacka ran toward the horses, shouting and waving, trying to get their attention. The first of the guard had passed but the second or third row was not so attentive, one soldier letting his horse shy and finally rear up, causing a chain reaction in the animals. The procession stalled for a moment, the horses snorting and rearing. Giant lethal hooves flashed in the air while their riders shouted and reined in the beasts.

Izzy, fearing for the girl's safety rushed from under the shadowed eave of the house, snatching Klacka away from the blow of both horse hoof and gloved hand of the guard. Pulling the child against her, she shouted at the guard to keep his horse under control. The guard spat and cursed at her.

Then, the Earl King came into view. He was a great man, thick and broad with hair the color of sunset, red-gold and loose about his shoulders. His facial hair was a dark russet red and climbed his cheeks, obscuring the majority of his face and serving to highlight his slate-colored eyes. His horse slowed at the commotion between Izzy and the guard. The Earl King wearily signaled to the horseman behind him.

Instantly, a dark-headed man rode forward and after a moment by the Earl King's side, he trotted ahead to see what the trouble was. By this time, most of the residents of *Fotr Tíivar* had emerged from their homes to cheer and wave at the visitors.

"She is just a child," Izzy, proficient in the language now, slung words at the guard, whose horse was snorting and huffing. The dinner-plate-sized hooves stomped impatiently at the ground.

The top of Izzy's head barely reached the mid-flank of the animal, and the guard had to lean down to strike her. She moved backward at the swipe, pushing the girl behind her.

"Coward." She uttered the word low enough that only the guard could hear her. She stepped back and spoke louder, somewhat braver now that she was out of reach. "Are you protecting the great Earl King from a child's greeting? From us? His subjects who serve the temple, women, and children who want nothing more than—" She got no further, her tirade halting at the appearance of the black knight, atop a black horse, sleeker and finer boned than the war steed threatening to stomp her.

The man dismounted, sword drawn, and ordered the guard aside. The guard whirled, ready for a fight, but upon seeing who faced him, the big man grumbled and clucked at his horse. Horse and rider trotted to catch up to his place in the procession.

"I-so-bel," the knight said her name in the old way, with the long I sound and syllables acutely delineated. "I am glad to see you." He smiled, sheathing his sword, and beckoning his horse. The animal came to him immediately, nibbling something out of his hand. "Art thou well?" Marlowe's distinctive cadence made Izzy look twice at him. His beard was full and thick, obscuring his finer features. His brown hair had gold streaks from constant sun, and was pulled into a short braid in back. He was dressed completely in black, and the familiar cape was tied at the neck and thrown over one shoulder, opposite his sword arm.

Her heart skipped a grateful beat as she recognized him, his hazel eyes were the same, though everything else was different. He seemed larger, thicker through the shoulders and arms, but perhaps it was the ancient garb or the way he carried himself. No longer the poet, but a warrior.

"*Marlowe*," Izzy exclaimed and moved to throw herself into his arms, ecstatic at his well-being. He stopped her with a subtle shake of his head. His eyes indicating the people around them, and the Earl King who was almost upon them.

He moved toward a barrel of rainwater at the hut, liberally splashing the grime from his face. After several minutes of scrubbing, he looked back at her. By this time, most of the people had moved away from them toward the approaching leader. They were alone.

"I'll find you, tonight. At high moon, near the creek." His words came so fast and low she wasn't sure she heard them correctly. He mounted the horse with the grace of long practice, settling in the saddle before trotting back toward the Earl King again. The two men conversed with few words in the ancient language and rode side by side for a moment, but while Marlowe did not look at Izzy again, the Earl King did. Under his sharp gaze, Izzy hustled Klacka back into the shadows of the hut.

Flo gathered her unsold arrows to secure them in the hut. "The guard who cleaned his face at our rain barrel?" she asked. "Is this your brother?"

Izzy hesitated. Wanting to protect her benefactor from harm, she'd said little about Marlowe after her initial explanation. That had seemed like ages ago.

"Yes. I am glad he is well." She remembered Klacka's dream about a man on a black horse. Could it be that the girl had the gift of premonition?

"It appears he has fared well. The king's guard is a coveted position." Flo appraised Izzy as she had several times over the past months. "As your guardian, he should secure you a good marriage."

Izzy sighed. This conversation had been had many times. Izzy was young and of marriageable age, and Flo had pointed this out at every opportunity, for the older woman had appointed herself as a guardian and mentor. Apparently, now that Marlowe was back, Flo's responsibility for marrying her off had been reprieved.

Izzy's heart felt lighter than it had in weeks, seeing Marlowe alive and well. That in itself was a miracle. The mission, which had been cast to the background for stoicism and survival, was now forefront in her mind. Soon—tonight in fact—she and Marlowe would work out a plan to find the missing piece of her formula. Izzy's optimism bubbled from her, and her smile was brilliant at the woman who held several arrow shafts in one hand.

"I am most grateful for everything you've done for me. I would not have survived without you and Klacka. Do not worry for me. My brother is back, and all will be well."

It was time to get to work, to do what she was good at. Solve the puzzle, work the problem, be the guide that Tam needed. The new moon approached and in a week's time, the portal could be opened. Marlowe was alive. She had survived and they would be going home soon. A part of her would miss Flo and Klacka desperately, but this was their world and their life. Hers was elsewhere.

∞

Darkness had fallen on *Fotr Tïïvar*. The tiny outpost was filled to the brim with soldiers, hunters, and villagers, and the reveling had already begun, though the official celebration was not until the next day. Izzy was tired yet she could not sleep, the meeting with Marlowe foremost in her mind. At last, Flo bid her good night and went to her sleeping pallet. Izzy finally closed her eyes, thinking Marlowe had not been able to get away.

A tiny hoot owl sounded in the distance, and it nibbled at the edges of her consciousness. There were no owls in the area that Izzy had heard. She rose, thrusting her feet into the slippers she'd worn since her arrival. She stepped out through the door and into the starlight. A tiny sliver of the moon beckoned her through the trees and with the hooting of the owl again, she followed the sound to the half-frozen stream.

At first, she thought she'd been imagining things, but eventually, she spotted his caped outline heading uphill into the woods.

"Were you followed?" He spoke as she caught up with him. They'd come to a small clearing in the center of some giant Alder trees. Not too far in the distance, she could hear the raucous shouts of men as they celebrated early.

Izzy gathered her fur cloak around her. "No. At least I don't think so. I'm so glad to see you. I'd thought that..." she trailed off, not wanting to say it. They stood under the trees, and she hugged him impulsively, her face buried into a hard placket of leather and chest muscle. He hugged her back, and she allowed herself to relax for the first time in weeks.

"'Twas my fear as well. We both fared satisfactorily in this harsh time. Well done, Isabelle." He grinned at her.

"What happened to you?" Now that she assured herself he was fine, she swatted at him. "I waited for you, for two months! Not knowing if you were dead or gone or..."

His shrug was nonchalant, as though he traveled to strange times and places every day. Izzy shook herself. Well, of course, he did. She was the fish out of water here.

"They tossed me in the dungeon, which is nothing more than a dirt hole. And being no stranger to the gael, I bided my time. Fortunately, for me, a fellow prisoner taught me the language, a necessity while formulating an escape plan. Unfortunately, he was executed before we could make our way. Once I convinced the Earl King that I was no threat to him and that I had skills that would benefit, I was pressed into service." He pulled away slightly to see her in the moonlight.

"Sevorian is a strong leader, but a fair one and I rose through the ranks to become a confidant."

"You are on a first-name basis with the Earl King?" she asked.

Marlowe shrugged as if this was something he did every day. "He is a harsh man, but smart, and we've conversed much about the defense of his land, his people, even his vision for the future."

He moved back through the trees as he talked, his voice low enough not to carry. The stream ran faster through here, splashing and rippling its way toward the sea. He lowered both hands into the cold water and much like he had at the water barrel earlier, he rubbed them clean, scooping a few handfuls onto his face. He wiped it dry with a sleeve. "We've defended the realm from marauders and left a small contingent on the Eastern border to guard. Filthy business, war. In any time. I've seen it in many, and it does not change much." He climbed back up the bank toward Izzy.

She could barely make out Marlowe as he approached. Suddenly, his words sounded far away, and she struggled to hear him. Her head buzzed, sparks of light hitting behind her eyes as she struggled to breathe. Something was cutting off her airway, and she grasped at her throat. There was nothing. She bent over, choking as she felt the sting of water in her nose. The distinct smell and taste of chlorine flooded her senses. She flailed her arms trying to escape.

Hands grasped her shoulders, shaking her, and Marlowe's voice came to her out of a fog. "Isabelle, are you okay?"

Air came back to her, and she crouched on the ground, coughing and sputtering. Her mind cleared as her breath came back. "Yes. Yes. I'm fine. I just felt her." She looked into Marlowe's concerned face. His eyes widened at her words.

"You had a premonition? A warning of Tam?"

Izzy nodded and took a deep breath, the cold air stinging her lungs but clearing her mind. The moon had dropped behind the treetops, shrouding them in darkness.

Chapter 22

Tamberlyn

I was drowning. How someone manages to do this twice in a lifetime, I'll never know, but apparently, I had a knack for it. At least this time it was the clean, chlorinated, and slightly warmed water of a hotel pool. Infinitely better than the run-off ditch drowning I'd experienced a couple of years ago. But drowning is drowning, and it's not pleasant. The lungs burn in your chest. The heart races until the blood pounds in your brain. Nasal passages sting with the taint of chlorine gathering and gurgling at the back of your throat until you gag. Once the last bit of air in your lungs has been expelled, the urge to inhale becomes overwhelming. It's not a matter of want or ability, it is inevitable that the body overrides the will and you suck in water for air.

It shouldn't be happening again. But it was.

Theo and I had survived the Toxeute's arrows only to run headlong into the Redcap's frolic in the pool area. Due to the explosion at the other end of the hotel, guests had vacated the pool and fortunately for them, they had not returned. The only evidence of trouble was a few overturned lounge chairs and two cocktail glasses upended on a nearby table, their paper umbrellas soaking up fruit juice and rum. The isolated sound of bubbles from the hot tub jets on the other side of the room drew my attention, but no one was about. After we were inside I turned the lock on the glass door to keep random swimmers from walking into a possible homicide.

Theo and I had skirted the pool in opposite directions, searching for our prey. In spite of the warm room, the hairs on the back of my neck prickled, and I resisted a shiver. The unearthly presence of the Redcap was like the smell of rotten fruit, sickly, and sweet. Or maybe he really did smell that way. I followed my nose, edging around overturned umbrellas and tables. Theo turned off the Jacuzzi, silencing the bubbles. All was quiet in the large room. I listened anyway.

Gradually, sound floated toward me. Theo's dress shoes barely made a scuffle on the cement. A leaf blower sounded from outside the wall of thick glass windows. The slight buzz of fluorescent lighting hovered in the high ceiling. Drops of the spilled cocktails fell to the concrete floor in intermittent plops. A bubble popped and splashed in the pool. Then another. Then an indistinct gurgling getting louder toward the center of the water.

I walked to the edge, trying to peer under the surface. There was not a single shadow, nor movement—nothing at all. Until that nothing grabbed my ankle, yanking me off balance. I struggled against the unseen force as it pulled me into the pool. I clenched the useless gun in my hand until I realized I was still holding it and let it go. Thrashing under water, I opened my eyes, feeling the chemical sting of chlorine as I tried to see my attacker. There was nothing holding me, no one. I was held fast and drowning by an invisible force—a hugely powerful, very real, invisible force.

The inevitable time came for me. The need to breathe became my sole focus. My kicks against my assailant grew weaker, my hands clasping at nothing. I choked, expelling the final air from my lungs and sucking in water. I choked again, sinking, feeling the darkness close around me as I lost consciousness. Fading to black, I felt a sudden undercurrent of water pushing against me. Someone had jumped into the pool. I struggled out of my fog as my hand grazed something solid. Arms wrapped around my chest, pulling me upward.

My eyes closed in relief as my rescuer turned me, my back to his chest, a strong arm clenching me to him. I felt his very real flesh and blood legs kicking to the surface, and I went limp. A moment later my head broke the surface of the water. I heaved, ejecting pool water and spit, and the arms loosened around me as we moved toward the shallow end. I gulped in air and coughed some more. My feet touched bottom, and he released me.

"Jesus, Paradiso. You okay?"

I looked up into the dark face of Cobb, water dripping from his hair and beard. At my startled nod, he sloshed toward the steps, pulling me along. We exited, and I collapsed on the cement, retching out more water. "Where's Theo?" I gasped.

In answer, a strange croaking noise sounded above us. We both looked up. The Redcap was hanging from one of the rafters, dangling Theo over the pool, the back of his tuxedo shirt gripped in the Redcap's sharp talons. The former fae was choking in a very human way, his legs kicking, his hands clutching at his throat. The Redcap's laughter echoed through the big room. Cobb ran to the deep end of the pool where his gun lay on the cement. He grabbed it and aimed at the Redcap.

"Wait!" I coughed more at the words, unable to catch my breath. Cobb didn't shoot. Instead, he yelled at the Redcap to let go of his victim and come down. His command was met with more laughter.

I heaved myself upright, wiping chlorine and saliva from my

mouth and forcing my eyes open against the sting. I squinted into the rafters, helplessly watching the Redcap swing a couple hundred pounds of human like a rag doll.

"How the hell did he get up there?" Cobb muttered. "Better yet, what the hell is he?"

"A Redcap," I croaked out the words. "Aim for his head, but don't—"

"I can't get a clean shot."

Theo had quit clawing at his throat. He was giving up. He was going to die, right here in front of me, choked by his own shirt.

"Buttons," I yelled up at him. With a feeble hand, he unfastened his shirt cuffs and ripped open the buttons on the front. In the middle of a swing, he wriggled free, slipping out of the Redcap's grasp. The wizened elf flipped in the air like a monkey, his feet clinging to the rafter as he lunged for the falling Theo. Cobb fired three shots. His aim was good, but the bullets passed through the shadowy Redcap, and pinged against the metal roof. But the distraction caused the Redcap to miss his grab, and Theo belly-flopped into the shallow end of the pool. The Redcap screeched in frustration as he shimmered out of sight.

Theo's stillness at the bottom of the pool caught me off guard. I quit thinking of him as the lying, deceitful, all-powerful fae he used to be and realized he was as fragile as any human. I jumped back into the pool, yelling for Cobb to help me.

We drug a limp Theo from the water and laid him belly-down on the cement, his face turned to the side so he wouldn't choke. Cobb gave him three hard thumps on his back, and I was in the process of checking his pulse when he coughed. Water and blood and spittle splashed onto the pool deck. He heaved a great shuddering breath and rolled to his side. Blood oozed from his temple, and I brushed it away.

"You okay?" I asked.

"Did you get it?" He rasped at me.

I shook my head. Cobb came up beside us and held out a wad of cocktail napkins. I took them and pressed them against the gash on Theo's head. He winced but held my gaze.

"I'm sorry I tried to shoot you," I said. "Before, I mean."

Theo grabbed my hand and sat up. "Glad you held off for death by Redcap. That's so much better." He grinned and coughed again, holding his ribs. The hospital bandage from the other night was soaked, and he pulled it off, revealing a reopened arrow wound. I pressed another napkin to his shoulder.

Behind us, Cobb swore and pulled off his soggy tuxedo jacket.

"I'll never get my fucking deposit back on this thing." He balanced his big frame on a lounge chair and glanced at me. "He going to make it?"

"I'll live," Theo answered. "Thanks."

"Good. Now, does someone want to explain what the fuck is going on here?"

Theo said nothing, but his eyes wandered over me enough that I suddenly felt my cocktail dress was not the least bit waterproof and entirely too translucent when wet.

I moved, found some towels from behind the counter, looped one around me, and handed out others. We dried off as best we could as I explained to Cobb what I'd tried to keep secret for six months. Monsters are real. I can see them. One tried to kill us.

The investigators had found their way back to the pool area by the time I finished. Strangely enough, they hadn't heard the shots at all.

"Paradiso, the weirdest shit happens around you." One of the forensic team remarked. I shrugged and wrapped the towel tighter around my shoulders. "That your gun at the bottom of the pool?" he asked.

Cobb found a long-handled net and fished my gun out of the deep end. He dropped it into a gallon-sized evidence bag the tech held out. Cobb glanced at me. "You fire this thing?" At my headshake, he snatched the bag from the guy and held it out.

"Thanks." I took the bag as he sat down. "And thanks for fishing me out too. I'm glad you came back."

"Took me a while to break in." He nodded at the doorway. "You locked the door?"

"I didn't want anyone to walk into danger," I said.

"I still don't know what I was saving you from," Cobb spoke under his breath.

Theo joined us at the lounge chairs. "It was a splinter. Redcap's have the ability to splinter into another form of themselves. This one just happened to be invisible."

"Sure as shit felt real enough," I said.

"I'm sure it did." Theo interjected and turned to Cobb. "And since the bastard is still around, we need to go. I think he'll go after the senator in an effort to get to me."

"And why is it after you?" Cobb hadn't moved, and I knew from the look on his face he wasn't moving until he was satisfied with some answers. He'd processed the supernatural events with more calm than I'd anticipated, but knowing hostiles are out there and actually seeing one in action can throw anybody for a loop.

"An occupational hazard," Theo answered. "A former occupation, a former life. No, I'm not a—I'm not like Tam. But I've seen a fair share of things."

"You must have been an asshole of a co-worker," Cobb muttered, but the answer seemed enough for now. He looked at me. "After we dropped Balfour at the emergency room, I called a unit to escort Shepherd and his daughter to a safe house. We should head there if you're okay." He scrutinized me more carefully than he had in the six months of being partners. Apparently, I was interesting now.

"Yeah, okay. Let's go." I heaved myself off a chair as Theo weaved to his feet. "You should probably get to a hospital," I told him. "You might have a concussion."

"If the Redcap is where I think he is, I have to go. Trust me, you want me with you."

"Hell," Cobb said. "He's right. It's not like we can risk a swat team to go after this thing."

After answering brief questions from the investigators, the three of us headed back to the parking garage, and Cobb tossed my go-bag in the trunk of my car. He would take Theo to the safe house. Neither Cobb nor I were willing to let Theo handle this on his own, and we couldn't very well tell the officers on watch duty to look out for an evil elf in a red hat. I would drive past my house to change before meeting Cobb at the safe house.

It was into the wee hours of the morning, but I called Volpi for a status update anyway. His sleepy voice told me things were the same. He tried to keep the worried tone out of our conversation.

I changed the subject. "By the way, it was a Toxeute. We got it."

"We?" he asked.

"Theo and I." There was hesitation on the line, and I could almost hear the wheels spinning in his brain. "Yes. I know that sounds odd, but the situation got very intense, very fast. Theo shot our archer with my long-range rifle. Quite a shot, actually. You were right, this was totally supernatural. Get this—Redcaps were after him."

"Him?"

"Theo," I said again. There was a moment of stunned silence where I couldn't tell if Volpi was surprised at the mention of Redcaps, or Theo's name coming out of my mouth so easily. "Are still after him by the way. We got one, but there's another one out there. I'm headed back to meet Cobb at the safe house."

"Your police partner. So you've dragged him into this."

"Not intentionally, but he is in it. He saved my ass, actually. Look Volpi, it's a long story, and we can go into details later. I just wanted to ask about Izzy."

"The portal window closes at midnight tomorrow, or rather, today," he said. And the tone he used didn't give me much hope. If they didn't make the portal closing, it would be another two weeks for the appearance of the waxing crescent to thin the rift enough to allow travel. We let the conversation lapse after that. Both of us knew the facts, and neither of us liked them much.

Chapter 23

Isabelle

Klacka and Flo had told Izzy about all the traditions of harvest festival and the hearing of the accords. The next day their small group arrived at the temple's great hall early to help set up the long tables for the king's guard and prominent families.

Outside, roasting spits held two enormous boars—the fat from the meat dripping onto the coals and sending up delicious tendrils of flavored steam and smoke. On each table a large trencher of nuts for the taking, both beech and hazel. The massive stone ovens of the village had been baking for days.

Izzy held a great basket of barley flatbread while Klacka walked beside her, placing two loaves at each end of the tables. The traditional meal would be served buffet style and a giant board along the wall was filled with pickled eggs, smoked salmon, boiled turnips and parsnips, dried plums, and crabapples. A savory stew consisting of mushrooms, leeks, and wild celery—picked before the first frost had come and stored for the occasion—was bubbling away in a large kettle over another outside fire. The villagers had brought a lot of the meal with them, and a game hunter had killed and dressed two large bucks for roasting. Flo stood by one kettle, cutting onions for the stew. It was more food than Izzy had seen since she'd arrived.

Her young helper's near-trampling had not dampened the girl's mood, and she flitted from table to table, inside and outside the great hall, laughing with excitement. The villagers had brought their own children, and soon Izzy was abandoned for a game of tag. Izzy was in a fine mood herself. She hadn't realized just how worried she'd been about Marlowe's survival until she'd seen him alive and well. He'd had no explanation for why he'd not returned home, even though several waning crescent moons had come and gone.

The king's guard was a sought after occupation, and she'd been surprised to see him so well-positioned. She shouldn't have been. Working under highly unusual circumstances, Marlowe was adept at blending in, and probably much more comfortable with horses and swords than modern transportation and guns. These people were his ancestors as well as hers, and she made a mental note to ask him if the understanding of words, tasks, and customs were like also distant memories to him.

She had also explained the error in their arrival being several years later than she'd anticipated, as well as her failure to access the temple. They'd made plans to meet tonight. Before the feasting began, there was the accords—young men coming of age and swearing fealty to the earl. There were five of them, each followed by great shouts of pride from their parents. After the fealty oaths, came the settling of disputes—anything from trespassing to theft, during which, Izzy kept a watchful eye on the crowd for Marlowe's face.

Unfortunately, the one face she didn't want to see had become a constant. The enormous brute of a man, Mael, his younger brother shadowing him, had spotted her. She moved through the crowd, hoping to avoid him. It had been a while since their encounter, but she knew that Mael had been running unchecked in the clan for some time—Attila the Hun without the military strategy or discipline. He had no leadership qualities, but the others acquiesced because their very lives depended on his limited benevolence. At last, the disputes settled, the Earl King called for food and ale, and the evening's celebration had officially begun.

Izzy ate little, hoping for a glimpse of Marlowe and trying to stay far from the big dumb brute. Overly loud and obnoxious, Mael leaned against the wall near the head table, a tankard in one hand and a dripping slice of roast boar in the other. His dark beady eyes followed her through the throngs of revelers. His enormous shaggy head rolling on his shoulders, he leered at her from across the hall while licking pork fat from his fingers.

In the time before, events such as her assault had been nonexistent. The power and magic had surged through her the last time, and the people sensed it. That power was the reason the temple priestesses accepted her, and she was as protected as they were. This time, all she'd had was refuge with an old woman and a child.

By nature of their designation, temple maidens were off limits to the baser needs of men. But times were different, no longer revered as they once were, the temple maidens and priestesses kept to themselves and their temple. And Izzy was just an ordinary young woman, subject to whatever fate would befall her in a violent world.

"Isabelle." Marlowe stood in the shadows of the great hall, indicating she should follow him. He disappeared, and she stayed where she was, busying herself stoking one of the hearth fires. Surreptitiously, she watched Mael as his brother came to him, engaging him in conversation. Using the distraction, she slipped out.

The great hall had been dark, lit only by the hearth fires and a few sconces. But outside the bonfire was raging, and she could see outlines of people as they gathered around the fire pits. They paid her no attention, most of them having drunk a fair amount of wine and a hard liquor drink they called *Skellr*.

She followed Marlowe into the shadows, and they stood on the edge of the clearing, hidden from view by thick trees.

"I don't know that I can open the portal now, even if we find the *Varŏi-lokur,* the song. Before, I could open the rift from inside the temple. It was easy, but now—" She broke off again and searched his face. "This time I don't have the ability. I am useless."

His expression had a resoluteness, full of mission and purpose. "We shall find the artifact or the verse. When we do, the power shall come to you, Miss Isabelle. And if it does not, then we shall simply walk back to whence we came into this place and use that doorway to get home." He turned and gestured the way back to the celebration. The moon was close to its apex, signaling the beginning of the ritual.

"You say that as if it's the simplest thing in the world." She followed him up the path toward the fires.

"It is. Because we have no other choice. I intend to get home, and to get you home as well."

∞

The ceremony began as most ceremonies begin—with a sacrifice of a goat. Izzy didn't flinch at the priestesses quick slash of the knife, the animal's twitching, the blood running over the granite tableau. By this time, she'd seen so much blood and animal flesh that she'd become inured to the sight.

The temple consisted of several sections. A receiving room to one side, small and kept cozy with an enormous fireplace, it was where villagers came seeking advice or blessings from the gods. Several other outbuildings toward the back, at the base of the hill, held sleeping quarters for the priestesses and healers.

The cathedral, where ceremonies took place, was an open amphitheater, oblong and defined by carved wooden pillars along two sides. The night sky was crisp and clear with thousands of stars watching from their premier seats in the inky black.

Toward the front of the room, a large curtain of rich fabric formed a backdrop for the round platform serving as a stage, holding two large altars of semi-carved stone. The rough-hewn sides of the granite appeared in its natural state, but the stone had been chipped away to a flat top about the size of a toddler's bed. Small oil lamps illuminated the altar. Along one side were several drums in varying sizes, each manned by a young woman. There were other torches, some at the entrance, more of them lighting the stage and the drummers.

The Earl King sat in a place of honor, just to the right of the high priestess. The woman was tall and black-haired, the long tresses worn loose and full over her breasts. She wore a light-colored dress, tied at the waist with a silver cord. After her nod at the king, she signaled to the women and they started a slow beat on the drums, first one, then two, and finally all of them, and the deep bellows seemed to echo through the temple and into the sky.

The priestess stood and began her dance, bringing one bare foot against the stone stage and keeping to her toes as she moved. Her breasts undulated under the fine material of her dress as she swayed before the Earl King. Yet she wasn't dancing for him. Her movements were for the god of seasons, thanking him for the great bounty of fall harvest and his benevolence in the months to come.

Winter was harsh in the ancient north, but it brought necessary water to the lowlands during a rainless summer. Whales would migrate south during the early winter, and most years a beached whale could provide food and oil for several villages.

The dance of the priestess, similar to the movements of the tropical hula dance, told a story.

Izzy wondered if a descendant of the ancient northerners somehow made their way to the islands in the pacific, starting an entire generation of dancers. She studied the dance carefully, trying to commit the hand and foot movements to memory, though her gut told her this wasn't the formula she was looking for.

Beside her, Marlowe seemed captivated by the priestess's beauty and grace. Izzy pulled at his cape and whispered. "Look for an older woman. She's the one we need to talk to. She is called the mother-*the Móðir*, and she would be the only one who might remember Stjarna."

Marlowe shifted uncomfortably beside her, his eyes still on the priestess, the drumbeats ramping up in tempo and volume.

"I thought you said the priestesses were pure, virginal. This woman is no—" His words were cut off as the drum beats stopped. The priestess had stopped in front of the altar, her back to the majority of the audience. She untied the silver cord and let her dress fall to the ground, the firelight dancing over the curves of her nude form. Izzy held her breath. Beside her, she could feel the tension in Marlowe. The hush across the room was deafening.

The woman faced her audience, her hands held up to the stars as four guards came to her. Two on each side, taking her limbs, they picked her up and placed her on the opposite altar of the freshly killed goat. The guards retreated and the young women surrounding the altars resumed their drumming. The priestess did not lie placidly on the stone, but writhed and squirmed as if in the throes of passion.

From outside the pillars, a man appeared, stomping his way through the crowd. At his appearance, the crowd cheered and applauded, parting the way for his path to the altar. He was young, late teens to early twenties, Izzy guessed. He wore black kohl around his eyes like a mask, and she did not recognize him as one from the outpost. He must be from the village. On his head, an elaborate headdress of feathers, moss, and antlers waved in the air as he tossed his head back and forth like a stag scraping velvet off his rack. Other than a leather cloth tied at his waist, he was naked.

The night air was below freezing, and by morning, the standing water in troughs and ponds would have a sheet of ice covering them. But in the temple, the close warmth of human body heat and torches offered some relief. Still, Izzy wrapped her fur cloak around her closer as the young stag came to the altar. The drums beat wildly as he pranced back and forth in front of the priestess. The two alternately reached for one another and shied away in a ritualistic dance of the ages, until the young stag climbed onto the stone, and knelt before the woman's open legs.

Izzy looked away. Toward the side of the great hall, across the crowd, still in the semi-darkness where the torch light ended, a crone-like figure limped into view. She was hooded, her face obscured by darkness and cloth, but her gait and stature belied her age. Izzy nudged Marlowe.

"Come on. I've found her."

At the altar, the boy-stag had flung the leather covering away, and the drums fell silent as he lowered himself onto the priestess. Marlowe tore his eyes away from the stage.

"Now?" His voice rasped. "Your timing is—"

The drums started up again, and Izzy glanced back at the altar. The stag was now rutting earnestly in time to the beat. Izzy rolled her eyes and grabbed Marlowe's hand, pulling him across the room.

∞

Their journey was quick as Izzy took advantage of everyone's attention on the stage. They weaved in and out of the hushed crowd. Izzy spotted Mael toward the back, towering over the others, his eyes fixed to the copulation on the altar. Good. The last thing they needed was the brute stalking them.

They stopped in front of the old woman. She stood quiet as a stone, tiny in her massive dark cloak, yet her eyes seemed unfocused and somewhere else. Izzy was suddenly shy.

"Móðir." Izzy started softly. "We need to speak with you." She faltered. The woman seemed not to hear her. She continued in a louder voice "I was a temple maiden once. My name is Isobel."

The crone took in her words. Her thin brittle hair was like the rest of her, a fragile filament of light. She seemed about to break as they stood, huddled together near the outside pillars. A sudden breeze blew in from the west, and Izzy shivered at its touch. Inside, the drums were thumping to a frenzied rhythm, and she knew once they stopped, the spell over the crowd would be broken and their opportunity would be lost.

They could not hurry the old woman though, and Izzy stilled Marlowe's impatient restlessness with a glance. She knew the woman had heard her. She felt the connection strengthening between them. The woman turned, grasping her wrist with a gnarled hand, decorated with age spots and a faded blue-black tattoo. Móðir looked into Izzy's eyes as if trying to remember something so long ago it felt unreal. She was recognizably the oldest person in the camp, possibly even the village.

"Isobel," Móðir spoke, her voice as strong as her grip. Her fragile, wispy appearance was deceiving. "You have come back."

"Yes, mother. I have come back. I need your help. As Stjarna before me, I need access to the temple. The sacred writings. Can you help us?"

Móðir seemed to notice Marlowe for the first time, craning her ancient neck to look up at him.

"This man is not of here. Not of us."

"He is safe, mother. He is a friend."

"A traveler?" Móðir questioned. At Izzy's nod, she stopped for another moment. More time passed. Time they did not have. Finally, the woman inclined her head and beckoned them outside. "We can enter the living quarters from the back. From there, you can find your way to the writings."

Outside the temple, all was quiet. The few stragglers not in the temple stood just outside peering in to get a glimpse of the ritual. The old woman led the way to an opening on the far side, facing the woods. Móðir stopped at an enormous white pelt hanging on the wooden side of the building. She pulled the heavy fur aside and stepped through. Polar bears were only seen further north, and their pelts were thought to contain mystical powers. Izzy found the fur to be rough and not pleasant to touch, like the bristles of a hairbrush.

She hesitated at the fur-lined doorway, looked back to reassure herself that Marlowe was there. At his nod, she took a deep breath and entered the temple, feeling the energy of the sacred place as she moved.

Chapter 24

Tamberlyn

I found an open parking space in front of Cobb's beat-up Chevy. The safe house area was in the midst of gentrification, and the few local businesses had given way to chain stores and coffee shops.

"You stopped to go shopping?" Cobb glanced at my outfit as he opened the hotel room door. He had changed out of ruined tuxedo trousers and shoes and into a pair of sneakers and sweat pants.

"Shut up, I got you something." I shoved a shopping bag into his hands.

He pulled out a XXL sand-colored shirt with palm trees skirting the bottom hem. "Aw, you shouldn't have, Paradiso. That's so sweet—" I reached out to grab the shirt back, but he pulled it closer to him and stepped away from me. "Your guy is in the bedroom," he said, stripping off his still damp tuxedo shirt and pulling the tags off the new one. "No activity so far. I sent Reaves out for breakfast. Apparently whatever team was here last drank all the coffee." His eyes drifted toward the small dinette table in the corner where the senator sat.

"He's not my guy." I hissed at Cobb. "But coffee would be great."

"Detective." Senator Shepherd looked up from his laptop. "I'm glad to see you. I've been watching the news feeds about the hotel explosion. It's horrifying to think someone would do all of this."

"There are crazy people everywhere, Senator. How is JoAnne? Is she—" I looked around for the young woman.

"My daughter is in the next room." He glanced at the connecting door. "She was unharmed but quite upset. She took something to help calm her nerves." His eyes flicked over my form. I'd changed into jeans, a black T-shirt, and light blue button-down—actual clothes instead of the evening dress that had seen the last of its days. "Theo told me you had a bit of a scuffle at the hotel pool."

"You could say that." I smiled at him. "But we survived." And then I realized how he'd addressed his campaign manager. "Theo?"

The older man looked thoughtful. "That's what you call him, isn't it? It seems to suit him."

Wondering what Theo had told him, I moved toward the table. "Yes. I guess it does."

The subject of our conversation stepped out of the second bedroom, having changed into perfectly creased khakis and a polo shirt. He was barefoot, looked less frazzled than the rest of us, and had a couple of fresh butterfly bandages covering the gash near his hairline. I felt a rush of adrenaline and glanced away. No one should look that good after what we'd been through. Unconsciously, I drew my fingers through the tangles in my hair.

Theo opened the bar fridge and peered into the dim interior. "Coke, or water?" He didn't look at me.

"I'll wait for coffee. Reaves will be back soon, I think." I sat at the table. "How are you, Senator? Were things okay here?"

Shepherd closed his laptop. "Shep, please, detective. And yes, I'm fine. Thanks to you and Detective Cobb. Theo credits you with his life." Both of us glanced at the man standing in the tiny kitchenette, in his casual clothes, his throat moving as he drank and looking for all the world like a celebrity in a soft drink commercial.

I turned back to the senator and he gave me that knowing smile again. "Unfortunately the guy who knocked him into the pool got away," I said.

Theo ignored us and moved across the room toward Cobb, handing him a soda.

Sensing the politician's eyes on me, I tried to smile and make casual conversation—neither of which are in my wheelhouse of skills. Theo's easy demeanor with Cobb set my teeth on edge.

If I had found Marlowe at home waiting for me, I might not have come back here. It would have been so easy to crawl in next to Marlowe's warmth and just stay. But he hadn't been there, and it wasn't a choice anyway. This was not about Theo or our history or my desire for—whatever. This was about protecting life—Shepherd's, Theo's, even Cobb's. I had to get back in the game and quit daydreaming.

I shifted back to the conversation with Shep. "Yes, unfortunately, he's still out there. He may not find us, but we don't want to take any chances."

Cobb spoke from near the balcony windows. "We'll stay here tonight, Senator. After yesterday's events, our suspect is escalating." The shades had been pulled and curtains were drawn, leaving the seating area dark except for a lamp in the corner. Cobb finished the soda in several large gulps and tossed the can away. "Paradiso and I will check the perimeter as soon as Reaves gets back."

Shep nodded and pulled at his loosened tie. He rose, saying he had some calls to make, and disappeared into the bedroom. It was an obvious excuse to give the three of us some time to talk. He was more perceptive than I'd originally given him credit for. With a sigh, I joined Cobb near the couch where I'd dumped my duffle.

"Monsters, huh?" Cobb asked. I didn't say anything as I unpacked my go-bag full of weapons. I pulled the rifle barrel out, and Theo automatically held out his hand. Cobb's expression was worthy of a meme as I handed the gun parts over. Theo sat in a boxy chair next to the couch, and pulling a cloth from the bag, he started to clean the weapon. Cobb watched him for a moment before turning back to me. "Here I thought you were just quirky."

I smiled. "I am quirky, but when I disappear or seem to be distracted, it's usually because there's something else going on. Someone or something not normal. You understand why I couldn't tell you?"

"I'm not sure I would have believed you if I hadn't seen it for myself." He pulled a vial of red liquid from the go-bag. "You have enough shit in here for an army. What's this?"

"Consecrated blood. Used for demons, mostly. There's also salt, colloidal silver, iron and silver weapons as well as the modern ones. Guns don't usually do much against hostiles," I said.

"I see." He replaced the vial carefully. "How long have you been at this?"

I glanced at Theo. His lips pressed into a hard line, but he kept his eyes focused as he placed the cleaned gun parts back in my go-bag. He pulled out a Kampfmesser with a five-inch blade and inspected the balance.

"Since I was young. A teenager." I sighed.

Cobb frowned. "Did Hernandez know? Is that why he..."

I shook my head. "No, he didn't know. And no, it wasn't a hostile who killed him. It really was Munson." I fumbled in the bag and finally pulled out a packet of baby wipes. Taking one, I cleaned some of the gunk off a blade cover. "The case was mixed up with a hostile, something called a Strigoi Mort."

"A Strigoi? They haven't been around for ages. Are you sure?" Theo interrupted, not looking at me. I resisted the urge to flip him the bird.

"What's a Strigoi?" Cobb asked.

"An ancient vampire. A creature, really. Not like the movie kind," I answered. I turned to Mr. Judgmental. "And yes, I'm sure."

One of the things that allowed Theo to fool me all those years ago was his highly evolved use of body language and facial expression. Now I knew everything about him was a lie, and I could read his face like a headline. He made the connection between the appearance of an extinct hostile and time travel. To his credit, he did not bring it up in front of Cobb.

A sliver of sunlight streaked through a crack in the curtain, landing on the open neck of Theo's polo. Glistening in the light, on a chain around his neck, was a small silver disc about the size of a quarter. I couldn't tell what was on it, but when he caught my glance, he moved the disk to the inside of his shirt. "Okay," he said and rose from his chair, the knife still in his hand. He resheathed the weapon and tucked it into the back of his khakis, pulling the shirttail over for cover as he walked away.

"And him?" Cobb's voice lowered as he indicated Theo. "Hostile? Or hunter?"

"Something in between," I said.

Reaves was back with fast food and several coffees, and I sipped at the scalding brew while the guys dug into the breakfast sandwiches right away. I wasn't hungry. I felt like I'd filled up on prime rib only minutes before, yet behind the drawn curtains, the light was already high in the sky. I stretched and yawned, exhaustion radiating through me.

Just as the guys were cleaning up food wrappers, the lights flickered. I pulled a flashlight from my bag and handed it to Cobb. Theo came out of the bedroom, this time with shoes on. He nodded at me. This was it.

We opened the door, asking Reaves and his partner to stay until we cleared the perimeter. The three of us left the hotel room, and at the end of the hall, Cobb used silent military gestures to send us in different directions.

We would look at anything and everything, bags left unattended, covered dinner plates from room service trays, housekeeping carts, or suspicious individuals. I was armed with my small Sig Sauer, a knife strapped to my calf, and a flashlight. Cobb had his standard Glock, and Theo had unsheathed the combat knife from its hiding place as he moved forward.

I had just opened the stairwell door when the flickering lights died out completely. After waiting in vain for the emergency lighting, I flipped on my pocket flash, shining it down the stairs.

Behind me, a fierce whooshing sound billowed down the hall, and I turned back to see Theo and Cobb knocked on their asses. Like an idiot, I rushed out to help them and was caught in the wind tunnel, tumble-weeding right along with them until a very solid wall stopped me. The flashlight fell and flickered as it rolled. I crawled on my hands and knees, feeling around for the light and my partner. I heard him groan some distance away.

My hand landed on a patch of fabric, and Taser strength shocks jerked up my arm. I yelped and rubbed my tingling fingers. I sat there, my eyes adjusting to the darkness until I could make out the Redcap's headgear, a boxy, blood-red hat with a small front brim and billowing cap as it sparked on the floor. The sparks died away and I jumped as the cap slid away from me in the semi-darkness.

Farther down the hall, I heard Cobb's grunts as he struggled and thrashed on the floor, locked in a fierce battle with an unseen entity. The splinter. The same thing that tried to drown me in the pool had followed us to the safe house.

There was no sign of Theo, or the evil sprite intent on killing him. For some reason, I could not get my mind off the hat. The headgear shuffled in spurts and stops down the carpeted hallway as though it held a rabbit trying to escape. I got to my flashlight and crawled along the floor in pursuit—the hat always just out of my reach, not that I wanted to make another barehanded grab. I had to think of a new tactic.

Cobb seemed to be winning his war with the invisible foe. At least he was upright and had grasped something in one hand while he punched at it with the other. Everything was in shadow, lit only by my small light and the exit sign at the end of the hall.

Just behind me, a room door opened and daylight flooded the area. The hat scooted away from me. I shouted at the curious guest to get back inside and shut the damn door. The hallway was drenched in darkness again, and the cap stopped its jerky progress. The dirty hat must gain power from the light. I focused my flashlight away from it, pointing the beam toward Cobb and his opponent as I crept along the wall.

The hat lurked beside a small desk, a sideboard that held silk flowers, and a lamp designed to make the hotel look homier. I sincerely hoped there wasn't an innocent rabbit stuck inside the proverbial hat as I pulled my knife. The thing was seriously creeping me out, and inanimate object or not, I was going to end it.

"Cobb. You okay?" I called over my shoulder. His response was a grunt and a thump as something hit the floor. "Where's Theo?" Not that Cobb would know this, but I wanted eyes on Theo before I did anything drastic. For all I knew, the Redcap could have shrunk my former flame to the size of a kitten, and it was he trying to escape from under the hat.

"End of the hall." Cobb's teeth clenched as he spoke, punctuating each syllable with a jab of his closed fist.

I spun the light around, shining it toward the exit sign. Theo's back was against the wall in a death clinch with the Redcap, hands around one another's throat. The small elf's back was to me, both feet planted against the wall on either side of Theo's hips in a seemingly impossible stance. His clawed hands gripped Theo's neck, and in the beam of my light, I could see Theo was losing this battle. I hunched my legs under me in a crouch. Knife in one hand, light in the other, I launched, ready to stab the Redcap in the back. Out of the corner of my eye, the hat jerked back to life at my feet. I flipped the knife in my hand, catching it in an overhand grip, and stabbed the cap, securing the little beastie to the floor.

The resulting shock knocked me back several feet and into Cobb who fell under me, cushioning my fall. My head rocked back against his chest with such force my teeth rattled and his arm came around my middle, securing me to him, much as he had in the pool. We lay sprawled on the floor for a second. I lifted my head to see if Theo survived.

The Redcap seemed to lose his footing against the wall and his grip on Theo's neck at the same time. He fell flat on the floor with an angry grunt. Theo lost no time in falling on him, knife in hand. With almost an identical motion to mine with the hat, Theo plunged the knife into the Redcap. It was a big weapon, a German-forged WWII blade, meant to cut down all enemies. The weapon was too large and unwieldy for me, and I left it in the bag most of the time, but tonight it seemed to do the job. Theo heaved the blade out and plunged it in again, the Redcap squirming under his weight.

Beside the hallway table, the hat stuck under my knife was still sparking and twitching as though alive and lit with dying sparklers. The Redcap, having lost a measure of its power with my hat trick, was ineffectual under Theo's attack. He could no longer manifest the splinter self, and the unseen force that Cobb battled was gone. We sat on the floor. Theo pulled the knife free from the Redcap's chest and with several hacking blows, cut the elf's head from its body.

It took some time. It's not like in the movies where the good guy makes a nice clean swipe of the sword and heads roll. This was bloody and tough and brutal, more like butchering than an honorable beheading.

I wasn't sad. I wasn't about to stop him. The bastard had tried to kill the senator and us. The vicious elf had killed an innocent woman in the process. Marcy Jackson's death was appeased, and I truly believed this would end the threat to Senator Shepherd. This was a hostile. It invaded our world with evil intent and it was dead. Drinks all round.

Theo rose from his task. Within seconds, the bloody mess on the floor dried up into ash and the lights came back on, blinding us.

Blinking, I sat up and realized Cobb's arms were still around me. He seemed to notice this at the same time and released his hold. We both stood, somewhat uncomfortable at our close proximity, and immediately stepped back to re-establish our personal space.

I walked down the hall with care and after a prolonged effort, pulled my knife out of the hat on the floor. The hat, its crown perforated with a knife gash, now seemed innocuous. I picked it up and finding a laundry bag on the doorknob of someone's door, I dumped the clothes and stuffed the hat inside. Volpi would appreciate the item. Theo, his breath coming in gasps, staggered back and bumped into me. I put a hand on his shoulder, and he turned, pulling me to him. "You okay?" he murmured. I nodded into his shoulder. We had survived. Not only supernatural forces but each other's wrath and long-held grudges.

"It's over," he said, his face into my neck. I figured he meant more than the attack on him, but whatever resentment he'd held for me, and me for him was over too. I pulled away.

"Let's hope so," I said.

Cobb came up to us and looked over at Theo. "You good?" Theo nodded and coughed in his hand. A puff of gray dust flew around. Cobb grinned and clapped him on the back, creating a bigger dust cloud. "What are we going to tell the senator?"

Theo's shirtfront and hands were covered in fine gray ash. He resembled a modern chimney sweep minus the hat. He brushed himself off.

"Shep knows whatever this was, it wasn't after him. I told

him that much." Theo shrugged and brushed stray ash from his forehead with the back of his hand. "I'll tell him the truth. That someone from my past wanted retribution and he won't threaten us again. I'll convince him not to pursue it."

"That's all well and good," Cobb said. "But we have an open murder case that we can't solve. We can't even say we got the bad guy because he's nothing more than a pile of dust waiting on housekeeping."

I looked at Cobb. "Welcome to the hardest part of my job," I said.

Chapter 25

Isabelle

Out of the shadows of the chamber, the soft muttering of the Móŏir floated to her, and Izzy shook herself to in the stagnant air.

"You have the sight," Móŏir said in her native tongue, ignoring Marlowe's halted reassurances and directing her comment to Izzy. "I sense this power within you. You have come far. Far beyond my humble understanding. I see you. I feel your energy. But you are lost. Untrained in the ways. You should stay here and learn. We can teach you the ways of the goddess."

Izzy bowed her head. "Thank you, Móŏir. But I must return home. My sister is also—" She hesitated, "different. She is a hunter of evil beings, and she needs me. And this man." She grasped Marlowe's sleeve. "He must return as well. He is a traveler of great import. We have a duty to—" Móŏir waved her hand impatiently.

"Yes, yes. I know. He travels with the moon. I feel his energy also. My grandfather's sister was a traveler on the moon's light. Only the Exalted Priestess was allowed to confer with her when she returned from such journeys."

"Stjarna?"

"Yes. And after many travels, long after she went to meet the gods, Exalted Priestess sang her mysteries and remembrances." The old woman closed her eyes in memory, and for a moment Izzy thought she'd fallen asleep. She didn't want to be rude and startle her, but she couldn't wait forever. She was about to speak again when the woman grabbed her arm and thrust the loose-fitting sleeve up to reveal one forearm and then the other. "You have not the markings. How is it you have the gifts without the mark of Stjarna?"

"I don't know." Izzy remembered her old friend's tattoos— intricate designs starting from her delicate wrists, writhing and twisting like braided rope up to her shoulders. The markings were part of another memory. In her dream of the family, the dried blood had been inking up her own skin. Until now, she'd never thought the tattoo was significant—beautiful, yes, but unimportant. "Móðir, can you tell us where to find the *Varði-lokur,* the song?"

It was several minutes before Móðir moved or gave any sign of life. So long in fact that Izzy started wondering if she should check for a pulse, or make a plan to escape. Being found with a dead village elder in the temple would not bode well for her future.

When Móðir stirred and lifted her head, Izzy breathed a sigh of relief. The woman's gaze focused on Izzy's face. "There are many songs. If you stay, I will teach them all to you."

"God's blood," Marlowe exclaimed. "We have not the time, Isabelle. Please make her understand."

"I cannot stay, Móðir. I don't belong here. Please. The Song of Tími. The ancient one that tells of Swords and Charms, of travelers on the moon's light."

In answer, Móðir moved away from them. A deep sigh

erupted from Marlowe as he let Izzy go ahead of them to follow her. Farther into the depths of the temple, the wood gave way to stone, and Izzy knew they were in the caves.

They traveled in silence, the torchlights flaming to light in front of the old woman and extinguishing as they passed.

It was some time before she stopped, and they found themselves in a large room. When the torches flickered to life on Móŏir's command, Izzy could make out the huge bas-relief along the wall. The Tree of Life. Covering the entire wall, its carved branches leafed out and held tiny runic symbols. The roots of the tree extended down and out onto the stone floor.

"I've been here before," Izzy spoke low to Marlowe, so as not to disturb the Móŏir's concentration.

"With Tamberlyn?" Marlowe asked.

"Yes. But we had no idea of what we were looking for."

The old woman ignored their conversation, humming to herself as she studied the wall.

Izzy and Marlowe stood idle in the center of the room. Móŏir started from the massive center trunk in the middle of the wall, shuffling her feet to the side as she traced a large branch with her fingers until the branch rose above where she could touch. She started to sing. The syllables and notes lifting and descending in the massive chamber. Suddenly she stopped, shook her head, and went back to the starting point of the tree trunk. This time she went in another direction, another branch, singing as she went. That too ended abruptly.

"The Earl King will start to wonder about my whereabouts. I must go soon." Marlowe's gaze never left the old woman as she sang and traced the words in yet another branch. "This tree has hundreds of branches."

"She's going to find it. Just a little more time, Marlowe."

After several minutes, and stops and starts, Móŏir turned to them. "The Song of Tími. A remembrance of my own relative and of all travelers in our past." The old woman looked at both of them. "And our future. It fuels the blood with the will to walk into the moonlight." She beckoned them over and they came to stand at the far side of the room. Isabelle followed her gnarled finger as it pointed to a branch—tiny and intricate, almost unseen, its relief flush with the stone wall.

"This is it?"

Móðir nodded. "It begins here." She touched the wall closer to the main trunk. "But the ending is..." She trailed off.

"Where?" Izzy asked.

The old woman sighed, her shoulders hunched as she splayed her weathered hands out in defeat.

"Okay, it starts here, right?" Not waiting for her answer, Izzy moved toward the center of the wall.

Móðir left her side to sit tiredly on a stone bench carved into the wall. "No one sings the song. I don't know the melody, and the words have disappeared back into the tree."

"No, but they're here. You said this was it." Izzy's tone became desperate as she searched. This couldn't happen. Not after all she'd been through. The waiting, enduring Mael's assault, the harsh climate and exhaustion she felt, and for what?

Marlowe grabbed a torch from its holder on the wall and moved closer to the carving. He held the light as he followed the branch Móðir had indicated. "Can you remember these symbols, Isabelle? These words. I will also commit them to memory."

They both studied the etchings. When they got to the end— the smallest part of the branch—the scratch marks were blurred and hard to read, finally fading to nothing.

"There's more, but we can't see it." She and Marlowe looked at each other and then turned to Móðir.

The woman sighed again, sadness stretched across her wizened face. "I am sorry *Sannligr barn*. The Song of Tími is no more." The woman rose and headed out of the room.

A sob caught in Izzy's throat as she glimpsed Marlowe's expression. He said nothing, but anguish pained his handsome features. He closed his eyes, his hand still gripping the torch. Replacing the torch in its holder, he and Izzy followed the old woman toward the front of the temple again.

Far from them, echoes of the celebration bounced off the stone walls. The ceremony must be over, and soon the night air would crackle with the sound of drunken revelers.

Móðir spoke again. "Here is the safest place for you. The *Messa* was once a sacred and beautiful spectacle to thank the goddess for her bounty and fertility. But now it has become an excuse for much drunkenness and *vígaferli*." She used the word for violence and mayhem. "You, Warrior, you may fend for yourself, but the *Sannligr barn* would be in danger were she to be caught up."

Marlowe frowned for a moment, and Izzy knew he was translating the strange language in his head.

She blushed. "*Sannligr barn* is a fairy child. It could be a common phrase or a term of endearment."

"Mayhap." Marlowe pursed his lips. At another shout from the outside revelers, he looked worried. "She is right. You should stay here. At least until the celebrations die down. I will be missed." He gathered his cape about him, his hand reaching back for Grim in the old world scabbard. After satisfying himself of its presence, he looked at Izzy. "I will be back for you at dawn."

He stood at the entrance, the flickering candlelight illuminating his tan cheeks above his beard. His murky clothing blended with the dark side of the polar bear skin at his back. "Have a care, Isabelle."

With him here, she felt safe and less alone. In the past two months, she'd had no idea how lonely and scared she'd been until she wasn't lonely and scared anymore. With Marlowe at her side, she felt like she could accomplish anything. Was this how Tam felt? A weight of loss came on her suddenly, thinking of her sister's life without Marlowe. How she must have missed him. Izzy launched herself into his arms, hugging him fiercely. "I'm so sorry," she whispered.

He unwrapped her arms, his hands gentle. "I must see to the earl. We don't wish to alarm anyone."

"We'll keep looking. We have some of it at least, maybe..."
She looked up at him.

"I have every faith in you, Isabelle." He bent down and
kissed her cheek.

After Marlowe left, she turned back to Móðir and the
inner chamber. Izzy took the older woman's arm and helped
her through another curtain and into a black hallway. They
navigated their way by memory, Izzy's free hand running the
length of the skinned log of the wall.

At the mother's command, Izzy found the materials for the
makings of fire and she worked in the dark for several moments.

"*Bruni.*" The woman commanded, and sparks flew from the
flint in Izzy's hand. She whispered the same mantra over and
over. *Bruni, bruni, bruni,* and finally *eldr.* The sparks caught
and the tiny flame burned quickly through the delicate tinder.
The container for the fire was an earthenware pot about the size
of a cookpot, but the friendly flame was warm and inviting and
threw light into the room. They were in the sleeping chamber of
the elder.

Móðir shuffled to the corner and in a slow and tedious
process lowered her old body onto a bed of furs not much higher
than six inches off the ground. Izzy lit a tallow dish and the flame
brought more light into the room. She knelt beside the woman
and put a hand on her knee.

"Móðir, what do you mean I am *Sannligr?*"

"The night is long, *Sannligr barn,* and I intend to sleep
for some of it." The old woman pulled a fur up to her chin and
closed her eyes. Beside the pallet, Izzy sat on a small fox fur and
leaned back against the cold stone. Móðir's breathing became
regular and heavy almost immediately, and Izzy relaxed, trying
to commit the few symbols she'd seen to memory. She knew in
her heart it wouldn't be enough but she had to do something.
If she were anxious about it, the memory would slip away, or
she'd interchange syllables or cadence. Her mind made up the
melody, turning the notes into numbers, the beat into words

and she felt them fall into place in her head. In her mind's eye, she could see the half-finished mathematical formula written on Volpi's whiteboard.

Angelo's hands were around her waist as she stood in front of it. She loved his hands. They were strong and reassuring and knew all the pressure points for both pain and pleasure. Angelo whispered in her ear. She didn't hear the words but rather felt his warm breath against her. She was warm and comfortable and wanted to stay. She turned in his arms, murmuring for more time.

Wake up. The voice said, no longer Angelo's. Izzy blinked in the darkness. The tallow had burned off, leaving only dim firepot embers to light the room. She fed some dry chunks of wood to the kettle and stirred it to flame again.

Móõir's pallet was piled high with furs and coverings, and Izzy shivered in the cold, wanting to dive under them. Or at least take one to put around her shoulders as the old woman slept. She crept to the bed and her hand sank down onto the empty pallet. Even inside the caves, they had heard the revelry outside. Now, there was nothing, not even the sounds of Móõir's relaxed breathing. Izzy was alone.

Pulling a fur from the pallet, Izzy draped it around her before scraping the bottom of the tallow dish and lighting it. There wasn't much, but maybe enough to get her through the labyrinth of stone to the outside temple.

She crept upward along the path, the tiny flame barely lighting her way, and realized they had traveled deep into the cave the night before.

The light flickered out just as the stone wall ended and wood began, the rounded tree trunks notched together for a weather-tight enclosure. Ahead of her, the dim light of dawn shone through gaps in the fur-lined doorway. Setting the vanquished tallow light down, she pulled aside the polar bear fur.

The camp was asleep, drunken guards and villagers huddled near the fires. Someone had been awake enough to stoke them as they still burned strong, and Izzy could smell the wood smoke and boar grease lingering in the air. Not wanting to wake anyone, if that were at all possible, she tread lightly across the camp, looking for the old woman.

She'd intended to glean as much knowledge as she could from Móðir, but exhaustion had won out.

A soft tread to her right and she turned to see the old woman hobbling toward her.

Móðir stopped some feet away and squinted at her. "*Sannligr barn?* Is that you?"

Izzy smiled and approached her. "Yes, Móðir, it is I. I was worried about you."

"Why? It is morning, I am alive still. There is no need for worry."

"I suppose not. Do you want *fruhstuck?* Using a modern word for breakfast, Izzy frowned. Where had that come from? Her mind searched for the word breakfast in the north language. It was gone and panic started to set in. "Móðir, please, I am forgetting. The Song of Tími—I need it." At the woman's helpless shrug, she continued. "You met Marlowe last night, and you know he is of the travelers. My sister is the same, and without the song, without the knowledge I get from you, she will be lost. Please."

"How is it that you do not know this? You have the sight, the memories. You are *Sannligr barn,* yes?"

"I don't know." Izzy was frustrated. "Am I? You keep calling me that, but I don't know exactly what that means. I'm human, just like you." She looked into the woman's dark knowing eyes. Eyes wise enough and old enough to have seen many things in the land where magic still existed merely because people believed it did. "Aren't I?"

"Not like me, child, but human. Yes. Your power stems from your love, your need to help, to nurture. The Song of Tími is a way of bringing that power to the surface. Sing. Sing and think of those you love."

Sing what? Izzy thought, turning away to gather utensils and food stuffs for a small meal.

After they'd eaten and the old woman returned to her living quarters, Izzy headed toward the creek. She splashed the icy water on her face, hoping it would bring her mind back to sharpness. Things were foggy in her brain. She heard a sharp howl of protest, a child's cry of pain. The sound came from the village, and she recognized Klacka's voice. Izzy had lost track of the girl the night before. Most of the children were asleep before the ritual, and Izzy assumed Klacka had done the same.

Down the hill toward Flo's house, Izzy ran, leaping over downed trees and stumps and sliding on frost slicked ground. People were stirring by the time she emerged from the woods. The further from the temple she got, the more early risers she encountered. As she came closer to Flo's hut, Klacka's cries grew louder. Some of the villagers looked up in alarm, but they kept to themselves, going about their chores—no one moved to help. She rounded a corner to find Mael's meaty hands gripping the girl's thin shoulders

Izzy could not stay on the sidelines any longer. "Stop," she shouted. Mael whirled, the girl still with him as he sneered at Izzy. When she made no other move, he turned away, ignoring the nonexistent threat. Izzy felt the blood pounding in her ears, her heart thumped in her chest and she couldn't stop now. *In for a penny.* Her sister's voice floated in her brain. She ran full speed into Mael's back shoving her hands into his solid muscle. "Let her go." She commanded. He'd barely budged with her impact, but the girl slipped from his grasp. "Go, Klacka."

Klacka moved out of his reach, but only as far as the doorway of her hut. Flo emerged and pulled the girl toward her. Izzy tried to follow, but Mael snatched her by the hair, yanking her back against him.

"I warned you, witch. Stay out of my sight." His breath was in her ear and stank of strong ale and greasy meat.

Izzy's eyes flooded with tears at the pain. He released her, and before she could recover, his open palm slapped her across the face. She hit the dirt. Dust filled her mouth and gravel stung her chin. She wormed along the ground, trying to get her legs under her, trying to remember all the techniques Tam had shown her for escape. Instinctively she knew the man's large boot would soon impact her stomach or ribs. When the blow came, she'd managed to roll away, avoiding the force of it. She got to her hands and knees, crawling away. Waiting for another blow, she heard his heavy footsteps behind her but the second kick never came. Instead, she heard a thud of flesh on flesh and a grunt of effort. Once out of the way, she looked up to see Marlowe dodging a blow.

Izzy backed up as the two men squared off. Brute's hulking stance towered over Marlowe, swinging wildly at his head. Marlowe ducked and punched the bigger man's gut. He barely flinched.

Turning toward the gathering crowd, Izzy implored them to please help, get someone from the king's guard. One man started to call out but was silenced by a growl from Mael.

Grabbing Marlowe by the neck, he tossed him to the ground, throwing a harsh jab to his throat. Luckily, Marlowe was able to roll to the side, kicking out and unbalancing the man. The brute's fist landed heavily in the gravel.

"Isabelle, leave now. Quickly." Marlowe spoke in modern English. A language neither had used for some time. He dodged and weaved like a professional boxer, trying to stay out of Mael's reach. The big brute tired of the chase and pulled his great sword, slashing out at Marlowe.

Marlowe in turn had drawn his own sword and stood in an *engarde* position.

"I'm not leaving without you," Izzy replied and launched a fist-sized rock at Mael's head. It missed, sailing over his scalp by a few inches. He laughed at the idea of her trying to hurt him, but it was enough of a distraction to allow Marlowe the advantage.

Mael, larger and more powerful than Marlowe, also fought with a different technique. One prone to the long sword rather than the broad. Marlowe was on the constant defensive, and only his speed saved him from a death blow. Soon men from the king's guard had gathered, shouting and calling, but they made no move to stop either man. Izzy wanted to call out, but she feared any distraction could result in Marlowe's death.

Marlowe attacked with several lightning-quick cuts to the man's upper arms and torso. He could have killed him, his battle armor had been discarded during the night, leaving his vulnerable midsection open to attack.

But killing one of the king's best warriors over an argument in the street would not bode well for either Marlowe or Izzy. His chance was lost in a matter of seconds anyway as Brute returned the attack, putting him on the defensive. He parried, deflected, and his expert swordsmanship saved his guts from spilling.

Marlowe blocked an overhead blow from the tall warrior, his hands on the hilt and lower blade. The larger man used his namesake strength, pressing the blade down on the other as Marlowe went to his knees.

"Stop them, please." Izzy cried out, beseeching the soldiers. "He'll be killed. He's the earl's captain. You must help him."

She ran toward the two men but a guard caught her by the scruff of her dress. "The warrior must save himself. No one dares against Mael."

"I do," Izzy said. And stealing a knife from his belt she lunged toward Brute, intending to stab him in the neck, the back, anywhere. She may not make it, but she had to try. She'd failed to find the solution, but she could not return through the portal without Marlowe.

The guard grabbed for her again, and she evaded his grasp, charging the big man. Her fear giving her strength, her anger a force that propelled her forward. Marlowe was weakening under the strain, his face reddening with effort, his arms shaking under the onslaught of the heavy battle sword. All she had to do was distract Brute and he could slip to the side and escape. Attack again. She raised the knife high, one foot already in the air as she made a spectacular leap at the giant man. In her mind, she was already there, coming down across him, blood spurting from under the knife blade.

But in reality, a rock, a tiny pebble rolled in just the right way, shifting between the hard ground and her foot. She fell, hands outstretched, face forward into the dirt.

They'd come so far. Home was within reach. Angelo would have a fire going and music on his turntable. Her sister would arrive, wanting pizza and arguing with Angelo about inane subjects, complaining until Marlowe would say something charming. A vision of life and happiness that faded as she realized none of it would happen. Instead, she was going to die here in pain and filth, and worse than that, the love of her sister's life would die with her. Tam and Angelo would never know what became of them.

Chapter 26

Tamberlyn

We left the two officers at the senator's hotel door, and I headed home. Assured that the primary danger had been dealt with, I was anxious to get to my other concern.

In my car, I pressed down a curling corner of an old bumper sticker on the glove box. It was a very plain sticker I'd found at some expressway gas station. White background, black words in Latin: *Illegitimi non carborundum*. My father used to say it all the time—only in English, of course.

Don't let the bastards get you down. I usually heard this little nugget of wisdom as he sat at his desk, mulling over a case file. The room he used for an office at our old house had been an add-on sunroom in the back. It was cold in winter, hot in summer, and cooled by a wheezing AC unit hastily tacked into the corner window casement.

The room itself was not spacious, barely big enough for an average-sized desk, which was always messy, covered with Post-it notes and cheap stick pens that never worked. His office chair was a creaky faux leather number inherited from one of the aunts. I remembered my academy days, where I'd come home and flop into Izzy's college cast-off—a fold-out sling backed chair, so I could vent to my father about my fellow students.

"They're just assholes, Dad, all of them. They're too lazy to do their own homework and figure I can help them on the written exams. One guy even said. 'You're the girl. You're supposed to be good at this stuff.'" I finger-quoted the last words.

"And you're not?"

I gave him a look. "Of course I'm not. Tests are Izzy's thing remember? I get high marks in defensive tactics, weapons, and investigative procedures." Dad's mouth twitched as I talked. Two out of the three subjects I'd mentioned were things he'd taught me before I ever entered the academy. "But criminal law? I gotta study, same as everybody else." I made a face. "And handling emotional situations—why do they think females should be good at this? I'm not. I screw it up—same as they do. Yet, I'm the weird one."

"Typically." My father's patient lecture voice settled into the small space. "Female officers are better at diffusing situations than males. They're less threatening and more diplomatic. So it stands to reason your fellow recruits would assume that you would fall into that category."

"Have you ever known me to be diplomatic?"

As I sat across from him, I was tempted to tell him exactly why I found some of the course easy. Sure, some of it was his tutelage. But the field training had been nothing compared to what I did on the side. It was all targets and dummy tackles, nothing remotely like giant snakes or fire-breathing trolls.

He sighed. "You have a talent for being decidedly undiplomatic. Your directness is warranted in lots of cases, but it won't always be appreciated. You have to work as a team and with a partner, and to do that you have to learn to get along." He brushed a hand over the stubble on his jaw, a habit he had when he was tired or mulling something over. "There may come a time when you have to decide which you want to be, well-liked, or a good cop." Something about how he said those words made me think he was talking more for him than for me. "Until then..."

"I know Dad. Don't let the bastards get you down."

I heard the words in my head as sharply as if my father was speaking to me now instead of years ago. I missed him. I really wished he could have met Marlowe.

I stopped at a traffic light when X appeared in my passenger seat. "So you told him," he said, his ephemeral body hovering lightly above the vinyl seat.

"*Jesus*. Don't do that." I snapped. "Scared the crap out of me, X." He looked more transparent than usual. I squinted at him across my car. "Are you disappearing? You look different."

"I'm tired."

"Ghosts get tired?"

"Yes, apparently," he said, his voice glum. "This world is fading for me."

"That's a good thing, isn't it? Means you're off to wherever you belong."

"Let's hope it's not hell. I get all wilty in the heat."

I chuckled as I crossed the intersection. My partnership with Cobb had shifted from awkward unease into a comfortable exchange, but I missed Xavier's easy-going nature. I glanced toward the shotgun seat, seeing through the bulky outline of him to the red smart car in the other lane.

"X. I'm sorry. Sorry for all of it. You getting killed. You getting stuck as a ghost. I appreciate your being here with me and all, but it's got to suck for you, man."

"It does," he said, and he paused for so long I thought he was going to disappear again. "But it gives me time to think. And I'm okay with it. Everything works out for a reason, and we know that it does. No coincidences, right? Then there's a reason I'm here—probably, just to keep your ass in line." His words rang true. "And now, there's no reason for that."

"There isn't?"

"You've grown up, I guess. You resolved whatever issue you had with the ex-boyfriend, and not by beating him up. That's maturity. You confided in Cobb. You finally started treating your adult sister like an adult. I think you're on your way."

X had always adopted the big brother role in our partnership. I never minded. He was right. I'd had no idea I'd even needed to do those things. "Don't forget I've also saved a senator and a retired member of upper fae royalty. All in a day's work, Partner. All in a day's work."

"Marlowe?" he asked quietly.

I nodded. "On my to-do list. I suppose you know they've gone through the portal. You know about the portal? Pinkie's bar?"

He chuckled again. "Yes, I have a vague idea. Your sister is a big girl. And your man is more than capable of taking care of himself and her. Trust them."

"Tonight the gate closes for two weeks. If they don't come back tonight, then..." My words faded. I didn't want to think about it.

I looked across the car to see the ephemeral specter of the man who truly taught me what it meant to have a partner. Someone who had your back. Someone you could trust.

X was quiet for a second, and when he finally spoke, his voice had lost its jovial tone. "This is probably our last time together. I want to say—"

"Don't." I stopped him. "Don't get all mushy on me."

"Shut up and let me talk, will you? You never truly lose people if you have them in the first place. And you have them now. Volpi, Ziggy, your sister, and Marlowe—even me. You won't lose me, Tam. Not really."

"X," I said tiredly.

"We didn't get to—before. Say goodbye, I mean." His outline shimmered—the ghost-version of an uncomfortable shrug. "Going is not a bad thing. Like you said, I'm off to wherever I belong. Because we both know I don't belong here." His gaze went out to somewhere I couldn't see. The car was too quiet. The road too barren. My eyes couldn't focus. "It's okay, Tam." His words hung in the cold air.

I knew he couldn't stay. He shouldn't stay. But I'd come to depend on him, yet again. His snarky comments, his overprotective, brotherly concern. It brought me through a lot of shit, including the grief over his own death. Wherever his spirit was going, I hoped it was beautiful. He deserved that at least.

"It's not okay by any means," I said, my hands gripping and relaxing on the steering wheel. "But maybe it's tolerable. Maybe that. You know, Cobb—he's all right. A good cop. A little grumpy maybe, but—"

"Like you got room to talk."

"Yeah." The words came to a halt when I stopped for another light. As if I couldn't speak without the car moving, going somewhere. If we were stopped, then too much would be heard, too much could be said. My chest hurt where the seat belt crossed, and I pulled at it. The light turned green. "He ain't ever going to be you, X."

"Copy that. I'm unique in all the world, baby." In the dim of the car, with his barely-there presence, I could see the gleam of his teeth as they flashed his usual grin. He laughed and my breathing eased. "Yeah, you got this. You're going to be fine."

He wavered and shimmered in the sunlight streaking through my dirty windshield. If ever there was an exit line, that was one, and yet he did not go. Maybe he couldn't. Maybe he was waiting on me to say something else, but there were no other words.

He sighed. I was sure breath wasn't exhaled, but the sound was deep with disappointment. "You know what you have to do, right? When the time comes?"

"That goes without saying."

"No. No, it doesn't, Tam. Because I know you. I know how

you are. Think of how angry you were with Marlowe because he let me die. He did what he was supposed to do. It was my time."

I didn't say anything. I didn't want to finish this conversation. The car radio crackled from the static of X's presence. I turned it off, listening to the blower of the heater until I turned that off too. It didn't help the angry spatter of voices in my head—the rat-tat-tat of a semi-automatic conscience. X would just echo Marlowe's words about timelines and duties. What did he know about it? All of a sudden, everyone's an expert.

I blew out a long breath as I pulled into the parking lot of Volpi's loft. I shifted the car into park and sat there.

"Yes, I know," I said, hoping he'd go away.

X waited. He didn't ask, but he didn't leave either. He just hovered there, waiting for me to say the words. I kind of hated him for making me say it.

"I have to let Marlowe die."

I got out of the car before X left, my words thundering in my head and heart. I'd known this simple fact. Marlowe had tried to tell me as gently as he could, but saying it aloud made it real. My steps were heavy. I glanced back at my car before opening the massive door to Volpi's building. X had disappeared. I knew I would never see him again.

Volpi was waiting for me in his apartment, his hat, and coat at the ready.

"Look," I said, and gently took the Fedora from him, placing it back on the rack by his door. I hung his coat on the hook and placed mine next to it. "We need to talk."

"Tonight is the last night to travel," he said. But he deflated, knowing that neither of us were going anywhere, that we were relegated to waiting like Izzy had with us so many times before.

"It's going to be fine," I repeated X's words. "We're going to be fine."

∞

I barely slept, but I did eventually pass out, exhaustion

overtaking my body and finally shutting down my mind. I was determined to keep busy, trying not to worry about how much trouble my sister had gotten herself into and trying even harder not to miss Marlowe so damn much.

I met Cobb at the office, and we went over Shepherd's and Theo's statements before adding them to our report. To Theo's credit, his official accounting of incidents was good, even to the point of not absolving himself of all wrong-doing. Someone from his former employer had been wronged, and this mentally unstable person had been out for revenge. The Redcap's bodies had disintegrated, but we still had a dead Toxeute, and he was our fall guy, killed by return fire at the Palomar Hotel. It was a plausible if weak, explanation of events.

Needing only a few more bullet points to close the case, Cobb and I headed to Ziggy's lab.

"What about werewolves?" he asked from the second stair landing. Apparently, he'd taken it upon himself to research a lot of supernatural mumbo jumbo and was now all into the hostile hunting gig.

"What about them?" I asked.

"True or not?"

"True. Sort of. I mean, they exist. Have I seen one? No." I replied as I moved ahead of him on the stairs. I remembered the battle only days ago at Pinkie's. "Maybe."

"How do you know?"

"I have a C.I." I smiled as enigmatically as possible. If Cobb was going to bug me about hostiles, I wasn't going to make it easy for him.

"A confidential informant? About hostiles?"

"Yes." I got to the stairwell door, and his hand landed above me to hold it closed.

"Paradiso." Cobb scowled at me. "If I'm in this gig, I need to be prepared. I don't want some fucktard monster eating my brains for brunch."

"Brunch? Nice alliteration. I have a friend who'd appreciate your choice of words." I smiled. Marlowe's cadenced language filtered through my memory. *My words shall be as spotless as my youth. Full of simplicity and naked truth.* The man had a way with words.

"A friend, huh? Does he *know* about you?"

I chuckled. "Yes. He does. As a matter of fact..." I moved away from the door, facing Cobb on the landing.

After a moment, Cobb's aha-moment voice came out. "So is this about Theopolis? You guys reigniting the old flame?" His bushy eyebrows waggled.

I gave him my best glare. "This is not about Theo. And it's none of your business anyway."

He opened the door and ushered me into the hallway. "If it's not Theo, why not? He's a good-looking guy who obviously overlooks your irritability and unreasonableness, so..." He let the words drop into the dead air between us. I said nothing, letting his dig pass over me. Because in a way, he was right. On the surface, Theo seemed like a perfectly good choice. In another life, I may even have forgiven his past manipulations and given him a chance. But that was before Marlowe.

I continued walking, but I slowed as we approached the double doors of the forensic lab.

Cobb brought me back to the conversation. "But if it's not him, then someone else. Someone who also knows the dark side of your sunny disposition."

"Yes," I said. "And why would someone not like me? I'm perfectly likable." I sighed at his chuckle. "Yes, someone else. He may be in danger, I don't know because I haven't heard from him. And..." I trailed off again. I wasn't at all sure I wanted to get into this.

"And?"

"And my sister is gone too. With him."

"Ah, okay." Cobb had the most irritating way about him when he thought he knew something.

"It's not like that. My sister is not like that. They're—he's honorable. He wouldn't do that. Nor would Izzy for that matter. I'm just worried about them. That's all."

"Do they need help? Can we—"

"No, Cobb. We can't. And I suppose that's what's got me in a snit."

He shrugged at my words. "Well, let me know. And if there are werewolves involved..."

I left him with that thought as I pushed open the lab door.

Ziggy stood at her gleaming white counter, a lab computer in front of her, and her always present coffee cup just to the side.

She looked up and pulled her glasses off as I came through the door, her smile widening when she saw Cobb behind me. So wide in fact that I had to glance behind me to make sure it was just Cobb and not Idris Elba, Clooney, or Pitt who entered her lair. Nope, just Cobb.

Zig was more social than I was but only slightly, and her circles ran more to 90's rock and strobe-lit dance clubs, so I couldn't imagine her and Cobb ever having anything in common. But then imagination wasn't my strong suit. Cobb's usual scowl had evened out into a semi-pleasant expression as he saw Ziggy. Not quite a smile, but closer than I'd ever seen.

Izzy would have called it a vibration or energy between them. I frowned, thinking of my foolhardy sister and hoping she would be home soon.

Ziggy finally took her eyes off my partner to see me. "Hey, it's all good, Tam." She rushed to reassure me, thinking my frown had been for the body on her table. "Fortunately, this guy looks human enough to pass. And the bullet wound can be explained by your report of the altercation in the parking garage." She moved toward the sheet-covered body on her table. "Nice shot by the way." She pulled the sheet back to reveal a once handsome creature, with a large gap on one side of his skull. The dead Toxeute.

Not thinking, I almost corrected her on the nice shot comment. But then I'd have to explain how a campaign manager got a hold of my sniper rifle. Ziggy didn't know about Theo. Cobb didn't know about Marlowe. I had too many secrets.

I signaled Cobb with my eyes, hoping he wouldn't correct her assumption. I needn't have worried. He stood on the other side of the corpse, watching everything Ziggy did as she talked.

"The body was tagged into the system, so we can't just lose him. I could alter the report to say he died in the explosion. I think he's too intact for that though. Shepherd's security team was the only other casualties. Everyone else was far enough from the blast radius and sustained minor injuries." Her eyes flickered between Cobb and me. "Is there something you're not telling me?"

We had done this before, me withholding the full story, and I trusted Ziggy, I really did, but Theo's story was not mine to tell. At least not here. I made a mental note to fill in the gaps next time she and I had drinks.

I cleared my throat. "And we need a suspect, so he'll do. I'll get Volpi to come up with one of his identikits so it matches up with Theo, er, Theopolis' account of events."

Finally, Cobb found his voice. "You know what this is?" He jerked a thumb toward the body.

Ziggy frowned slightly, but her eyes gave her exuberance away. "Not exactly, but I know he's not human." Another smile for Cobb and the cold lab had a temperature spike. "I heard you saw some weird shit go down."

Cobb's mouth dropped open, but he recovered fast and looked at me in silent accusation as if I'd been holding out on him. I rolled my eyes.

"Okay, so yeah, Ziggy knows about a lot of this stuff. Who do you think helps me with cover stories? I can't just leave supernatural bodies all over the city, and they don't all collapse into dust. Ziggy has been on the team for a while now."

It was like a light opened up under Cobb. "Last year, the dead guy with six fingers we pulled out of the river? Not human?" He bypassed me and spoke directly to Ziggy as she covered the body. The two of them chatted as they moved to her workspace at the counter, Ziggy fairly sparkling at my partner's attention. Was this new? Had I been so preoccupied with my own shit that I'd missed the budding attraction between my best friend and partner? I was often accused of being less than observant of my fellow humans. Too busy canvassing the world for evil, I often missed the good. At least I hoped this was a good thing.

Jenny from upstairs called my cell to tell me I had a visitor. My first thought was Marlowe. Izzy wouldn't come to the station, but Marlowe had found me here once before.

I left the lab in a hurry and ran up the stairs to our floor, bursting through the double doors to reception where Jenny sat transfixed behind her desk, talking to Theo.

"Theo."

He turned. "Hi. Could I have a moment?" He wore faded jeans and a leather jacket over a dark T-shirt. This was the most casual attire I'd seen him in. His glasses were back for the first time since we'd met in Harrisburg.

Standing in front of me, his hands jammed in his pockets, he looked like a grad student, tired from all night cramming for finals or recovering from a long day-drunk. The sheer humanness of him struck me. The medallion I'd seen earlier around his neck glinted. In this light, I could see it was a St. Christopher medal. He moved toward me as I stared at it, thinking it was odd that a former fae would wear a religious medal. His hand closed around the silver, and when he released it the etching had changed to something else—a dragon in a field of lightning bolts. I blinked, and the thing changed back into good old St. Chris.

My sightline traveled from his midline to his face. He waited for a response, his expression tentative and ...hopeful? I wasn't sure.

"Can we talk?" He indicated the outer door, and as Jenny was not even trying to look busy, I nodded and led him down the main hall. Central booking was, as usual, complete chaos—

dealers, pros, and delinquents competed with each other for the loud and obnoxious award as overtaxed officers entered them into the system.

Theo followed me out through another set of doors and onto the steps of our building. It was cold, but not bitter, and we could shelter out of the wind and away from most observers.

"What are you doing here?" I got right to the point. "Did something else happen? Is Shepherd okay?" I didn't ask about Theo's well-being. He appeared so physically fit it made me a little ill.

"Yeah, yeah, He's fine. We're headed back to Harrisburg today. I just wanted ...so, are we good?" The dark eyes behind the hipster frames expressed that hopefulness again. "You believe that I'm not here to harm, well, anyone?" he asked.

I sighed. "You saved me in the parking garage, killed the Toxeute, and helped us with the Redcaps. Though—" I frowned. "It was your fault they showed up in the first place, so there's that. But I believe you are without the power of the fae. You may be fierce still, but you have no magical hoodoo to mess with me."

"Hoodoo? I never used it on you when I had it." Irritation crept up in his tone. Unhinging his hands from his pockets, he put a palm up to stave off any retort from me. "Not because I'm noble. But because I couldn't reveal what I was. And—" He faltered, another human quality I hadn't noticed before. "Look, can we not talk about the past? It just gets me into trouble."

I laughed. "You're the one that brought it up." I noticed his hand had gravitated to my shoulder and his warmth was more welcoming than I was comfortable with. "But the past is just that. The past."

"Speaking of, has it happened yet? You traveling?"

I shouldn't have been surprised, but I was. "No. How do you know that I—"

He put on a ridiculous smirk. "Former fae. It's a known thing. Not a fae gift, but we know about it. If you ever..." He stopped as a couple walked past us into the station. "Never mind. Look, the senator's campaign will be in full swing soon and—" He cleared his throat, hedged some more, and finally went on. "I'll be in Philadelphia, a lot. We could have dinner."

It wasn't a question. No inflection at the end of the sentence. No imploring look.

"No, we couldn't." I smiled though. It was kind of fun, seeing him squirm.

"I mean, would you? It was meant as a question. Would you have dinner with me?"

I held up my hand. "Theo. It's okay. Don't pretend we're all normal and shit."

"I'm not pretending. And we'll never be normal." He blew out a breath and shoved his hands back into his jean pockets. "Normal is not really our thing, is it? That wasn't what I was trying to say."

"I have someone." I rushed to say it before he went on. Because if he went on looking at me that way, and talking all soft and sweet, the memory of him would crush whatever good sense I had, and I'd be screwed. "He's like everything for me, this person. Whatever you and I were, we aren't that anymore."

He took a moment before speaking. A whole lifetime flickered in his eyes.

"Okay, I get it. Whatever we had, it's in the past. And we don't talk about the past. Or the future, apparently. I should be happy we're not killing each other in the present." His lips curved into woeful expression as fleeting as the idea of a rekindled romance. "Goodbye, Tam." He stepped back.

I nodded and turned toward the entrance again. Before he could leave, I tugged at the sleeve of his jacket He stopped. I dropped my hand.

"May the gods guard your well-being," I said.

There was a genuine smile now, his mouth opening into a laugh—a bright silvery thing that caressed air and ears and made me smile in return.

"After yours." He gave the standard reply, before jogging down the steps and blending into the crowd of pedestrians.

Chapter 27

Isabelle

Izzy heard shouts from behind the crowd and screamed, hoping to draw the attention of the guard. Soon four men in full armor stood between Marlowe and the brute. Marlowe lowered his sword cautiously.

The head guard disarmed both men, and the others restrained them.

"Put them in the *borg fang*," he ordered. "The earl will decide what to do."

"The girl started it." The temple guard pointed at Izzy. She glared at the man, his face turned toward her in a savage scowl. When she recognized him as Mael's brother, the guard who'd beaten her at the temple entrance, a wave of fear went through her. But the fear passed and was followed by something else. Her jaw hardened and she straightened her shoulders. Another guard stepped forward to grip her arm.

"Coward." She spit the word toward Mael's brother with

as much venom as she could muster under the circumstances. The guard holding her pulled her away, and she cast one more glance at her accuser. To her surprise, the man cringed in fear.

Hustled into the long house, Izzy found the interior surprisingly tidy. The man pulled her along the length of the building, past the bunks and the cordoned off area for eating meals. At the back of the room, there was a trap door and rudimentary stairs that led to a small space that smelled of excrement and death. Izzy did not move for several minutes after being tossed in. Her mind was busy analyzing and plotting an escape. She wondered where Marlowe had been taken.

Gradually, as her eyes adjusted, the tiny cracks of light through the trap door allowed her a view of her new quarters. She was grateful she was the only human there, as the smell gave the impression of a pile of corpses in a corner. The place was also devoid of varmints, no rats or mice as there was no food to be found. She settled herself into the lightest corner of the space and waited, determined to not let her imagination run off with her sanity. She tried to keep her mind occupied and away from worry for Marlowe. Eventually, the trap door opened and a wineskin was tossed down before it closed again. There was nothing else for long while.

Her deep-set sense of time allowed her to estimate she'd been in the hole almost two days before the guards came for her, dumping her form unceremoniously on the floor of the Earl King's hall. The meeting room was dim, but Izzy blinked and her eyes watered against the light. She felt like a mole, blind, and afraid above ground. The darkness of the hole had become her friend, and she was surprised at how quickly she'd adapted. The cellar prison had also been quiet, with only an occasional sound of the heavy boots tramping overhead. Her legs were shaky and probably would have been more so if she hadn't forced herself to work through forms of Tai Chi several times a day. The earl gestured at her.

"Give her some ale. She has to live long enough to be

executed."

His guards laughed but someone handed her a cup. She drained it gratefully, the strong ale burning down her parched throat. The wineskin they'd given her had only been half-full. She calculated that by this time the pull of the crescent moon would be in full force. As she was finally able to look around the room, she spotted a badly bruised Marlowe bound and held between two guards.

"What is your name?" The Earl King asked.

Izzy croaked, her voice giving out a few times before she could speak. "I-so-bel."

A boom of thunder sounded in the distance, but it was far enough away that everyone ignored it. Everyone except Marlowe. As her friend flinched, Izzy turned her focus onto the earl who stood at the head of the table. Once again, she noted his coloring, the auburn hair, and gray eyes, same as hers. When she was young she'd often wished for dark hair and eyes like her sister and father, indeed, most of the Paradiso family had. But her mother had been a fair-skinned ginger, and Izzy took after her. Perhaps that trait had transcended eons of generations. Izzy scanned the rest of the room. Several men were gathered around and one woman, presumably the earl's wife as he addressed her as *Drottning My*.

"What say you of this female, my queen?"

The woman was more finely dressed than Izzy had seen in the entirety of her time there. Wrapped in fine colorful cloth and jeweled rings and circlets on her hands and wrists, her blue eyes were intelligent and bright as she gazed at Izzy.

"She is a pretty thing. Perhaps she could be of service. Entertainment for the guards?"

Izzy tried not to let her shock and horror show in her expression. When the earl had inquired of his wife's opinion, she'd hoped for empathy or kindness. She sagged under the woman's gaze and the guard's leers. Tam would say something snarky, probably. At the same time, she would be kicking the kneecaps of the guards and stealing a dagger to throw into the cold woman's eye socket. Izzy could barely stand, let alone kick anyone, and her brain failed to come up with an adequate retort.

Thunder boomed again, closer this time, and Izzy felt a tingling in her fingertips. She flexed her hands, trying to get the blood flowing back into her extremities. The nerve endings crackled. Refusing to look at the woman next to him, she raised her eyes from the floor to the Earl King's chair. Looking at the queen would be an acknowledgment, and her fate was in the Earl King's hands anyway.

He chuckled as he returned her gaze. "The girl has more spirit than we'd thought. Perhaps you are right, my queen."

At this, Marlowe struggled and cursed. A guard cuffed him on the ear—a glancing blow that sent him to his knees.

"Who is this woman to you, traitor?" He demanded.

Marlowe looked up, first to Izzy and then to the earl. "She is my *systir,* my liege. I beg of you. Please do not harm her. She is—"

The earl cut off his words. "Your sister attacked one of my warriors." He squinted at Izzy again. "Twice now, I believe. She is the one who stopped our procession into the village, is she not?"

Izzy raised her chin. "I am."

The earl furrowed his brow at her words. She held his gaze, trying to channel her sister's stubbornness and courage. He sighed and gestured tiredly. "Speak then, woman. Tell us why you should be spared."

Izzy's thoughts whirled in her head. What would Tam do in this? Or Angelo? Or better yet, Maurelle? But she didn't have Tam's quick wit, Angelo's intellect, or Maurelle's power. All she had was a hollowed-out belly and a static spark or two as it came off of Marlowe. She squared her shoulders and faced the Earl King.

"I should not. By your standards, I am worth nothing. But my *brudr.*" She indicated Marlowe. "Is a great warrior. This you have seen for yourself. He has value. Spare him."

The red-haired leader chuckled. "You are of the same lineage. Both courageous and reckless—qualities of a warrior, true, but undesirable in a female. Still, my warrior Mael has been affronted, and I cannot allow dissension in the ranks."

"Mael *attacked* a child." Izzy fumed. A guard hastened to silence her, but she avoided his fist. The sudden movement made her dizzy. "Some great warrior." She scoffed, her anger getting the best of her. "He bullies because he is weak. He is large but slow. He is angry, but his anger gets in his own way. You know this, my liege." She addressed him in the customary way as she drew herself up to her full height of five and a half feet. The tingling in her fingers drew up into her hands, making her palms itch. A burning sensation prickled on the back of her left hand. "Yet, you let him get away with terrorizing your own people." She pointed her chin at the men around the table. "All of them turn away at this. Are you all afraid of him?"

The subject of her tirade erupted with a roar, shoving his heavy chair back and lumbering toward her.

Izzy flinched. She couldn't help it. Cringing backward to avoid Mael's attack, she missed the other action in the room.

Mael's actions distracted the guards at either side of Marlowe, and within seconds he had knocked one of them to the side and stolen the knife from the guard's belt. He launched himself between Mael and Izzy, his bound hands holding the knife steady as it slashed Mael across the torso. Mael stepped back in pain, his hands pushing at his bleeding chest.

The place erupted in chaos. Cursing men came to their comrade's aid. Marlowe backed toward Izzy, the knife in his hands small in comparison to the swords being drawn.

"Enough." The earl's voice boomed over the raucous. Everyone fell silent except for the hiss of pain from Mael as his men attempted to staunch the bleeding. "Everyone *out*. Take Mael and see to his wound." He had risen from his chair, his hand on his own sword. "Leave them." He indicated Izzy and

Marlowe. "You cannot control them anyway. Go." Everyone exited through the door to the main living quarters where the queen's voice could be heard commanding her servants to bring her hot water and herbs for the injured man.

Marlowe lowered the knife in his hands but didn't let it go. He turned to Izzy.

"As we are about to die, I would say that your sister would be proud of your courage, Isabelle."

"It is a shame to execute you." The earl spoke to Marlowe. "Even injured and bound, you still outmaneuvered my guard. Your loyalty is misplaced, however, in this scrap of a girl."

Marlowe looked at Izzy. "She is family," he said as if that explained all of his actions.

The earl sighed. "Yes. I have a younger sister as well." He peered meaningfully at Izzy. "But mine is very quiet and does not cause trouble."

"You have good fortune, my liege," Marlowe said. The earl laughed.

"I have always liked you, *Finngailler*. But you've put me in a difficult circumstance." He slowly took the knife from Marlowe's hands. He cut the binding on his wrists. "You could have killed Mael, yet you did not. For that, I will spare your sister." The big man gently pushed Marlowe and Izzy ahead of him.

"Wait." Izzy implored.

Marlowe stopped her. "Quiet Isabelle, you are not helping here."

"But—"

Marlowe's arm went around her waist, and his palm pressed against her mouth. "Trust me." Static electricity buzzed against her lips.

As the three emerged from the long house, the sky had darkened with storm clouds, and dust kicked up in swirls in the open square in front of the barracks.

Several soldiers gathered outside the barracks, the villagers standing in the square, waiting to hear the fate of the two foreigners. One of the guards came out of the long house behind them and spoke to the Earl King.

"Mael will live. The cut was deep but too high to do much damage." The guard glowered at Marlowe. "Your aim was bad, *Undarligr*-stranger." The guard muttered as he walked by.

"It was never my intent to kill Mael. Only to stop him." Marlowe replied, more to the earl than to the guard.

With a raise of an eyebrow, the Earl King dismissed the guard and turned toward the crowd, raising his hands for silence. As the crowd jostled for a view of the proceedings, lightning lit up the sky. Several people ducked at the closeness of the strike, the flash followed almost immediately by its shadow of thunder. Even the Earl King was startled for a second or two.

"Isabelle, step away from me. It is time," Marlowe whispered.

Izzy stared at him. She could feel the static in the air and strands of her hair lifted in a halo around her head. Almost involuntarily, she stepped to the side. A faint blue light glowed around Marlowe's head and body as if he stood in front of a neon sign. The light flickered and wavered. It tricked the eye into not quite seeing what was visible. Thunder boomed again, followed by more lightning flashes and harsh fat raindrops pelted the dust around them. People who'd stayed put to hear the Earl King's words now darted toward enclosures.

The previous tingles in Izzy's hands had bloomed into a burning pain and she rubbed them together. The strange blue light grew with increasing strength and only one guard dared to stand close to Marlowe.

"I have ruled in this dispute. This man—" The earl indicated Marlowe without looking at him. "Will be executed. May he die with courage."

"Courage," the crowd shouted and then ducked at another flash of lightning. Their words almost drowned out by the thunder.

"The girl will be spared and taken to the long house as a slave." The crowd cheered again. Izzy gave no notion that she even heard the proclamation. Her focus was on her left hand as she held it in front of her. Starting just below her wrist a white-hot line writhed on the back of her hand and burned its way up her forearm, twisting and turning as its stinging heat seared her skin. She fell to her knees from the pain of it, but she could not look away. Someone from the crowd shouted out the ancient word for witch. With the guard watching her, Marlowe seized the opportunity, and whirling on the man, he ripped the sword from his belt.

It was Marlowe's sword after all. He held Grim aloft in a battle stance as the blue lightning sparked around him. The guard, initially on the attack for having his prize stolen from him, stopped as the blue sparks danced along the weapon and the man who held it.

The design on Izzy's skin was beginning to cool, leaving a thin vine of intricate knots—a nexus of spirals and whorls along her arm. Rain whipped around them, soaking their clothes, their hair. Izzy's newly branded skin steamed in the cool drops. The symbols taking shape as they had in her dream.

The guards and crowd rushed toward them, stopping suddenly as another bolt of lightning struck. Marlowe shouted. "You must run when the chance comes."

"I can't leave you," Izzy shouted back. The wind was howling. A vortex of rain and air and dirt swirled about the two of them. Izzy swept her tattooed arm toward the crowd. "Leave us be."

Her intent was to protect, not only herself and Marlowe but the people as well. At her words, the crowd lurched backward onto each other as if a strong gust of wind had picked them up, tumbled them dry, and set them down again.

The Earl King shouted. Children cried. The guards picked themselves up for another charge toward Izzy and Marlowe. A massive bolt of lightning streaked down from the dark sky and struck Marlowe, bathing his body in a blue-white light. Izzy was thrown to the side. The crowd panicked and ran for cover, nearly trampling Izzy in the process. Someone grabbed her hand.

"This way." The little girl had slipped through the crowd unnoticed. Izzy grasped Klacka's hand and got up. She hesitated a moment, looking back for Marlowe. There was only empty space where he had been. "Come on." Klacka urged her and they ran.

Klacka knew all the back ways through the village, and she took them, guiding Izzy along the narrow mud-filled alleys. When they stopped, Izzy saw that they had emerged on the outside of the tall timbered gateway. Flo was there with a small satchel. She thrust it at her as she noticed the thin blue lines against Izzy's reddened skin.

"Móðir was right. You are a *Sannliger*. You have the mark." The woman smiled at Izzy. "This gives me hope. Here is some food for your journey. Go past the first rise and stay out of sight. Móðir will be there."

Izzy's eyes brimmed with tears as she touched the woman's scarred cheek. Flo cried out, her hand flying to the scar. When she drew it away, the mark had faded. Not gone, not completely, but faded enough that it was visible only upon close inspection. Izzy bent to hug Klacka, whispering a soft blessing onto her hair. She took the offered satchel, and slinging it over one shoulder, she ran.

Her energy was ebbing fast, but the mark seemed to give her strength as she clawed and crawled her way up the sharp rise and down the other side. Móðir was there, partially hidden by a clump of trees, holding the reins of a horse.

She thrust the reins into Izzy's hands. Izzy stopped, pulled a wine sack from the satchel, and drank great gulps of cool water. It was the best thing she'd ever tasted in her life.

"Móðir, you should not have come. If they catch you helping me, you'll—"

"Shush, child. They think I'm harmless. An old woman with an addled mind." The woman brushed aside Izzy's concerns. "As much as you would learn here, you can no longer stay. Your traveler has left on the lightning, yes?"

"Yes." Izzy startled as the great beast stomped and snorted. She recognized the same horse that Marlowe had ridden into the outpost.

"Then you must leave also. Go now, *Sannligr barn*. You know of the gate?"

Izzy nodded and then looked at the horse. His great patient face turned toward her and he snorted, blowing air and spittle onto her hand holding his tether. She swallowed. "I can't ride. I've never even been on a horse."

"You will remember. Now, go." The woman gestured for Izzy to mount the warhorse. Izzy took the reins, and after a few terrifying moments where the horse did his best to sway her memory of knowing how to ride, she managed to climb into the saddle.

"Thank you Móðir. You have saved me."

The old woman uttered no words of profound encouragement. She simply gave a vague and tired wave as she made her way through the trees. Izzy kicked her legs awkwardly until the horse moved. He took three steps and stopped. She heard shouts from behind them, deep in the woods. The thunder had eased with Marlowe's departure, but the rain was steady, relentless.

"His name is Reykr." Móðir's voice did not travel on the air, but Izzy heard it in her head. She leaned down over the beast's neck and stroked his mane.

"Go, Reykr. Go."

She breathed a sigh of relief as the horse moved into a slow walk at first, allowing her to get the feel of his flanks under her legs until she was confident enough to stay upright, then he slid smoothly into a gallop.

Chapter 28

Tamberlyn

My sister arrived home three weeks ago, skinny and bruised, tattooed, and speaking in a mix of Ancient and English. She was devastated about not finding the formula, apologizing to me again and again. I think she felt worse about it than I did.

I'd always known it was a long shot—a chance that we'd hit upon the exact combination of words, symbols, or talismans that would allow Marlowe to travel at will and return to me. I also knew that if given the opportunity, he would return. Which may be why the whole traveling deal should be left to chance. Human will and desire would always interfere with destiny, subverting the true motion of time and space. Us insignificant humans thinking that our miniscule lives mattered in the scheme of the universe.

My sensitive little sister had not fared well during her trip to the ancient world. She showed signs of PTSD—nightmares, lapses in short-term memory, often spacing out during a conversation.

After Volpi called, I'd gone straight to his loft and found her curled up on his couch, a drink in hand. She'd rocked back and forth as she told the tale of Marlowe saving her, of his lightning-induced departure, and her failure in the caves of the temple. Tears choked her words.

After days of rest and food, her language returned to normal for the most part, though often she would suddenly stop as though in another world—stillness and memory taking over her. Freya had been concerned enough to reinstate our weekly family dinners, which now included Volpi.

As instructed, I stopped at the corner grocery to buy hard rolls and white wine to go with Freya's meal plan and arrived a few minutes late to Izzy's apartment. The tiny room felt overly warm from the heated oven, and the delicious smell of roasting chicken permeated the space. My stomach growled, almost never satisfied of late. I handed off the wine to Volpi and sat on the couch near Izzy.

"Hey, how are you?" My words were low, though it was an innocuous question. I listened vaguely to Freya and Volpi as they bickered in Izzy's kitchen. Freya had made no bones about her displeasure at the relationship between the older man and her youngest granddaughter, but Volpi, who had never cared about anyone's opinion, worked hard for her acceptance over the last few weeks. He seemed to be making progress as I heard a faint chuckle from Freya at something he said.

"I'm okay." Izzy's answer was determinedly cheerful. "I just ...it's weird being back. Sometimes, things don't match, you know?"

I didn't, but I nodded anyway and yawned. The warmth of the room and the relaxed atmosphere made me drowsy. I plopped my head back on the couch and put my feet up on her coffee table.

Next thing I knew, Izzy was nudging me awake. "Tam. You've been asleep for almost two hours."

I blinked and stretched. "Did I miss food?" I sat up and looked around.

"We saved you some." She headed to her kitchen, and I heard the low hum of the microwave. I looked across at Volpi who sat in a ratty plaid rocker in the corner. He closed his book and squinted at me.

"You okay?"

"I'm fine. Just tired. And starving." Izzy handed me the warmed-up food as she sat next to me. "You guys could have woken me up." I picked up a roast chicken leg.

"I tried. You weren't having it. You hissed at me and went back to sleep."

"I did not," I grumbled as I chewed. A glance at Volpi told me I had. "Sorry." I continued wolfing down the food. "Where's Freya? This is great stuff." Another bite of cheesy mashed potatoes—my favorite growing up.

"She stepped out to take a call."

At that moment, the subject of our conversation came back in Izzy's front door.

"Duncan, you bad thing. I may hold you to that, next time you're in town." She giggled.

My eyes met Izzy's across the couch. I rolled mine and turned to watch my grandmother as she crossed the room, still smiling. She put her phone into her large leather bag and took a seat.

"Berly, are you coming down with something?" She used her nickname for me. "You fairly collapsed on the couch."

"I'm fine," I said again.

"You look tired. You're sure?"

"Yes, who was that?" I tried to change the subject, and in doing so made the ultimate taboo. My sister's foot stretched across the couch to kick me lightly. As soon as I said it, I realized what I'd done. Freya had no compunction about revealing the details of her romantic relationships. I had no idea who Duncan was, but I knew from previous experience, that I didn't want to know.

"Well, I—" Freya started, a dreamy look crossing her features.

"This is just like my dream." Izzy interrupted her.

"Yes?" I jumped at the opening, knowing both of us would be anxious to change the subject.

"Yes. Well, kind of. We were all together, at Angelo's loft, and it might have been Christmas, though I'm not sure. But we had Freya's roast chicken and it was nice, and everyone was..." She stopped and looked at me. "Marlowe was there, with us."

I sat back at the mention of his name. Freya paid close attention. She'd met Marlowe some time ago, but I didn't speak of him often.

"Berly's gentleman?" She asked. "I'd assumed he'd gone back to England ages ago."

"He was here briefly, a while back," I answered. "What else, Iz?"

"Not much, it—" She stopped again. And there were several quiet moments before she spoke. "And there was laughter, a child's laugh. A baby."

Silence in the room. Like tomb silence, quiet as the grave, pin dropping, dead calm silence.

After several agonizing seconds, I laughed. "Nice dream," I said. "What else?"

My sister studied me a moment more before muttering something vague about how the dream ended. My mind drifted as she and Volpi discussed the lucidity of dreams and their ramifications on the human psyche.

My thoughts turned to Marlowe and our encounter during his short visit here. As I sat there on the couch, every minute of those glorious hours came back to me. It was suddenly very hot and closed in. I needed to move.

I busied myself taking my plate into the kitchen and rinsing it. I gazed over the counter at the three people I trusted the most. Volpi I'd known for a dozen years, and while we didn't always like each other, I trusted him. My sister and I had grown much closer in the last couple of years since I finally, at Marlowe's urging, trusted her with my darkest secret—the things that go boo in the night. And Freya, my wild and crazy grandmother who helped raise us in her unconventional way. I missed my old partner, X, but knew he was in a better place, as they say. I missed Marlowe and tried to maintain the hope that someday he'd return to me. This was my team and these were my people.

After a few minutes, Freya appeared in the doorway, her purple cloak thrown about her shoulders, her large tote over one arm.

"Look after your sister, won't you, Berly? She seems very distracted lately."

"Of course. Thanks for dinner. Good night." I walked her to the door.

After loading my extra plate in the dishwasher and wiping down the counters—Izzy the clean freak would go over them later with antibacterial solution—aching tiredness had me searching for my own coat.

Izzy came into the kitchen, and after checking to make sure I'd loaded my dish properly, she started the machine, humming softly to herself.

"That sounds so familiar, what's that song?" I asked, searching my own brain for the latest pop song I'd heard.

"Um, I don't remember." She faced me. "Oh, I know. It's a kid's song. A little rhyming thing that Klacka taught me."

"The girl from the ancients?" I paused, folding my coat over my arm. After her initial tale of event, Izzy hadn't spoken of her time there, at least, not to me.

"Yes. I taught her a couple of old Beatle's tunes, and she taught me this. It seems to be caught in my brain somehow, which can be annoying."

"I get that all the time." I smiled at her. "Sometimes, only singing the words will get it out of my head. This has words, right?"

"Yes." She pulled the damp kitchen towel off the hook,

replacing it with a clean towel from a drawer. "Something about a winter fox who chases a mouse through a magical door." She blinked at me. "The fox's name is Timon."

"Okay," I said, glancing at Volpi.

Outside the high window, snow had started to fall, muffling the city noise, blanketing the ugliness with white crystals. It was beautiful and peaceful, and like most good things in my world, it wouldn't last.

Volpi rose from his rocker and came to stand at the counter facing us. "Timon the fox. Isn't that similar to Tími?"

Izzy stared at him for some moments before speaking. "I was so sure the Song of Tími would be in the temple. When the symbols we found were too faded to decipher, I'd thought it was lost forever." Izzy's face lit up, her gray eyes glistened with tears. I blinked at her, still trying to figure out what the hell she was so happy about.

She grabbed my shoulders. "Don't you see? The song that Klacka taught me. It's in the form of a child's riddle, a nursery rhyme, but the melody is there and the right components. The magical doorway, the brave fox who travels through it. The moon that guides his way."

"You have the formula? A solution for Marlowe?" The concept of time travel wrapped inside a child's nursery rhyme. A slim chance, but enough that my sister was bursting at the seams with the possibility.

"Well, it will take some work. But—" Volpi mused.

"But the framework is there. We have something to start from," Izzy said.

I laughed and swung her around the kitchen. Volpi grinned from across the counter.

"And just in time, too," Izzy exclaimed.

"What do you mean?"

"You have to go back right away. Marlowe saved me, Tam, back in the world of ancients, he saved me. And now, we can save him."

"Iz." I didn't want to talk about this. "I'm not sure we can," I mumbled. Knowing his fate also meant that I had to leave him to it. I had wrestled with this idea for months. Ever since X had died.

"You need rest, Iz." Volpi cut in.

"No, it's not a dream, but a vision. Marlowe's death. It's all wrong. I know it is. And it changes everything. You have to go back, Tam."

"Go back where?"

"To England, to Marlowe's time."

"Okay, okay. Let's just take a breath here, and we'll talk about it in the morning, okay?"

"Marlowe was hanged for treason." Her voice was low, breaking on the words.

The words chilled me, but this wasn't news. "Yes, I know, Iz."

"No, you don't. He shouldn't be. His history has been re-written and you are the only one to—" She closed her eyes again, the blue shadows cast beneath her lashes. "We have to send you back to fix it. To fix the timeline, or..."

"Or what?"

"I don't know exactly, but it's bad. Or wrong, things are just wrong."

Volpi pursed his lips. "What do you mean?"

Izzy's troubled gaze flicked back and forth between us. "This is more than just saving Marlowe. It's about saving us. This—" She gestured vaguely about the room. "This time, this world, it has changed and will continue to change until you fix history."

"I have to go back," I said. "And do what exactly?"

Izzy's eyes became unfocused again, as though seeing something other than her tiny basement apartment.

"First," she said, her voice soft and far away. "You have to break Marlowe out of the Tower of London."

Acknowledgments

Many thanks to all my readers for sticking with me through three books, and hopefully more to come. To my critique and writer's groups for their continual perusal of this work and sound advice for making it better: Nancy Young, Jack Lloyd, Kelly Jones, Renae Sutton and Jan B, Parker. Also thanks to my publisher, Susan Brooks, editor, Kylee Howells, and cover artist, Pozu Mitsuma at Literary Wanderlust.

Writers find support in all kinds of ways and these are often aside from typical critique groups and literary functions. A special thank you to beta reader, Danielle. Much gratitude to the ladies at the pool: Anne, Susan, Joanne, and the two Judys, the gaggle of Castle Pines: Sue, Martha, Joan, Sheila, Charlotte, Prissy, Belinda and Judy again, as well as the Boxcar coffee regulars: Adriana, Patty, Renae, Annie, Kelly, Jennifer, Jaime and Sheon.

Coming Soon

Nightfall in Deptford
Book 4
Crescent Moon Chronicles

April 5th, 1593

A spring squall swept in from the channel, lashing Christopher Marlowe in whip cracks of half-frozen rain. Visibility was scarcely a man's length in the darkness, and the traveler used the faint glow from sputtering lamps and torches to guide him into London.

As Kit trudged up the muddy path, he was grateful for his heavy leather tunic and trousers, his long boots and full-length cloak. After his time in the ancient realm where the sun hung low on the horizon for several months of the year, the cold barely affected him. But the walk was long, and after an hour with his waterlogged cloak dragging through the mud, he looked forward to a warm fire, mulled wine and a bed. A meal wouldn't hurt either.

He made an imposing figure. Plentiful food and hours of battle training turned his usual wiry frame into hard broad muscle, but he hadn't eaten in almost three days and his belly complained.

"Hail, friend." A hearty voice called out from several yards away as a horse and rider approached. Marlowe stepped further into the shadows, his hand reaching to his hip for Grim. The broad sword's grip rested reassuringly against his palm. "Kit Marlowe, how fares thee?"

The fellow's horse stopped and Marlowe looked up into the thin face of his old friend, Thomas Nashe.

"Good eve, Master Nashe, what brings you out at this late hour?" Marlowe's rough voice was lost in the wind and rain and Thomas leaned down over the horse to hear him.

"I could ask of thee the same, Marlowe. I am here but a moment. I must retrieve my belongings from near Bayarde's and then back to Norfolk."

Marlowe remembered Nashe's recent play, The Isle of Dogs and the havoc it caused the playwright. "Under cover of night goeth the playmaker of controversy. A wise decision, friend. And a fine work compiled if dangerous in these uncertain times," Marlowe said.

"Alas, my papers had been seized as I fled to avoid the rack. My dearest Anne has recovered a few for me. These are dangerous times for all, but for especially for some." Nashe's voice dropped, though there was little chance of being overheard. "Thy reputation is growing, Marlowe, and not always in thy favor. Talk of heresy and sedition. I for one, do not believe a word, but some do, and they are the ones who count."

"Worry not for me, friend, though I thank you for your faith. I have been away, and no play of mine is in Southwerk. I have just returned, finding myself without funds or horse and still some distance from town."

"Come." The man held his hand out to Marlowe. "Old Sadie is weary, but a good strong steed and we can take you as far as

St Paul's."

Marlowe mounted behind Thomas and Old Sadie gave a soft whinny at the added burden. Thomas clucked at her and the horse resumed her steady gait, turning at Grace Church onto Thames St.

"'Tis an inopportune time to be afoot. The thieves are thick as the Black Death in London these days. From whence do you return?"

"Up North," he replied vaguely and hoped the matter would drop. Thomas questioned him at length on the news of the day and was disappointed Marlowe had nothing to impart. For all his months spent in the ancient world, his absence from his own time and city had been scarcely three weeks. Thomas offered him a place to stay and as tired as he was, he gladly accepted.

They arrived at Thomas's friend's and woke the mistress to allow them entrance. Marlowe thought of his many journeys where his survival depended on the kindness of strangers. His travels often had him hunting a supernatural creature of some sort, and thus, fraught with danger, but he also found kind and able people to help.

He trudged up the stairs behind his friend, listening to Madame Danby's gentle scolding over late night visitors as she set a kettle to warm over the hearth. The garret consisted of two rooms, a larger sitting area with a squat fire pot in the corner opposite a desk and chair, and a much smaller room with only a spoon cot and a chamber pot.

Inside the tiny room, Kit hung his cape on a peg and quickly pulled the dragon-embossed tunic over his head before Nashe could observe his unusual attire. He shed the thick-furred boots and leather trousers as he heard Thomas open the outer room door to admit the tailor's wife with her kettle of hot water and blankets. Wearing only his long muslin shirt, Kit collapsed onto the cot—wide enough for two bodies to sleep if slotted together like spoons. When he awoke in the late morning, Nashe had already gone, making his escape back to the country. He washed himself with the water provided and even cold, it refreshed him somewhat.

Prevailing on the good Madame Danby yet again, Kit went down stairs in search of a meager meal and some ale to wash it down. Revived enough to travel through the streets of his city, he set out to start his life over and ambled up Fleet Street toward St Paul's and the booksellers.

Amid the busy streets of London, his thoughts wandered to his most recent journey to the world of Tamberlyn and Isabelle's ancestors. He and Isabelle had sought out the final clue in the formula that would allow him control over his travels, but he had traveled home before the mission completed. He felt the failure keenly, as time travel was not just his destiny, but his love, Tamberlyn's as well.

He turned and headed east, toward the market square and Master Gomfrey's apothecary shop. As he did so, he noticed a shadow moving just out of his line of sight. He slowed, pretending to peruse the street vendor's wares. Holding up a knife blade as though to inspect it in the sunlight—he watched the reflection of someone making their way down the other side of the street. The small hunchbacked woman appeared not to notice him, but the hairs under his short braid rose and he rolled his shoulders in response. He reversed the knife in his hand with old expertise and handed it back to the smithy, hilt first. Crossing High Street, he continued until he caught sight of the woman's cloak as she ducked down a tiny alley. Marlowe picked up the pace and turned into the dark, dank path, his long knife drawn from its sheath at the small of his back.

The figure still wore the ragged cloak of the old woman but underneath the hood was darkness—a deep unfathomable emptiness, interrupted only by glittering yellow eyes.

Marlowe halted. He glanced back to assure himself they were alone. "Be gone from here, demon." The only response was a deep raspy chuckle as the hooded figure approached, slowly at first, and then seemingly without footsteps, it swept toward

Marlowe in a rush.

Within a second, Marlowe drew Grim from the scabbard and swung it in an arc forward, slicing through the hooded neck and shoulder at an angle, sliding through the figure like butter. Only the hood fell away, revealing naught but a wispy blackness, the eyes narrowed to mere slits. As his sword made another swish through it, the oily smoke invaded Marlowe's throat and stung his eyes. Choking, he could see nothing but darkness as it swooped in. Overwhelmed by a sense of foreboding and dread, he jabbed with the long knife as he whirled Grim through the invisible foe. His balance upended and his head woozy with lack of oxygen, he dropped the knife, gripped the sword with both hands, and swung the weapon in a great arc as he spun. The blackness dissipated as he fell to his knees, gasping for breath. When he wiped at his streaming eyes and looked around, there was nothing but a shredded cloak on the ground.

Coughing, he rose unsteadily to his feet and staggered from the alleyway into the traffic of London.

Marlowe stopped to recover himself in front of a house with the delicious aroma of baking bread.

A woman stood in the doorway, her long grey hair coming loose from its cloth covering and wisping about her face. She squinted into the sunshine.

"Mistress Sutton, good morrow." Kit bent in a short greeting.

The woman wiped her sweaty brow with the back of her hand and beamed at him. "Hail, Marlowe. 'Tis been some days since I seen you. Art thou well?" Her thin lips pursed with worry.

"Yeay, Mistress. I am well," he replied, aware of his winded state and reddened eyes from the demon's putrid essence. "I have been up North and the morns up there are bleak and cold for they are without thy brilliant smile. London is most fortunate to have you in her midst. As well as your baking. The bread's very scent makes the angels hunger."

The woman, twice Marlowe's age, had the giggle of a debutant. "Thou jest with me by thy pretty words."

"Nay, Mistress, I mean every word."

"I bid you wait." She retreated through her open doorway, returning with a round loaf that she handed over. "For Master Gomfrey as thanks for the burn salve he provided last week."

Marlowe offered a deep smile and breathed in the earthy scent of rye bread. "Delicious. He will be most pleased." He tucked the bread into his satchel.

Gomfrey made his living with tinctures and salves, but on the sly, he was known as a conjurer for the more superstitious folk. For Marlowe, he was a friend and confidant who'd become somewhat of a father figure, and the only one who knew of Marlowe's special abilities.

"Good day Mistress." A short bow, another smile, and Marlowe had a spring in his step as her distinctive laugh followed him down the street. He turned, raising his hand in farewell and halted his step. Several doors down from the bakery, another cloaked figure slid into the shadows.

Kit's shoulders sagged. Barely at home a day, and already there had been one hostile vanquished, and now another in the offing. He kept walking, weaving to avoid running children, old men with carts and basket-laden women. Occasionally, he'd catch a glimpse of his follower, a man quick enough to scurry out of sight, but not so fast Marlowe missed his peculiar lurching gait. Marlowe sighed and veered down an alley. He intended to lose his stalker before arriving at the safety and warmth of Gomfrey's apothecary shop.

About the Author

L. E. Towne is a self-proclaimed reluctant traveler and a continual student of the human condition known as real life. Her work has been published in Welter, Legendary, Zouch, and Main Street Rag, and Foliate Oak Literary Magazine. In between novels, she has written and produced several short plays. Crescent Moon Chronicles is her first Urban Fantasy series. She currently resides in Raleigh, North Carolina, with her tuxedo cat, Kat Marlowe. You can read more about her on her website, www.letowne.com, or find her Instagram, le.townescribe or @LETowne on facebook.